After You've Gone

Austin Starr Mysteries by Kay Kendall

Desolation Row
Rainy Day Women
After You've Gone—An Austin Starr Mystery Prequel

Praise for *After You've Gone*

This charming historical adventure features a protagonist readers will warm to. Bootlegging, newfangled motor cars, prodigal family members with shady backgrounds...all create an enjoyable set of temptations and tribulations for our heroine, who always tries to remain ladylike however challenging the circumstances.
—**Cathy Ace**, Bony Blithe Award-winning author of *The Cait Morgan Mysteries* and *The WISE Enquiries Agency Mysteries*

Kay Kendall's Austin Starr mysteries are great reads, and *After You've Gone* follows right in the family footsteps. Readers will love the story, and Kay is a master of drama and historical accuracy.
—**Pamela Fagan Hutchins**, USA TODAY bestseller and Silver Falchion Best Mystery winner

Sweeps us from the sudden reappearance of a prodigal scoundrel to family secrets, bootleggers, murder, and a young woman's yearning for adventure and independence Whether exploring one family's past or showing life in 1920s Texas, clearly to Kay Kendall, history matters.
—**Helaine Mario**, author of *The Lost Concerto* and *Dark Rhapsody*

Southern manners meet their match with irrepressible Wallie MacGregor, a charming belle who dreams of road trips, flapper hairstyles, and using her brain like her hero, Sherlock Holmes. She gets her chance when a long-lost uncle's reappearance leads to tragic consequences.
—**Lisa Alber**, award-winning author of *Path Into Darkness*

After You've Gone

An Austin Starr Mystery Prequel

Kay Kendall

After You've Gone—An Austin Starr Mystery Prequel

Reach out to Kay on the Internet
www.facebook.com/KayKendallAuthor

STAIRWAY PRESS—APACHE JUNCTION

Cover Design by Guy D. Corp
www.GrafixCorp.com

STAIRWAY≡PRESS

www.StairwayPress.com
1000 West Apache Trail #126
Apache Junction, AZ 88120 USA

Dedicated to Carole, Glenda, and Nancy—

in gratitude for your enduring friendships that

began when we were four-year-olds.

After you've gone and left me crying
After you've gone there's no denying,
You'll feel blue, you'll feel sad,
You'll miss the bestest pal you've ever had.
There'll come a time, now don't forget it,
There'll come a time, when you'll regret it.
Oh! Babe, think what you're doing.
You know my love for you will drive me to ruin,
After you've gone,
After you've gone away, away.

After You've Gone (1918)
Music by Turner Layton and lyrics by Henry
Creamer

CHAPTER ONE

1962

BEING A GIRL with a boy's name caused me to hanker after adventure. Maybe. All I know is that for as long as I can remember, I've always craved it. And for just as long, I danged near got none.

My parents expected a son. That explains their naming me Walter—after my father, the judge. As a male, I could've gotten away with daring adventures. Instead, my parents kept the male name and my family saddled me with endless rules of decorum. They groomed me to become the proper wife of some pillar of our community. But a nice married matron who ran a beautiful home was nothing I aspired to be, believe me.

What's in a name? Shakespeare asked in *Romeo and Juliet*.

To that question, I always answer, "Plenty."

Like me, you, my darling granddaughter, received a male name.

While my *Walter* is usually softened to *Wallie*, you are and remain simply *Austin*. That name is tough to shorten. It stands strong, just as you do.

I've always thought this trait we share explains the grounding for our compatibility. Neither of us could be accused of being overly feminine in the traditional manner. We both like to speak our minds and go our own way. Despite getting lots of pushback, we keep going. I hope my example has helped you.

My dear Austin, you don't know how much it pleases me that you also share my overriding curiosity. I like to solve puzzles and dig for the facts to explain them. Like me, you've become haunted by the story of our relative, Rory MacGregor. Although you've begged me for the full account of his adventurous life, I never felt the time was right. You were too young.

I decided to wait until you could understand my uncle's complicated history. With your sixteenth birthday coming next week, I believe you're mature enough now to handle the details of this exciting yet sad tale.

Poppa and Aunt Ida used to laugh and call me nosy. They thought it was cute when I grilled Poppa about his day at work. He'd comply and describe wild and crazy cases that came before him at the courthouse. However, he was not forthcoming about the disappearance of his brother. In fact, I never knew that he had a brother until I was eight years old. That was when I spied a photo in a fancy frame hidden behind a potted fern in our parlor.

I peered at the striking young man in a cowboy hat.

"Who's that?"

My aunt said, "Put that back."

Her sharp tone startled me. Nevertheless, I picked up the picture and handed it to Poppa. He looked down at his feet, then over at his sister-in-law.

"My brother, Rory, was younger than me and a real handful. I haven't seen him since he left home at seventeen."

I knew what that meant. How many times had Aunt Ida called me a real handful?

Poppa rose from his armchair.

"I won't discuss this further. Now let's go in for supper."

Aunt Ida followed him into the dining room.

This deliberate silence intrigued me. Here were real-life mysteries for me to solve. What made Uncle Rory leave? Where had he gone? And why wouldn't my relatives talk about him?

Despite my best efforts, digging up bits of information about my uncle was surprisingly challenging. Even our housekeeper would say little, and she was ordinarily one to gossip. People around town didn't seem to know much. I acquired a few meager facts and jotted them down in my daily journal. Although I eventually quit asking about Uncle Rory, he remained in a back corner of my mind, lurking.

Last night I dug up two relevant volumes of my personal journal, dusted them off, and read through my notations. The first volume was written when I was eight. After a hiatus of fifteen years, Uncle Rory's name returned to my pages. That volume covered the month of November in 1923.

Going through the old entries refreshes my memory for the detail you've longed to learn. Many years have passed, filled with those adventures I yearned for, and I want to ensure I get the record straight.

My notes for Thursday, November 1, say that Uncle Rory returned that morning to our hometown of Gunmetal, Texas. Those days I spent with him were the best time of my young life. The escapades he shared set my imagination galloping.

All too soon, however, just as suddenly as he had appeared, my uncle was gone.

And after that, the mystery of Uncle Rory consumed me.

CHAPTER TWO

1923

LOUD POUNDING ON the front door echoed through the house.

My beagle puppy, Holler, scurried into a corner and tripped me on his way past. Then, lickety-split, I landed hard on my bottom with my bathrobe tangled up in my legs.

Darn it. Not a great way to begin a Thursday morning.

The loud bangs continued. I'd been ready to wash my hair, and here I was lying on the bathroom tile, nose to nose with Holler as he cowered beneath the bathtub. But I couldn't ignore the door. Poppa was out back, and Athalia had the day off. No one else could stop the incessant racket. I'd either have to let the door go unanswered—not very mannerly of me, although I was tempted—or show up in my pink chenille bathrobe.

Who on earth had the audacity to pester us at eight o'clock in the morning? Folks in town knew that wasn't proper. Out on our ranch, drop-ins were common at all hours. Not here in town.

My curiosity finally won out.

I rose slowly. My ankle ached, but it held when I put my full weight on it.

"I'm coming," I yelled. "Hold your horses."

Aunt Ida detested my yelling but that never stopped me.

I scooped up Holler, wobbled along the hall, and managed to reach the front door. My puppy lived up to his name, yelping and wriggling frantically. I clutched the little escape artist against my chest. He liked to leap from my arms and dash outside as soon as I opened the door.

I checked to ensure my robe was closed. Satisfied that I was minimally presentable, I reached for the door handle.

A towering stranger stood on the porch. Beneath a gray Stetson, his face was streaked with dirt, but his eyes were a deep blue and his lashes were long. When he smiled, his eyes crinkled in a pleasing fashion.

"Howdy, ma'am. I need to speak to Walter MacGregor."

He breathed out hard and jiggled one leg.

While Holler kept barking, I considered my options. The caller didn't wait for me to reply.

"Please, I must talk to Walter MacGregor."

"I'm sorry. My puppy doesn't know how to behave yet." Speaking into Holler's ear, I said, "Hush now. I can't think." To the man, I said, "Sir, my name is Walter MacGregor. How can I help you?"

"But you, you're—"

I drew myself up tall and spoke in a terse voice.

"My name is Walter, like my father's. To be clear, we are both named Walter MacGregor."

The caller stepped back and whisked off his cowboy hat. "Oh, mercy, beg pardon, Miss, umm, Walter. Maybe your, perhaps your, uh, father is at home, yes?"

His stammering speech and confusion were endearing, and his eyes sparked brighter than ever.

5

The cowboy might be unkempt and a trifle dirty, but he certainly didn't lack for charm.

Curiosity bubbled up in me.

"I don't mean to be rude, but who are you?" I drew my words out slowly, unsure of how I should proceed. At the age of twenty-three and unmarried, I shouldn't have been wearing a pink chenille robe in front of this scraggly male stranger.

"*Should* I know you?" I added.

The man laughed, a ragged, high-pitched sound.

"Heavens to Betsy. We're kin."

I cocked my head. "Do tell."

"I'm your uncle. I left town before you were even born, about the time your parents got hitched." A shadow passed across his face.

My spine tingled. "*You're* Uncle Rory?" I set Holler on the floor and eased myself out the front door. "You've no idea how I've longed to meet you."

He dipped his head and took a step back.

"I trust your parents are both well." His tone was polite, although a touch perfunctory.

My shoulders sagged.

"You have been out of touch if you don't know about my mother. She died when I was a baby."

Uncle Rory paled and stammered again.

"I didn't know. I'm so sorry. You have my, my deepest condolences and—"

I had to cut him off. Not wanting to be drawn into a discussion of Mama's death, I stuck out my hand. He shook it.

"Poppa will surely be surprised to see you after such a long time."

"I know, I know." He rested against the doorframe and stared into the distance. "Shoot. I reckon that's entirely my fault. And I regret my absence. But truly, I need to see your father right away. Don't mean to scare you, but, well, it's a matter of life or death." He looked over his shoulder at the street, then back at me. "Please."

What on earth? How was I supposed to take this ridiculous assertion? If this man really was my uncle—and he did resemble the photograph—I should comply. Circumstances called for a fast judgment.

"Why don't you go around back? You'll find Poppa there with his hunting dogs. I'll join you as soon as I change clothes."

His head bobbed, and his appealing grin returned.

"Thank you, Miss Walter."

Clapping his Stetson back on his head, he dashed down the steps, then ran around the corner of the house and disappeared.

My goodness, I was unaccustomed to so much excitement. I surveyed the street in front of our house—no horse or motorcar in sight.

So many questions crowded my head. Where had my uncle come from? How had he landed on our doorstep? And why had he appeared after years and years of absence? He piqued my curiosity, that was for danged certain.

I went back inside, where Holler's patience was at an end. I scratched behind his ears and shushed him.

"You *must* behave. And I must dress fast and see how Poppa and his long-lost brother are getting along."

I rushed down the hall to the kitchen and tossed Holler a biscuit, one left over from last night's supper. The window over the sink overlooked the backyard, and through it I could see how close Poppa and Uncle Rory stood together. Poppa had his hands on his hips, never a good sign. My uncle's hands were waving in the air. He also stamped his foot, while clutching his Stetson and working his jawbone. I couldn't judge whose mood was worse.

Three of Poppa's hunting dogs sniffed at the visitor, behavior Poppa usually didn't tolerate. Now he paid them no heed whatsoever.

What on earth were they saying?

I couldn't join the men immediately; I had to ditch the chenille. I shut Holler into the kitchen and ran upstairs to my bedroom. My desire for speed warred with my training—to always look presentable for guests. I grabbed an old work shirt and riding pants from the dresser and pulled them on, then added boots.

A glance in the mirror showed my hair was unruly, but the top of my head was ready to explode from curiosity. The mere touch of a brush would set it off for sure. I *burned* to discover why Uncle Rory had returned to our family manse in Gunmetal after so many years away.

Here was a dream come true, a day I had longed for but never expected to see.

When I hurried out to the back porch, I immediately caught the sour tone of the argument ensnaring my father and his prodigal brother.

I inched down the steps from the porch. I specialized in eavesdropping, and I didn't want them to see me and stop talking. As I drew closer, I caught fragments of their speech, although it was difficult since they started to whisper. They didn't look up, yet they must have sensed my presence. Finally, when I was maybe ten feet away, I made out an entire sentence spoken by Uncle Rory.

"But, Walt, I can't help it. It ain't my fault. They're fixin' to kill me."

And then Uncle Rory broke down and cried.

I gasped and clapped a hand over my mouth. Maybe he wasn't joshing after all when he claimed his problem was a matter of life or death.

CHAPTER THREE

POOR UNCLE RORY. I'd never seen a grown man cry before. My heart went out to him.

Of course, I probably had exalted expectations of men. Poppa, the gentleman whose ways I knew best, was a paragon. I would never use *him* as a yardstick to measure a *regular* fellow, even his own brother. Nevertheless, my woman's intuition, if you could call it that, told me Uncle Rory might not be a straight shooter. Then again, perhaps I was influenced by his saying someone wanted him dead.

Uncle Rory was rubbing his eyes with a red bandana that he pulled from his back pocket. When he noticed me, he returned the bandana to its original place, took off his hat, and bowed.

"Beg pardon, Miss Walter. I'm so upset about my situation that I lost control."

I saw my chance. I took it.

"What exactly is *your situation*, Uncle Rory?" I leaned forward. "Who's trying to kill you?"

Poppa reeled to face me. A fierce glare replaced his usual gentle expression.

9

"You're presumptuous to ask. My brother and I are holding a private conversation, into which you have intruded. I thank you to return to the house and go about your own business."

Poppa never spoke to me so sharply.

Now tears welled in my own eyes, but I blinked them back.

"That's not fair. Uncle Rory told me he's afraid for his life. I know that's why he's come to us. So you see, I'm already involved, and I—"

My uncle said, "Don't be hard on her, Walt. She's right. I did tell her I've got enemies out to get me."

Enemies plural? Good heavens.

I shot Uncle Rory a quick smile, then faced Poppa. "Seems to me if he stays here with us"—I gestured at Uncle Rory—"then it's prudent for me to know what I can expect—and who I should look out for."

Poppa reached down and patted his favorite dog, Jigs, a white English pointer with liver-colored spots. When Poppa looked back at me, his eyes no longer blazed and his mouth had relaxed into a half smile.

"Perhaps I spoke too harshly, Wallie. Rory's news has undone me a bit and—"

"But what *is* that news exactly?"

He raised a hand to cut off my speech. I complied.

"I must think on this," he said. "Your uncle and I have many things to consider. Now, please, be a good girl and go about your plans for the day. At suppertime we'll discuss what's to be done and how much detail you need to know."

My impatience rose like bile in my throat, but I choked it down. Usually Poppa was an inherently patient man. One of his preferred sayings was *Rome was not built in a day*.

I would copy him and play at having patience. But I would not abandon my quest to uncover Uncle Rory's dangerous secrets. After all, my two aunts—Ida and Hazel—often noted how my tenacious spirit made me behave like "a dog with a bone." Although I suspect that their observation wasn't meant as a compliment, I took tenacity as a fine quality to have.

I feigned a meek tone.

"Yes, Poppa. I'll be busy for several hours shampooing my hair." My spirits lifted. "So I won't be in *your* hair."

I tossed my blond hair to emphasize my point, turned, and walked a few paces toward the house. Then, realizing that supper would be a problem, I hurried back to the men.

Poppa eyed me, one eyebrow raised.

"What is it now?"

"Shall I ask Athalia to return to make supper? What she made for this evening isn't enough for company."

Uncle Rory's head snapped up.

"Athalia's still with you? You're one lucky son of a gun, Walt." He punched Poppa's arm. "She was always the best cook in the county."

"You knew her?" I squealed.

Oh, there was so much to learn about my uncle.

"Sure did," he said. "Her man came to us first, to work with the horses." Uncle Rory turned to the old carriage house. "Walt, is Moses still around?"

Poppa shook his head, and a look of pain shot across his face. "Moses died in an accident about the time you left town."

Good golly, here was more surprising news. Why didn't I know all these things?

"So Athalia's husband once took care of our horses?" I looked first at Poppa and then turned to Uncle Rory. "Now there's only one horse out at the ranch. We use the Model T."

Poppa gave me a gentle push toward the house.

"Go take care of your hair. Rory and I have important things to talk about."

"Bye, Uncle Rory."

I forced my tone to sound merry, unwilling to give my

game away. My plan was to discover every iota of information about my uncle and how he fit into the history of our lives. History I had known very little about, it now appeared.

Oh, this was going to be such fun.

My very own mystery to solve.

CHAPTER FOUR

WHAT AN ONEROUS job, washing and drying my hair. It was heavy and fell almost to my waist.

As my arms grew weary, I thought of film actresses with their shorn tresses. Bobbed hair must be a snap to care for, and the only thing holding me back from following their lead was the conniption Poppa would throw—not to mention Aunt Ida's wrath—if one day I chopped off my blond mane.

By noon I had forced my unruly hair into submission and was ready to visit Athalia. What a pity I couldn't telephone her. I made a mental note to myself: Must discover if one of her neighbors had a phone. That could come in handy when another surprise popped up in our lives. As long as Uncle Rory stayed with us, daily shocks seemed likely.

I released Jigs from the kennel out back, and we began to amble to Athalia's house. Holler was too young to take for a walk. With all his nervous energy, he had a long way to go before he would behave as well as Jigs.

Athalia's house was located in the colored part of town. Gunmetal, with only two thousand residents, had a compact layout, so Jigs and I didn't face a long stroll. The first five blocks featured sidewalks and paved roadways, with wooden frame houses situated on large, well-tended lawns. Although none were as fancy as Poppa's house—a three-story Queen Anne Victorian—the other homes were comfortable and tidy. The live oaks along Orth Street provided shade, and a slight wind ruffled the hard leaves of the magnolia trees and made them crackle. The few people I saw nodded and smiled. We all knew each other.

Then we arrived at the town square and commercial district—all four blocks of it. After we passed the courthouse, we came to Brown's Shoe Store, where Herman Brown was changing his window display. When he saw us, he brought out a treat for Jigs. Jigs wolfed it down, his tail wagging merrily.

We walked along to the next block, passed over the railroad tracks, and entered the colored section. I was glad Athalia's house stood on the edge, because streets in this area weren't paved and the dust from the roadway coated my boots and kicked up on my legs. My cowboy boots and riding pants had been a wise choice. Years ago I'd learned that wearing a dress and soft lady-like shoes was a bad idea when I walked to Athalia's.

Several children played in the dusty road, and as I passed they waved and grinned.

"Howdy, Miss Walter," they sang out.

I reached into my pocket and pulled out a few pieces of hard candy that I carried whenever I strolled around town. Children were always happy to see me.

I had walked to Athalia's house on my own since I was in grade school, but when I was fourteen, Poppa surprised me by talking about it. He joined me on the sofa where I was reading.

"Wallie, there's something we must discuss."

I laid my book aside and folded my hands in my lap. The story he interrupted was *The Hound of the Baskervilles*.

"Yes, Poppa?"

He liked to explicate the ways of the world, a habit I loved. Because he mostly talked to me as an equal, his attitude gave me confidence in my own judgment.

"The customs people follow in small towns are often different from those of inhabitants of big cities. If we lived in a metropolitan area, then—"

I jerked forward. "Are we going to move?"

He patted my knee. "Rest easy, we're not."

I sank back against the cushions. "That's a relief. I like it right where we are."

He grinned.

"As I was saying, we'd have to change some habits if we lived somewhere different, a town with a much larger population. In Gunmetal we know almost everyone."

Where was he going with all this?

"Let's say we lived in San Antonio, for example. In that case I could not allow you to go into the Negro area—or the Mexican one either, for that matter. Not by yourself."

"And why not?"

I went wherever I liked in Gunmetal.

"For one thing it might not be safe for you, and for another, well, white folks in cities just don't do things like that."

I considered this. The practice he described ran counter to the way I'd spent my life.

Slowly I said, "When we visit our relatives in Houston, I notice their manners seem more, umm, formal. I just try to watch myself more closely and try not to be too...*free,* I guess I'd call it." I glanced at my book, then back at Poppa. "So from now on I'll keep watch on those other people—our friends and relatives—and follow what they do."

Poppa's expression relaxed. "Very good."

I held up my hand. "But wait, I'm not finished. If after watching our relatives I agree with their habits, then I will

15

behave the way they do. Otherwise, if I see that their customs don't make sense to me, well then, I will *not* follow their lead. I always watch folks anyway, so this won't be anything new."

How else would a detective like Sherlock Holmes gather so much detailed information? He watched everything and everybody all the time.

Poppa pushed himself off the sofa and strode around the room, mumbling under his breath. He stopped a few paces in front of me.

"Oh, Wallie, if only your mother were here to help with you."

I stood, looking him straight in the eye, determined to make an important point.

"I'll always aim to make you proud of me, Poppa. Don't you fret. You raised me right—you plus Aunt Hazel, Aunt Ida, and of course dear Athalia."

I sat and resumed my reading.

I recalled this incident as I stepped up on Athalia's front porch. Her home was a traditional shotgun house. The wood was weathered and needed repainting, but bright curtains hung at the windows, and flowering potted plants lined the small porch. I knew Athalia was proud of her place, and she kept it up herself. Her son and daughter, both older than me, had moved out, and only her mother lived with her now.

When I had asked Poppa a long time ago, when I was small, why Athalia's house was like a shotgun, he had laughed. "The rooms are lined up one behind the other. So if you opened the doors and blasted a shotgun through them, then your shot would go clean through the house and out the other side."

I always wanted to check his theory, to see if the doors would line up like that, but to my dismay, I never had the chance. I never got past the front room.

Now I knocked on the front door and waited. Soon I heard footsteps shuffling up, and the door opened. Athalia's mother, an elderly and tiny colored lady, stared through the screen.

"What you want?"

"Is Athalia here?"

The woman left, and soon Athalia appeared.

"Pleased to see you, child, but I hope your daddy knows you're here."

"Yes, ma'am, he does, and we have a favor to ask. A surprise guest dropped by and we need a more substantial supper than the fixin's you left us. I know it's your day off, but could—"

"Sure enough, I'll be right over. Been to the doctor this morning and that's outta the way. Just let me get my shoes on."

She bent to pat Jigs on the head, and he licked the hand that so often slipped him treats, much to Poppa's consternation.

Before she could leave, I said, "Do you by any chance remember my father's brother—name of Rory?"

"Indeed I do." She pursed her lips. "Why're you askin'?"

"He dropped in on us this morning."

"Lord a mercy. Has that bad penny turned up at last?" She used her apron to fan her face. "This will be somethin' to see."

I swear that if my ears had been bigger, they would've flapped right along with Athalia's hands. Before me stood a potential source of information, a veritable diamond mine of historic details. I bet she knew *all* our family secrets, even if she never admitted that to me when I was younger.

"You get your shoes on," I said. "I'll wait here, and we can walk back together."

Our journey, however, turned out to be a disappointment. I could pry nothing much from Athalia's firmly set lips. Only one small gem of information.

"Mister Rory be younger than your daddy, and your daddy threw big shade. Mister Rory never got out from it. They squabbled somethin' awful too. Their ways be different." Athalia slowed to catch her breath, then picked up her pace again.

"No'm, I can't say nothin' else about your uncle. He be here a long time ago, and maybe now he be changed some." She shook her head. "Lord a mercy."

What had my uncle done to deserve such disapproval? I vowed to pester her another time. Never Say Die is one of my mottos.

Later that night Poppa, Uncle Rory, and I sat around the dinner table eating Athalia's incomparable chicken fried steak. Sadly, I was too keyed up to do the food justice. Underneath the table, my knees jiggled up and down as I tried to outwait the men. Surely one of them would broach that most tantalizing subject—the dangers Uncle Rory faced. My impatience was bound to leak out through my ears if I had to endure another minute of talk about boring old cotton futures and rice fields.

I wiped my lips with my damask napkin and slowly laid it beside my plate.

"I'm wondering, Uncle Rory, what—"

"Miss Walter, I just can't get over what a fine young lady you are." Uncle Rory eyed my shiny, newly washed hair falling in curls down my back. He sat straighter in his chair and cleared his throat. "I reckon you must, umm, sometimes dress like a lady. I mean, you do live in town, in our fine house, no more out in the country at the ranch."

Poppa coughed. "Wallie only wears dresses for special occasions or when her Aunt Ida threatens her with bread and water for supper." He stroked his gray beard. "Growing up without her mother took its toll."

He lapsed into silence.

A grimace marred Uncle Rory's handsome face. "I hope you realize I'd no idea you'd lost your beloved Martha. I only found out when your daughter told me this morning."

Poppa twisted the napkin in his hand so hard that I imagined he wanted to strangle Uncle Rory, who in turn looked at Poppa's hand and ducked his head. Both men began to fiddle with their cutlery, leaving me time to regret my mama's death for the thousandth time.

If only she had lived. What would my life have been like?

I couldn't rightly complain, though. Poppa was the best father in the whole world. He made sure I loved to read and play classical music on the piano. He even indulged me in most of my less than feminine pursuits. Truth to tell, many young women in Texas knew how to shoot, hunt, and fish. He said it was part of our pioneering heritage. He said it made sense because Texas had been a tough place to live. However, he'd also enlisted my mother's two sisters to provide feminizing influences after Mama passed on. Trouble was, for many years my aunts had canceled each other out.

Aunt Ida was a strict disciplinarian who took me on as her life's work. Her ideas for proper behavior often clashed with Poppa's. They also went crosswise with my own inclinations and butted up against the rules of deportment, such as they were, of her own sister, Aunt Hazel.

If only the latter had taken charge of me, I would have become a truly modern woman, perhaps even a flapper—like those women in the newspaper photographs—unencumbered with old attitudes and free in my ways. In other words, I *might* have become a wild hellion, the perpetual fear of Aunt Ida.

Alas, Aunt Hazel had passed on from this mortal coil fifteen years after Mama vacated the scene. During the following eight years—dreadfully contentious ones at that—I was left to the untender care of Aunt Ida. She tried to undo the influence of Aunt Hazel as well as the brooding indulgence of Poppa and Athalia. They had a habit of spoiling me silly while at the same time keeping me swaddled in complete safety. My knowledge of the real world was limited to Poppa's tales from the courthouse and my own reading of mystery novels. I feared I would live with Poppa until a husband freed me from his stringent care, at which time my spouse would become my protector.

What a bore. That was not the adventurous life I read about and craved.

When I broke free from my reverie and turned my attention to the situation at hand, I saw that my father and uncle still could not meet each other's eyes. To break the somber mood that had settled over the dining room, I resorted to an attempt at feminine wiles. Indeed, I had picked up one or two tidbits from the exhortations of Aunt Ida and deployed them as I judged necessary.

I looked at my father's downcast head and decided to change the subject from my mother's early demise.

"Surely, Poppa, you remember the new dress I had made for the dance on Saturday night?" Addressing Uncle Rory, I said, "I'm not against wearing a dress if the occasion calls for it."

Oh happy day. My ruse worked, and the topic changed.

Poppa's gloom broke as he beamed at me—his full smiles were a too-rare occurrence—and then at his brother.

"Wallie is going to chaperone the high school dance. In fact, she has two suitors jockeying to accompany her. They both drop by often these days."

Darn it. Here was another subject I didn't care to discuss.

My ruse hadn't been successful after all. However, my uncle created a welcome diversion.

"No offence, Wallie, but you ain't quite the ticket to chaperone high school students. You're unmarried. On the other hand, guess you're almost old enough to be on the shelf."

Poppa slammed his fist on the table so hard that his silverware clattered.

"Hell's bells, Rory. We'll have none of that. Your views on the fair sex are not compatible with my own, something you well know."

Poppa glowered at Uncle Rory, who glowered back.

What was that all about?

Undercurrents of family history hovered over the room.

Furthermore, Poppa never swore. His brother had gotten his goat for sure. I didn't like what Uncle Rory said about me, but I wasn't nearly as upset as my father was.

"Never mind, Poppa. It's all right." I sipped my sweet tea. "Perhaps what you said, Uncle Rory, would be true under ordinary circumstances—that I'm not *quite the ticket* to be a chaperone—but I agreed to help out in a pinch. You see, I used to teach at the high school, but I quit two years ago and I—"

"*You* had a job?"

Uncle Rory's voice squeaked. His voice had also squeaked when he talked to Poppa in the backyard; that high pitch was a giveaway to strong emotion. I nodded to myself. The lessons I'd learned reading Sherlock Holmes were already serving me well.

You could never know when minute morsels of information gleaned from a person's habits would come in handy.

Rory was still talking.

"You let her *work,* Walt? Y'all need the money that bad?"

Mercy me. He certainly wasn't afraid to speak his mind to his disapproving older brother. Maybe if he gave Poppa some respect they might get along better.

Poppa's face had grown redder by the minute, and now loud, angry words burst from his mouth, filling the room.

"Damn it all, Rory. Wallie wanted to use her education in a useful way, and I agreed. She has a fine mind, for a woman. However, when Wallie turned twenty-one, she came into an inheritance. She chose to use the opportunity to become a writer."

Athalia peeked her head around the corner from the kitchen, but I motioned her away. I smiled to myself, recalling how she'd told me that the two brothers often argued in the old days.

"I don't know why I'm telling you this, Rory," Poppa said. "After all, it is none of your business. I really don't know why I ever try to explain *anything* to you."

Uncle Rory's eyebrows arched skyward, and his mouth fell open. His comical look made me want to laugh, but I stifled myself with a cough.

He set his fork down on his plate and spoke more slowly than he had before, choosing his words with care.

"And what are you trying to write, Miss Wallie?"

When I heard Uncle Rory use the word *trying*, my anger flashed, but I stuffed it down. Maybe he didn't know how condescending he sounded. I tried to reply in an offhand manner.

"I write poetry and short stories. I also keep a daily journal. That's what serious writers are supposed to do."

When Uncle Rory made a choking sound, my anger flashed anew. I might not be able to squelch it much longer.

"Do tell," he said. "Not many ladies are as lucky as you. This gentleman who left you his fortune, did I know him when I lived here?"

He looked pointedly at Poppa, who opened his mouth to speak, but I proved quicker on the draw.

Poppa had had his turn at expressing his displeasure. Now I got to take my shot.

"Why do you assume my benefactor was a *man*? Actually, it was my mother's sister, Hazel Nutter, who left me an inheritance. Perhaps you knew her? She was a wonderful woman who dearly loved me. She always worried about my having enough freedom so that I could make choices most people of my sex never have. I'm thankful to be so fortunate."

"But I did not—" Uncle Rory began.

I held up my hand to cut him off.

"When Aunt Hazel was on her deathbed, she gave me her favorite book, *Jane Eyre*. She flagged one passage and told me to live by its creed. I have it memorized. Would you like to hear it?"

Poor man. What else could he do but bob his head in agreement?

"Charlotte Bronte was the author," I said. "She wrote 'I am no bird; and no net ensnares me: I am a free human being with an independent will.' And just like Jane Eyre, I try to live by that credo."

I sat back in my chair and rubbed my hands together. "Now then, Uncle Rory, let's get down to business.

"Why have you returned to Gunmetal after such a long absence?

"Why did you leave in the first place?

"And if someone chased you here, have you put us in danger too?"

CHAPTER FIVE

UNCLE RORY EYED me for a second, then his gaze darted wildly around the dining room, settling on the sideboard beneath the windows.

He licked his lips and wiped his mouth with his hand.

"Walt, have y'all got any, uh, well—" He scooched his chair back, stood, and lurched to the sideboard. Tapping it, he said in a squeaky voice, "Got any liquor round here? I can't tell all about my crazy business straight up, you know. I just can't."

Ah, so he understood my aching curiosity after all. I hoped some liquid courage would set his tongue loose. I was eager for him to begin.

Poppa sat still as a boulder before he too pushed back his chair and slowly approached his brother. "I have some whiskey stored up from when it was legal. You sit yourself back down, and I'll fetch it."

Uncle Rory slouched into his chair. His demeanor reminded me of Holler when I chewed on him something fierce after he misbehaved.

Poppa left the room for a few minutes, and in his absence, I didn't speak. I sensed Uncle Rory needed to calm down before he launched into a litany guaranteed to show him in an unfavorable light. I was all atingle, eager to hear a good yarn. What had he gotten up to in the decades since he left Gunmetal?

Poppa returned carrying two cut crystal tumblers. Each held an inch of amber liquid. After Prohibition became the law of the land in 1920, three years earlier, Poppa no longer kept a decanter full of good Kentucky sour mash on the sideboard. He took his position of judge seriously. He didn't have to tell me this bourbon was purchased before the law changed.

Uncle Rory grabbed the glass Poppa offered and inspected the short pour.

"You're kind of stingy with your hooch."

Poppa scowled.

"Be advised that's all you're getting tonight. Better sip it."

Uncle Rory set his glass down with a thump and made a face that would've curdled cream.

"What about killin' the fatted calf when the prodigal returns home?"

Poppa didn't reply, merely returned to his chair.

A silence with the weight of a heavy blanket fell over the room. I needed to pierce the gloom and get my uncle talking.

"What have you been up to, Uncle Rory, in the last twenty-five years?"

"Must I really listen to this again?" Poppa grumbled.

My sainted father was certainly a different man around his brother.

I pressed on. "Twenty-five years—is that how long you've been gone?"

Uncle Rory drank from his glass, then began his spiel.

"I left these parts right before the new century started up. Kicked around doing odd jobs east of here. When Spindletop blew, I moved over to Beaumont. Learned how to work on oil rigs. Started as a roustabout and moved up to roughneck. It was hard and dirty work, great pay, and great pals too. Guess workin' in the Spindletop field suited me. But then, hell, as luck would have it, those wells started to play out. Put aside my dreams of moving up to tool pusher. Decided to try my hand at something different. I wound up in Arkansas."

"What about having a family—a wife and children?" I said. "Seems everybody wants those sooner or later."

"That's enough." Poppa's voice was grim.

"Naw, let her be," Uncle Rory said. "She said nothing to upset me, leastwise not yet anyhow." He took a sip of his whiskey and winked at me.

His smile was magnetic, flying across the table. The hairs on my arm stood straight up.

"Nope," he continued. "Couldn't settle on just the right woman. They all looked as delicious as Athalia's apple pie."

Poppa emitted a low groan.

But I was more intrigued than ever with my uncle and his mysterious past. This man had *lived*. Why, he was just like the swashbuckling actor Douglas Fairbanks in *The Thief of Baghdad*.

I returned his smile, though mine could only be an unworthy imitation of his. How did he put so much pizazz into a smile? Did he have more teeth than normal? Maybe I could learn his secret.

"Do go on, please."

How many secrets could one man possibly have?

"Is that why you moved around so much, Uncle Rory?" My voice poured out like the honey meant to cover Athalia's biscuits. "You wanted to find more women?"

"Dagnabbit, girl. Your daddy was right. You do have a good head on your shoulders for a female. You're gettin' close enough to the truth, and that's a fact. My movin' around did have lots to do with the ladies, but sometimes it was more about their menfolk chasin' after me that sent me on my way. I'd say that's why I'm sittin' here with y'all tonight."

He drank from his glass and shifted in his chair. From the look of him, he wasn't used to refined dining in polite society. No wonder he'd left Gunmetal for adventure.

After another sip, Uncle Rory said, "There was a right perky little miss I took a shine to a while back. By gum, she took a shine to me too. Her husband wasn't right pleased, though, and he and I almost got into a scuffle last week. Next thing I know, he was fixin' to kill me. Forced me outta a danged good job too."

Whoa there. So his dazzling smile often got him into trouble. I contemplated the two brothers and how different they were. While Poppa was serious, Uncle Rory smiled and joked all the time. I bet he often used that smile to get what he wanted.

Oh my. Before me sat a possibly wicked man. How extraordinarily scrumptious. Even better than the moving pictures. *This was real life.*

I wasn't satisfied with what I had uncovered.

"Are you still a tool pusher? I didn't think Arkansas had much oil."

"Naw, that's not it. Haven't worked on oil rigs for quite some time. Never made it to tool pusher. They're the ones that run the rig crews."

Poppa looked down at his plate. If he thought his brother hadn't risen very far in the world, I had to agree.

Uncle Rory went on. "Up in Arkansas, I went into the booze business. Then Prohibition hit, and I moved up north a bit to Missouri. Those caves around Branson were mighty good for hidin' the odd barrel or two."

"What an exciting life you've led."

I regretted my words soon as they burst from my mouth. I didn't want to show my hand to Poppa. My uncle might not have made much of himself—especially compared to his brother the judge—but he had certainly seen more of the world.

Poppa frowned. "My brother always leaned toward the exciting and the forbidden, to his great detriment."

"Might could be," Uncle Rory said, "and for once you make a good point, Walt. A year ago I had to hightail it outta Missouri and ended up in Galveston. Then I—"

"Where I bet you hooked up with rumrunners, didn't you?"

I beamed, feeling learned and up-to-the minute in my knowledge. After all, I followed the news in the papers. Galveston was notorious for its wild ways and was less than two hundred miles from Gunmetal. When we visited our relatives in Houston, only fifty miles north of Galveston, they always shared the latest rumors out of that port city. I hung on every detail and thought the rumors sounded thrilling.

"Yep, hooked up with them rum-runnin' sons of guns. We had us some fine old times stayin' just a step ahead of the Coast Guard. But then I found out the doll I shacked up with—"

"Watch yourself." Poppa's voice rolled out across the dining room table like thunder across the grasslands.

"Sorry, Walt. What I meant to say was, uh...I found out Vivian had a husband, and he came down to Galveston from Houston to find her."

I hunched forward. All caution left me, and I could no longer hide my hunger for details of his daring life. Here was another difference between the brothers. Poppa loved the law and carried it out while Uncle Rory flouted the law and bragged about breaking it.

As a county judge, Poppa picked up on plenty of dirt in his job and often shared some tales with me. He declared the details would help me understand human nature, leaving me with few illusions about the righteousness of humanity. While Aunt Ida poo-pooed his logic, he continued to educate me about the foibles of mankind. The minor scandals he exposed me to had only whetted my appetite for more.

"What about Vivian's husband?" I said. "You didn't say

what happened when he hit town. Did you come to blows?"

I tried to control my enthusiasm, but still Poppa sent me a warning look.

Uncle Rory squirmed in his chair. "Let's skip all that, but I'll admit a pal put a bug in my ear. He'd been at a gin mill and overheard Vivian's guy swear he was lookin' for me so's he could bump me off. Once I heard that, I took action. During a run over to the Hill Country to deliver some booze, I stopped off here. Don't think I was followed. Leastwise, sure hope not."

Uncle Rory eyed the remains in his glass and downed it in one gulp.

Dozens of questions swirled in my head, begging for answers. I couldn't keep quiet.

What would one more little question hurt?

I eyed Poppa, who was looking over my head, staring out the window. He looked like he wished he were anywhere but in his own dining room.

"Let's see if I understand. Your *job* is to deliver bootleg goods around this part of Texas—is that right, Uncle Rory?"

"You got it, girl. As long as the coast is clear, then I take the boss's Lincoln and deliver bottles from Galveston out, oh, maybe some three hundred miles. Top speed of eighty miles an hour from that high-quality V-8 engine. Best job I ever had. See the scenery, meet the ladies, and all the while earn mighty good dough."

Jiminy, I couldn't believe my ears. What a life my uncle led. A quick glance at Poppa showed he wasn't as entertained as I was. His red face looked ready to explode. A vein throbbed in his neck.

I quickly said, "Did you drive the Lincoln here? I didn't see it out front."

"Nah. I hitched a couple of rides." He sat back in his chair and chuckled. "Now I reckon I'll stay here a spell with y'all, if that's okay. After a week, if no one's on my trail, well then, I'll move on." He reached out and jabbed at Poppa's arm. "See, I won't stick around long. You'll be rid of me soon."

"What does Vivian's husband look like?" I said. "I want to recognize him and tell you if we see him hanging around."

Poppa heaved another massive sigh. "A reasonable question, but I nevertheless detest thinking about it. Surely you exaggerate the danger facing you."

Uncle Rory shook his head hard. "Afraid not. Vivian's husband is a real son of a—"

"Watch it," Poppa growled.

"Beg pardon." Uncle Rory picked up his napkin, moving it to his nose as if he were going to blow. Then he seemed to think better of that, placing the napkin back on the table. "Vivian's husband is named Herschel. He's tall, about my height, but skinny, like a toothpick. That is, if a toothpick had a carrot top."

"If he has red hair and doesn't wear a hat," I said, "then he'll be easy to spot."

Uncle Rory considered this for a minute.

"Come to think of it, he usually goes around bareheaded. Also, he's not smart enough to figure he needs to be sneaky and wear a disguise. Not my sorta fellow, I must say."

Bull's-eye. I knew it. Uncle Rory possessed a lot of guile. He must have gotten an extra helping of it, leaving none for his brother.

Poppa's lip curled. Clearly his patience had reached its limit.

"I've heard more than enough for one day. You realize I cannot condone your actions, but I will endeavor to keep you safe as long as you're under my roof. Tomorrow at breakfast we'll discuss how we're going to manage this."

I wondered if Poppa knew even more about his brother's exploits than I did. Happiness and excitement surged through me, from my ears down to my toes. Tomorrow promised to hold more secrets and surprises. I even dared hope that the entirety of Uncle Rory's visit would turn out to be noteworthy. I vowed to watch for any bad guys that wanted to hurt him.

CHAPTER SIX

MUCH TO MY surprise, conversation at breakfast on Friday morning was not disagreeable. While Poppa's mood had lightened since the previous evening, Uncle Rory displayed what appeared to be an ever-cheerful nature. Holler was allowed into the dining room, and from his place on the Oriental carpet, he begged scraps of food.

Outside the sun shone, and air coming in through the open windows was mild for November. Athalia bustled in from the kitchen and laid a plate of venison sausage on the table.

"You always fed us good, Athalia." Uncle Rory helped himself to several sausage patties. "Walt, remember those picnic lunches she made when we went hunting? Best grub in the world."

Poppa's answering smile was so bright that I thought another sun had been invented.

"Those were great times," he said. "Did I ever tell you, Wallie, about the trips your grandfather let us take on his railroad? He was the conductor on the San Antonio to Port Aransas line, and he'd let us boys come along. When we got to a good hunting spot, he'd have the train stop, and we'd get off. When the train came back in two days, if we weren't on time, we'd miss our ride back to San Antonio. We shot quail and wild turkeys and deer when we were lucky."

Poppa almost smiled as he gazed at his brother.

Uncle Rory grinned back.

"Those were our best days. I agree."

"Remember when Pop smelled cigarettes on us that one time when he picked us up from hunting?" Poppa asked.

"And he made us smoke twenty cigarettes each as a punishment. I haven't touched a cigarette since. Just remembering makes me as sick as I was back then."

Poppa's roaring laughter was a delight to hear.

"That's right. I also don't smoke, and no one else in this house does either—even visitors. I can't abide smoke. You put your finger on why."

Peace broke out in the room. My breathing slowed, and I felt all warm and snuggly. I slipped Holler a tiny piece of the venison.

Athalia returned to the kitchen, humming.

This harmonious state of affairs was all too brief, however.

It was interrupted by determined knocking on the front door. Regret sliced through me as I recognized the heavy hand of Aunt Ida. Her appearance was sure to disrupt the amiable mood, yet I knew with equal certainty the trouble she raised would be diverting, perhaps even entertaining—at least to me, if not to the menfolk.

Aunt Ida barged into the dining room ahead of Athalia, who tried without success to usher her in with decorum. My aunt's face was as puckered as if she'd tasted a green persimmon. She marched to a vacant chair and took her place at the table without an invitation. Her eyes remained fixed on Poppa as she peeled off her customary white gloves and laid them on the table. She cast her gaze to the ceiling, as if seeking divine help.

I recognized the trick, one Aunt Ida used when she assumed the role of martyr. Poppa had seen this performance before many times too, and we both knew that the quickest way to end a scene was to allow her to rant unhindered. Trying to stop her mid-outburst only prolonged our exposure to her suffering.

Uncle Rory was uncharacteristically silent. I wondered how well he'd known her in the old days.

She addressed Poppa.

"And just *when* were you going to inform me that Rory MacGregor has returned to town, hmm?"

Oh, but he was wise, my father. He didn't deign to reply. I sat with my hands firmly clasped in my lap and waited for Aunt Ida's performance to reach gale force.

"Did you intend to keep the presence of *this*"—she waved an imperious hand at Uncle Rory, as if he were an inanimate object—"a secret, pray tell? If so, you are a foolish man indeed. Of course I heard from several friends last night that your brother was newly ensconced in your home." She waited, and when no response was forthcoming, added, "What do you have to say for yourself, Walter?"

"Now, Ida, don't be so foolish as to cast aspersions my way," Poppa said. "I intended to call you later this morning."

"Fiddlesticks." Aunt Ida's tone was harsh and sharp. She swung around to face Uncle Rory. "How long do you plan to stay?"

Uncle Rory opened his mouth to speak but wasn't quick enough. Aunt Ida motored right over him.

"I don't expect the likes of you to understand, but it's unseemly you're *sleeping* in this household where a proper young woman resides. A man the likes of *you* has no business being under the same roof with her."

Apparently Poppa had heard enough.

"I'll thank you to keep your views to yourself, Ida. I

manage this family and do quite well without your interference."

Aunt Ida's mouth fell open. Poppa had never upbraided her like this in my presence. I felt as shocked as she looked.

She straightened her shoulders and sniffed, nose high in the air.

"Well, I never. I've never been so insulted at my own table and—"

"You forget yourself," Poppa said. "This is *my* table and my home." He flourished a fork in Uncle Rory's direction. "And this is my brother."

Uncle Rory bobbed his head.

"How do you do, ma'am. I reckon you may not remember me. I was wet behind the ears when I was here last."

She sniffed again.

"Most certainly I remember you. The whole town does, and it's the gospel truth. That means I cannot sit idly by while your presence here could sully the reputation of my niece. Such a bad influence should be nowhere near an impressionable young lady."

"But he isn't—" I began.

Poppa's voice boomed out, cutting me off.

"Wallie, please take your aunt upstairs. I suggest that you show her the frock you intend to wear tomorrow evening."

"But, Poppa, I don't want—"

"At once."

"Yes, sir."

Aunt Ida threw her head back, nostrils flaring and eyes blinking.

"I won't be shunted off like some poor, some"—she hesitated—"poor relation."

As she looked into her brother-in-law's furious countenance, I witnessed a miracle take place.

Aunt Ida glared at Poppa. But after rising slowly to her feet, she left the field of battle.

"Let's go, Wallie. I know when I'm not wanted."

Although disgust dripped from her every word, she had suffered a major setback.

Aunt Ida and I climbed the stairs to my bedroom. We didn't speak until we were in my room and she had shut the door firmly. I wondered if she would continue to rail against my uncle once we were alone, but she was busy pretending she was unaffected by Poppa's dismissal.

She walked to a slipper chair—one I was told my mother had cherished—and sank onto it.

Rubbing her brow, she said, "Show me your new frock, please. And tell me, did you end up selecting the mauve one I preferred or that ugly blue thing you leaned toward?"

Did she sense she was about to face another defeat? We had battled earlier in the week over what dress I would choose for my chaperoning duties. Now she leveled her guns at the blue dress she knew I adored.

Getting the drop on me ahead of time, I'd call it.

My feelings for her at this point were mixed. Since neither Poppa nor I ever stood up to her so boldly, I did feel triumphant. Yet on the other hand, I felt some modicum of sympathy. I could see how hurt she felt, and that tempered my comments. There was no need for me to behave in an uncharitable manner.

I drew the blue dress from the wardrobe. "I did like the mauve one you preferred, but this blue seemed to suit my coloring better. I had to deliberate long and hard, Aunt Ida, since you do have such exquisite taste."

I fluffed out the skirt of the blue dress to display it better.

Her body made a little self-satisfied twitch, and her lips turned up at the edges.

"Thank you for at least taking my views into consideration. Not like some others in this house who I shall not mention."

I hurried on.

"I'm undecided about which shoes to wear. What do you think about these?"

I placed two styles in front of her. I preferred the Mary Janes. She chose the other pair, and I let her win.

I was so proud of my diplomacy that I felt I was ready to work at the new League of Nations, if America ever decided to join.

For the next ten minutes I kept her chatting about clothes. Then noting that her temper had cooled, I edged our conversation to a more important topic.

"And speaking of style," I began.

"Yes?"

"Poppa and his brother are very different." I spoke fast, making an interruption difficult. "For example, their speech is completely at odds. Poppa speaks so well, and Uncle Rory sounds downright, hmm, uncouth. How can that be when they were raised in the same family?"

When she closed her eyes momentarily, I steeled myself for a barrage of words. Aunt Ida did not disappoint.

"Rory MacGregor left high school without graduating. It's obvious, to his detriment, that he's consorted with people of the lowest character ever since. Believe me, he was not raised the way he behaves. Even at a young age, however, he was always such a——" She dropped her head and lapsed into deep thought. Finally she said, "*Scoundrel*. That's the mildest term I can use to describe your uncle with any degree of accuracy."

I placed my new dress back in the wardrobe and settled on the edge of my bed. No sooner had I stretched out in comfort than Aunt Ida berated me.

"How many times do I have to tell you not to sit on that bedspread? It is a treasured family heirloom."

"But there's nowhere else to sit."

"Then stand."

I looked away and rolled my eyes. "Yes, ma'am."

I stood and paced around my bedroom. "But why was Uncle Rory allowed to go off the rails? I don't understand; Poppa is such a fine, upstanding man."

To her credit, the expression on Aunt Ida's face softened.

"Child, as you mature, you'll watch the ways of male creatures and will learn that some cannot be guided, no matter how hard a concerned relative tries. Rory MacGregor was one such as that."

She shook her head sadly.

"He was a handful, no doubt about it. While everyone acknowledged how Walter MacGregor was always dutiful and had an easy nature about him, Rory was a changeling. Walter was older and tried to counsel his younger brother. Walter managed to corral Rory's wild instincts too, as long as Walter was here in Gunmetal. But after Walter started college at A&M in College Station, Walter's hold on Rory loosened. Maybe if Walter had returned home after college he could have saved his brother, but instead Walter moved on to Austin to get his law degree."

Here was more detailed family history than I'd ever heard. Perhaps I hadn't paid enough attention when I was younger. Then again, Poppa was mostly silent about the old days. I had come to suspect he avoided discussing the past because it hurt too much to think about losing my mother.

Such thoughts led to another question I burned to ask my mother's sister.

"Aunt Ida," I began cautiously, guessing I might be tiptoeing into deep waters. "Aunt Ida?"

"Yes, what is it? Spit it out. I won't bite."

I grinned despite myself. How could she say that in all seriousness?

"What did Mama think of Uncle Rory? Was her view as harsh as yours?"

Expecting a sharp retort, I was surprised when none came.

Instead, she seemed to ponder my question with total gravity. She smoothed her hair, gazed out the window, and bit her lip. This behavior was totally uncharacteristic, considering that her opinions were always as rapidly delivered as they were strongly expressed.

My leg jiggled, up and down—always a sign of my impatience—as I waited to hear her pronouncement.

At long last she let out a breath and began her explanation.

"Martha always focused on the best in people. If I remember rightly, she used to say that Rory would find himself one day, that the love of a good woman would help him settle down. I never heard her express a critical word about his actions. I do recall, however, she often tried to make peace between Walter and Rory."

Aunt Ida bent her head, then raised her eyes to me.

"Here is a puzzle that mystifies me, one I never have been able to sort out. About a week before your parents' wedding, Rory snuck out of town one night without warning. No one seems to know why, although I suspect that your father does."

I stopped pacing, my attention riveted on her.

"Over the years I've given this considerable thought, plus I've tried to get your father to explain Rory's sudden departure. He's said consistently that he has no idea whatsoever, and eventually I quit asking." She gave a woeful smile. "You know that's *not* my way. I don't give up easily, as a rule. You take after me in that regard."

Heavens to Betsy, could she be right? Was I really as dogged as Aunt Ida? As I contemplated the unwelcome idea, I slumped against the wall for support.

Aunt Ida sniffed.

"Yes, it's true, but never mind that now. What's important is that I began to suspect that your father and his brother had had some serious altercation—one so dire that it forced Rory to leave town and never return. I will go even further to suggest

39

that the incident may have had something to do with a young woman. I just hope it wasn't your own mother."

My eyes widened, and a tremor ran through me.

"Surely not Mama. But maybe some other girl. Could that be the reason Poppa's so hard on Uncle Rory even now?"

"Perhaps. You see, your uncle was always one for the ladies and—"

"He made no bones about it at supper last night."

She nodded.

"If he hasn't changed his ways—and I bet he hasn't—that's exactly why I'm upset about his being in this house, Wallie. I cannot stand by and have your precious reputation sullied. People will talk. They always do. And they will remember his wicked ways quite well. At least folks of my generation will remember."

I straightened away from the wall and walked to Aunt Ida.

"But I'm his blood relation. Besides, I can take care of myself. His exploits are fun to hear about, but they certainly aren't going to rub off on me. Never fear, Aunt Ida. Furthermore, from now on out, I'll be more on my guard than before."

"Oh, my dear child." She shut her eyes and swayed a little. "You don't realize the depravity some men can sink to. I don't want you to learn about their ways either. You're probably safe being with your two young suitors. They seem such decent, God-fearing young men, both of them. But I'm afraid Rory never was such."

She rose, crossed to the window, and stared out at the front lawn. With her back toward me, she said, "You have no idea what a tough world this is for women. That's why we campaigned so hard to make Prohibition the law of the land. So many men destroyed their families with their uncontrolled drinking. But now we have the Volstead Act together with the Nineteenth Amendment that allows women to vote." She rotated to face me. "We ladies will finally have our say about what happens in this country." She paused for emphasis. "And that, my dear, is a very good thing."

Who was this creature? I knew Aunt Hazel had held those views, but I'd had no inkling that Aunt Ida did as well. Perhaps they were not so different after all.

Abruptly she changed the subject.

"Speaking of men, which of your young suitors will accompany you to the dance tomorrow night?"

Oh curses. I hated when she started up about my suitors, as she called them.

Also, I felt confused. First she said men were a mess and had to be controlled. Next she did an about-face and hinted at her well-worn theme—how I needed a husband in order to be a complete woman.

Wasn't it ironic that she herself had none?

Then suddenly I remembered that one of my suitors was due to visit soon.

"Oh, good gosh," I gasped. "I completely forgot that Clayton said he'd drop by this morning. He and Dewey both want to escort me when I chaperone the high school dance, and I need to make up my mind what to tell them."

I expected Aunt Ida to begin interrogating me about Clayton and Dewey. The subject of my suitors fascinated her endlessly, but this time she had bigger game in her gun sights.

"That's nice, dear," she said, her tone indicating lack of interest. "Enough of that. What I really want to know is why your Uncle Rory has returned. After such a long time, there must be a significant reason."

Her remark amused me since it indicated we wished to use each other as an information source. While this seemed altogether fair, what she asked about now wasn't my secret to tell. I had to disappoint her, and this would be far worse than failing to choose the dress she preferred.

I was getting punch drunk from her twists and turns. She seemed to have much on her mind, and it was coming out in confusing chunks.

"Honestly," I said, lying through my teeth, "I have no idea. You'll have to ask my father or uncle. They talked all day long yesterday, and when I was around, they switched to discussing deer hunting. I think they plan to go hunting next week out on our ranch and—"

"I don't care about that. Come now. You must have some notion why Rory has returned."

Her stare was so intense that I had to look away.

"N-no, I really don't."

"Neither man is apt to tell *me* anything. I might as well save my breath, but I shall persist. I shall find out the answer." Aunt Ida spied lint on her dark skirt and bent to pick it off. "Now, let us go downstairs. I have other calls I must make."

Even though she was hard on me, I loved my aunt and even felt sorry for her now. Perhaps she was right. Perhaps some of my own nature—my pushiness, my curiosity—came from her. On an impulse, I hugged her.

"Mercy, what's all this about?"

She stiffened but sounded so pleased, she was almost giggling.

"You're very kind to fill me in on family history. Undercurrents swirl around Poppa and Uncle Rory when they talk, and I'd like to know what makes them behave so oddly. Surely they must have once felt real brotherly love for each other. As a matter of fact, right before you arrived, they reminisced about hunting together in their youth. The affection for each other was so touching that I almost teared up."

"It's sad when hard feelings tear families apart. Even though Hazel and I had different temperaments, we remained civil with each other. Your sweet mother was always a soothing influence—always." She edged over to the door, then swung around to face me. "You're an only child. You don't know the depths of sibling competition and ill will that can occur."

"I see my friends fight with their brothers and sisters, and the intensity of their animosity shocks me. I'm glad you and your sisters didn't suffer that." A sob caught in my throat. "How I wish I could remember something about Mama, but I don't."

The sudden outbreak of raw emotion shocked me. That wasn't like me.

Aunt Ida patted my shoulder awkwardly.

"I promise we'll talk of this another time. Now then, I really must go, my dear."

I brushed away a tear, and we walked downstairs together in a far more companionable silence than when we had gone up earlier.

Athalia met us in the front hall with my aunt's white gloves in her hands.

"Don't be forgettin' these, Miss Ida."

Aunt Ida dipped her head in thanks and pulled on her gloves, taking care to press away any wrinkles.

"I need these for my next calls across town." She gave me a determined look, and her lips puckered into a scowl. "Do be careful at the dance Saturday evening, Walter. Don't let those youngsters get up to any tomfoolery on your watch."

When she was at her most stern and determined, she always called me Walter rather than Wallie.

Squelching the urge to salute, instead I said, "Yes, ma'am. I'll certainly do my best."

"See that you do."

With that parting admonition, she marched out the front door.

I watched her progress down the front porch steps and her left turn at the sidewalk. As I ran through our recent conversation in my mind, I continued gazing after her, but in a haphazard way, without focus. That is, until movement caught my eye.

Across the street and to the right, a man rested against a live oak tree. He busied himself with smoking and staring at our house.

My breath caught in my throat, and I gasped. Holler whimpered.

Was I looking at Uncle Rory's potential killer?

CHAPTER SEVEN

MY FIRST IMPULSE was to find Uncle Rory and warn him that his nemesis was at hand.

But was this Hershel? What if I were leaping to conclusions? Poppa was forever trying to slow me down, rein me in. *Hold your horses* was advice he repeated over and over again.

The man across the street wasn't a local. True, he matched Hershel's description in that he was tall and thin, but his cowboy hat covered his head completely. Red hair under that hat would clinch the deal, meaning that he was Vivian's husband.

My view of the man's coloring was obscured by the dusty window pane in the front door. I opened the door a little and peeked through the crack. The view wasn't much improved. I opened it a bit more. Holler took the opportunity to nose against the door, pushing it open and rushing out to the porch.

"Holler, come back here."

He leapt in delight, and in a flash my puppy ran down the steps and frolicked around the yard. I flew down the steps after him, yelling all the while.

Ready for fun, my rambunctious beagle brought me a twig from our pecan tree. Here was a chance to seize him, but instead, I grabbed the stick.

"Good dog." I meant it.

Playing with Holler was a plausible reason to be in the yard.

I cast a furtive glance to see if the outsider still lurked. Then I threw the stick in the man's direction. When Holler ran closer to the street, I took out after him again.

Although this brought me closer to a possibly enraged, cuckolded husband, I still couldn't see his hair—or even if his skin color indicated red hair hidden under his hat.

Holler skittered up and dropped his stick at my feet again, his tail wagging. I scratched his ear.

"Good boy. *Very* good boy. Now, what should we do next?"

Holler answered by snatching the stick and racing across the street. Laying the stick at the man's feet, Holler proceeded to paw at his legs.

The man pushed him aside, not unkindly.

Now I had little alternative but to confront the stranger, whether I was afraid to or not. Heartened by Holler's friendliness, I crossed the street under the pretense of recovering my puppy.

I was breathless when I reached the man. I hadn't run, but my nerves were wearing me out.

Gulping air, I said, "I'm sorry, sir. My puppy isn't trained well yet, as you can clearly see." I stopped to see if he would reply, then rushed on. "Sorry he's bothering you."

The stranger grinned.

"No pardon necessary. I'm always ready to talk to a fine young tomato like you."

What? I had nothing in common with a tomato. What had that got to do with anything? If he meant to compliment me, it didn't work. Sometimes men were just plain screwy.

Still, his nonsensical reply gave me an idea.

I bent to pick up Holler. Cradling him in my arms, I looked over his head and batted my eyelashes.

"You're nice not to be bothered. Many folks would be."

"I like dogs."

"Do you keep them for hunting?"

"Sure do."

"My puppy was meant to be one of my daddy's hunting dogs, but he was the runt of a litter and needed special tending. When I got attached to him, I was allowed to keep him inside as a pet. Poppa says he wouldn't make a good hunting dog now anyways. He says I spoiled him. And say, I don't think I've seen you around here before. Who're you visiting?"

Butterflies fluttered in my stomach at my boldness.

He scuffed his boot in the dirt.

"Just passin' through on my way over to Austin."

"Have you been to the state capital before? You don't sound like you're from Texas."

Aunt Ida would skin me alive if she heard me being so forward, let alone talking to a man to whom I'd not been properly introduced. Still, someone had to look out for Uncle Rory.

The man raised one eyebrow.

"No'm, I'm no Texan."

"You don't sound like a Yankee either." I cocked my head. "Or are you?"

That brought a grin to his lips again.

"Now don't go hurlin' insults at me. I'm from the Show Me State."

I had no idea which state that was. At least he hadn't said he lived in Houston, purportedly Herschel's home. Perhaps he wasn't Vivian's husband after all.

Or perhaps he was lying.

The man made a sudden, sweeping movement with his

47

hand, and I jumped back. I looked up and down the street. Was there a rescuer nearby if I got into trouble?

But he had only whisked off his hat.

"Pardon me, ma'am. Where are my manners? I shoulda done this right away."

"Oh, please," I mumbled, trying to cover my embarrassment as I stared at a balding head decorated with meager wisps of brown "And thank you for stopping my dog from running away. Now I must get him back to the house." I waggled my fingers at the man in a lighthearted goodbye. "I hope you enjoy your trip to Austin."

He opened his mouth, but shut it without emitting another word. When I said goodbye again, he wished me farewell, and I crossed back to my own yard.

We'd had a friendly conversation. No harm done.

Once I was back inside our house, my racing heart slowed, but my thoughts were still disturbed. I peeked through a window beside the front door and checked to see if the man had left. I watched him turn a corner at the end of our block and disappear from view.

Just because he was no redhead didn't mean he wasn't out for Uncle Rory's hide. He could be a scout sent to relay information back to Herschel. I had no way of knowing if someone who looked suspicious or acted oddly was friend or foe.

When I giggled, Holler stretched and whined. I stooped to whisper in his ear.

"Maybe I've read too many Sherlock Holmes stories."

When he licked my hand, I fancied he agreed with me.

My beloved mysteries by Arthur Conan Doyle featured deviousness, violence, and death. Had they turned my thoughts toward farfetched possibilities of danger? Uncle Rory might well be exaggerating the peril that made him flee to his old stomping grounds in Gunmetal. But perhaps not.

So far his yarns indicated he'd led a life full of exploits, of willing women and angry husbands. He might be used to this, but Poppa and I certainly were not.

I should probably be angry with my uncle for going on the lam and drawing potential danger to our home. Yet I couldn't follow my aunt's example and condemn him. Despite my fears, I'd keep nosing around. Way down deep in my heart, I even thanked Uncle Rory for giving me an excuse to play consulting detective.

Maybe I could write my own Sherlockian stories one day. Uncle Rory's troubles could inspire me.

I tromped upstairs to write in my journal.

CHAPTER EIGHT

AN HOUR LATER I waltzed downstairs and found Athalia in the kitchen making a pecan pie, Poppa's favorite. I took a bottle of milk from the icebox and poured myself a glass.

Aunt Ida pushed me to learn housekeeping skills, but I resisted. Why bother when Athalia was perfection? Slowly I was winning this battle with my aunt, although she hadn't yet conceded defeat.

Hovering at Athalia's elbow, I cadged a fat pecan and plopped it into my mouth.

"Where's Poppa?"

"Mister Walter and Mister Rory gone out back. Mister Rory wants to work on the motorcar. Says he can save your daddy money."

Holler bounded into the kitchen and leapt up to grab food off the counter. One of these days I needed to teach my puppy some manners.

"Down, boy. Bad dog." I pushed him away with a gentle hand. "Let's go see what the gentlemen are up to. We'll try to dig some information out of them."

Athalia leveled a knowing look at me.

"Mmm-hmm."

That was all she said. It was enough.

I gulped down the rest of my milk and left the kitchen with Holler at my heels. While I plucked a jacket from the coat tree in the front hall, he ran in circles and barked, acting like he'd never been out of doors in his young life. Oh, the simple pleasures of a canine existence.

Out back in the carriage house I found Poppa and Uncle Rory, just as Athalia had predicted. They bent over the Model T's engine, their heads close together beneath the raised hood. Though their conversation was muffled, the tone was calm, and this mollified me. If Uncle Rory was staying all week, I had no desire to hear constant bickering.

Wanting to interrupt, I instead bided my time. Good manners ground into me for years told me to wait my turn to speak to my elders. I held my fire, fighting the urge to discuss my encounter with the baldheaded man. I suspected Poppa would disapprove when he learned I talked to a stranger. But for heaven's sake, I had to tell someone about my risky gamble. Perhaps it was only a tiny one, but in my limited experience, it felt bold to me.

Up to this point I'd led an awfully sheltered life. No wonder Uncle Rory's tales intrigued me. I longed for exploits of my very own.

Lounging against a stall once used for horses, I heard how the addition of a self-starter had improved the Model T.

"Those old crank starters were murder." Uncle Rory let out a loud laugh. "I sprained my wrist plenty a times workin' with those danged things."

"That's why I bought this new model, so Wallie could drive it. The kickback from the cranking was nasty. She wanted to drive, so we needed the self-starter. I prefer it too."

When they moved on to problems with the Ford's

differential, my mind drifted. Who would listen to my tale of the bald man and not jump on me? Maybe even help me with fresh ideas for sleuthing?

My friend Sue Ellen was an ideal choice. She had an adventurous spirit and shared my love of Sherlock Holmes. She was out of town for several weeks, however. As far as Clayton and Dewey were concerned, I never confided anything important to either of them. I doubted they'd support any derring-do that I might undertake.

Tuning back in to the discussion, I tried to follow it, but failed miserably. I could only comprehend a little and concluded I needn't bother to learn.

My curiosity fastened on all aspects of human behavior. It did not stretch to include *mechanical* behavior.

Holler pawed at my leg.

"You're right, boy. We don't need to understand rear axles and differentials."

All of a sudden, Poppa's loud voice interrupted my dog chatter.

"So that's why you wanted to make sure my car runs well. Well, sir, you cannot borrow it. I will not be a part of your dishonest activities. I will not."

No longer leaning inside the car to examining the engine, Poppa and Uncle Rory stood facing each other. Poppa's face was red like a beet—or a tomato.

Uncle Rory put out his hands in a beseeching action.

"But, Walter, I just—"

"I'll thank you to remember I am a *judge*. A judge committed to upholding the law of the land, and that includes the Volstead Act. I'm astonished you would want to place me in a compromising situation. This is low, even for you. You *cannot* deliver liquor in my motorcar, and that is final."

Poppa opened the door on the driver's side, leaned inside to get the key, and thrust it into his pocket. Then he marched to the front of the vehicle and banged the hood shut hard.

I jumped, and Holler whimpered.

Poppa stomped out of the carriage house without a backward glance. I doubted if he'd even realized I was standing nearby.

Uncle Rory stared after him, then he began to wipe his oily hands on his overalls. His manner was nonchalant—whether an affectation or real, I couldn't tell.

Twisting his head toward where I stood in a corner, he said, "Your pappy sure does get riled up easy these days."

Surprised to be spoken to, I nodded slowly.

"Your presence does seem to irritate him—you know, like when floodwaters wash a snake out of its hole, and it gets grouchy. Ordinarily Poppa is quite mild mannered, I assure you."

Uncle Rory spat on the dirt floor.

"You coulda fooled me. Now, listen, Miss Wallie. I didn't mean no harm. Just wanted to borrow this improved Tin Lizzie for a spell. I'd like to take it out for a spin, see how it compares to my boss's fancy Lincoln."

This was the second time Uncle Rory had referred to his boss, and I wondered who he was. A prosperous business man with an illegal operation on the side? Maybe a criminal who used Prohibition to boost his earnings? Although I was dying to know, I had more pressing issues to ask about. Unmasking the big boss would have to wait its turn.

"All right, I'll give you the benefit of the doubt even if Poppa won't." I sidled closer to where my uncle stood. "But I wonder if you can help me with something."

"Okay, shoot."

"Which state is the Show Me State?"

"I used to live there. Missouri. Why do you want to know?"

Hiding my distress, I tried to smile, but I couldn't for the life of me get my lips to turn up.

"I hate to tell you this," I began.

His tone was sharp.

"What?"

"A little while ago a stranger was standing across the street, staring at our house. I went over to talk to him and—"

"What? That wasn't right smart of you, missy. He coulda been a real bad guy."

"Yes, I considered that, but I still wanted to suss him out. He was tall and thin, but he wore a hat, so I couldn't see his hair. He *could* have been your rival, Herschel, and I just had to know. So Holler and I went across the street and talked to him. Turned out he wasn't a redhead." I laughed. "In fact, he was bald. He said he was from the Show Me State. I didn't know what that meant, so I decided to ask you."

Uncle Rory let out a low whistle.

"Damned good thing you didn't ask your daddy. It woulda proved I'd brought danger your way, and then he'd have given me the bum's rush after that." He shook his finger in my face. "Don't go messin' around and gettin' into trouble on my account, you hear me?"

"But I want to help."

"And I appreciate it, but—"

"Okay, okay, stop. I understand, but do you think it's important the man said he was from Missouri? He also said he was on his way over to Austin, but I couldn't get him to say what for."

"Missouri, huh? Sure enough, that makes me jump, like a bug dancing' on a red-hot griddle. Darn it, now I have to figure out if I should tell Walt. He won't be right pleased, and that's a fact."

He kicked the wooden stable door with his boot.

"But do you think you know him?"

"Who?"

"The bald man who hails from Missouri. Sound familiar?"

A pained look flitted across Uncle Rory's face.

"Might could be one guy I knew in the booze business back there. Can't be sure, though." He rubbed his jaw. "Now don't go gettin' any ideas to find him."

I beamed, all innocence.

"Course not, Uncle Rory. But can I ask you another question?"

This time he didn't seem as eager to answer. He drew out each syllable deliberately.

"About what?"

"What made you leave all those years ago?"

I waited, counting to ten slowly. He didn't answer.

"Well?" I prompted.

"A long and complicated story. Doubt if your daddy'd want me tellin' about such things."

I dipped my head in what I hoped was a winsome fashion and batted my eyes.

"Why don't you start up, and let me decide. Go on, try me."

To my chagrin, he laughed.

No, he guffawed.

"For Lord's sake, Wallie. That won't do the trick with me. No, and don't go sulkin' either," he said when my face drooped. "If you wanna hear about this so much, then I'll tell you, but first I better go find your daddy and straighten out why I want to drive his motorcar."

My mood brightened.

"And you promise to tell me? You really do?"

"You bet. Soon as we get the chance, I'll tell you about the whole deal. Not somethin' I'm right proud of either."

This was new, a different tone that I hadn't heard from him before. He'd seemed pleased with himself before when he talked about romancing the ladies.

Now my curiosity was truly inflamed. Had he participated

in something out and out illegal or so shady that even he was ashamed? Whatever the secret was, I could hardly wait to hear all about it.

Uncle Rory returned to the house, but I stayed outside. I waited for Holler to do his business in the yard, happy to stand still and mull over the mystery of Uncle Rory.

The two basic questions were still the same, and I had no answers. Not yet.

Why had he left Gunmetal in the first place, and what was the real reason he turned up again on our doorstep?

Perhaps he hadn't told the complete truth about that latter point yesterday. Had his boss turned on him, threatened him, and thrown him out? I bet rumrunners or bootleggers could be downright dangerous given the slightest provocation.

I was so deep in contemplation that I forgot all about Holler. That is, until I heard a high-pitched shriek from the neighbors' yard.

My attention snapped back in time to see Mrs. Carson run after Holler. She brandished a long stick in one hand and yelled at him.

I hurried toward her. When she saw me, she stopped and yelled at *me*.

"I told you to keep that infernal pup out of my garden. I just found him chomping on my prize squash. If he can't stay away, I'll set out poisoned food for him and then you'll both be sorry."

Before I could apologize for Holler's behavior, she turned on her heel and stomped back to her garden. She picked up a hoe and carried it to her back porch, then disappeared inside the house.

Lifting Holler, I cuddled him and stroked his muzzle.

"She's always been an unhappy woman. Don't feel bad. She yells all the time with or without an excuse. I don't know what her problem is."

Holler whined and licked my face.

On my trek back to the house, I saw Uncle Rory march out to the carriage house. He looked so determined that I didn't try to engage him in conversation. He disappeared into the building, then exited quickly carrying logs for our fireplaces.

Then I noticed Clayton coming around the side of the house and into the backyard. Uncle Rory eyed Clayton as he passed, but they didn't speak.

Clayton bounded up. "Who was that man? I've never seen him before."

"My father's brother, Uncle Rory."

Clayton's eyes widened. "I never knew your dad had a brother."

"He doesn't live in Gunmetal. Only passing through." Discussing my uncle with Clayton wasn't something I wanted to do. "So what brings you over today?"

I knew the answer, but that was the best I could come up with in a hurry.

"Ah, come on, Wallie. You know what I want. Are you going to let me take you to the dance tomorrow or not?"

"All right, if you insist."

I wasn't playing hard to get. I needed someone to go with me and didn't care who.

"I do insist."

When his face lit with a smile, his happiness gave me a pang. He was smitten with me, and I didn't honestly know why. I never encouraged him.

I had already rejected one suitor's proposal of marriage. I had a life to lead, one that needed to be unfettered. Most husbands wanted to control wives just as much as my family tried to control me. What a bother.

Clayton's parents were friends with my father and belonged to our Methodist Church. Aunt Ida declared him to be a good catch. He was a teller at his father's bank, so his job was steady. He was taller than me—a definite plus. When I looked at him, however, my heart never went pitty-pat.

I wanted to find my own Mr. Rochester and figured I hadn't discovered him yet. I'd read *Jane Eyre* at least five times. If I ever were to get hitched—many years from now—then the man needed to be interesting—not to mention tolerant of my headstrong behavior.

"Wallie, you listening to me?"

"Sorry, I must've drifted off. What were you saying?"

"I said I'll pick you up at seven o'clock. Is that jake with you?"

When I didn't respond, he said, "Well, is it?"

"Better make it half an hour earlier. Since I'm a chaperone, I need to be there before everyone else arrives."

"Fine. Then I'll get here at six thirty. Say, are you okay? You seem, uh, distant or..."

His words trailed off.

I adopted a brisk tone. "There's lots to do before the dance, that's all. So I'll see you Saturday." I wiggled my fingers at him. "Bye, Clayton."

I took off for the house, feeling his eyes on me as I walked away. I hadn't been very kind to him, but again, it was the best I could do under the circumstances.

I didn't want to get bogged down talking to Clayton for a long time. Not only was I dying to talk to Poppa and discover what he thought about the lurking presence of the baldheaded man, but I also was busting to hear Uncle Rory's story.

Waiting was infuriating.

CHAPTER NINE

BACK INSIDE THE house, I looked for Uncle Rory. Tarnation, I had the bit between my teeth and wanted some questions answered fast.

Perhaps Athalia could clue me in. I wandered into the kitchen. She'd finished the pecan pie and was working on chicken and dumplings.

"Have you seen my uncle?" I asked.

"Mister Rory went to his room."

I stamped my foot. "Guess I can go upstairs and—"

"No'm, Miss Walter." Athalia flung her hands to her hips. "Wouldn't be proper. Besides, we need to get your things ready for tomorrow night."

Oh, curses. I'd forgotten the need to get all gussied up.

"What a bother. Well, can't be helped. Okay, Athalia. I'll certainly need your help."

For the next hour Athalia cleaned my dress shoes, fluffed my petticoats, and perfected my new blue dress—the hem needed adjusting. Only Dewey Brandon's telephone call interrupted our preparations. With the excitement of Uncle

Rory's arrival, I plumb forgot that Dewey had wanted to take me to the dance.

"I can't, Dewey. I'm sorry, but I already promised someone else."

I really did feel bad. I'd made an almost-promise to him.

Dewey hesitated, then mumbled, "I see."

"But next time there's some kind of shindig, I promise you can take me. How's that?"

"I'd like to see you sooner than that. May I drop by for a visit this afternoon?"

I hated to disappoint him a second time.

"All right. Come over after two o'clock. Bye for now."

"Wait a minute, Wallie. Who's your escort to the dance? Who should I be jealous of?"

"It really doesn't matter."

"It does to me. Please tell me. I can find out anyway."

"Clayton's taking me."

"That's what I figured." His voice sounded tight. "Okay, then, I'll come round later this afternoon."

He hung up.

Athalia stood at the kitchen door, watching me, and her lips were pursed.

"That Dewey Brandon be a real nice fella, Miss Walter. You need to treat him better."

"I just forgot to follow up with him with all the hurly-burly happening around here lately."

We stared at each other. Her right eyebrow lifted.

"Okay. You're right," I said.

Smiling, Athalia patted the footstool I'd been standing on when I left the kitchen to answer the phone.

"Come back here. We got to finish that hem."

Before I hopped onto the stool, I spied a dress shoe hanging from Holler's mouth.

My shriek hurt my own ears.

"Bad dog!"

Holler slithered under the stove, and both beagle and shoe disappeared. Athalia put down her measuring stick.

"Stand still, Miss Walter. I'll get the li'l dickens."

Down on her hands and knees, she wrested the shoe from Holler. It was drenched with slobber and displayed a puncture on top of the toe.

I collapsed on a chair in a fit of giggles. Athalia stood over me, watching me wave the blue shoe in the air.

"What's got into you, child?"

"I've got a backup pair of shoes suitable for dancing. But poor Aunt Ida will think I ignored her and didn't wear the pair she suggested."

I returned to the footstool. Holler crept out from under the stove, then snuck over to a corner where he cringed, placing his nose under his front paws. He wasn't truly chastened, however. After a few minutes he happily returned to nosing around the room. As Athalia adjusted the hem on my dress, I watched his every move, imagining he was looking for the backup pair of Mary Janes.

Athalia surveyed her handiwork, and a grin spread across her handsome, lined face.

"Everything's ready now. Somethin' unexpected pops up tomorrow, you still set to go."

"Thanks. You're a peach." I hugged her.

During the time spent perfecting the costume that would turn me into a vision of femininity, neither my uncle nor my father had ventured forth from his room. I was still determined to talk to Uncle Rory alone as soon as possible—the sooner the better.

As luck would have it, as soon as I heard Uncle Rory walk into the upstairs hall, the doorbell rang. I peeked out a window to see Dewey's family automobile parked at the curb. Their Ford was new, and his father only took it out for short spins around town.

Athalia peeked over my shoulder.

"Be nice to that young man," she said, wagging a scolding finger at me. "I'll let him in. Go upstairs and put your clothes back on, then come straight back."

"Yes'm," I called over my retreating back as I she scurried from the kitchen.

When Athalia told me what to do, I didn't mind. She had a sense of humor. Aunt Ida had none. She was acted like the schoolmarm she used to be.

I threw on my cowboy shirt and men's trousers and raced downstairs to find Dewey chatting with Uncle Rory in the parlor. I put my brakes on, almost skidding to a stop, and stared from the hall.

They were engaged in an earnest conversation, the subject of which I couldn't make out. One would speak, the other would nod, then reply. I watched for several minutes, and neither seemed to notice me. Only when Holler escaped from the kitchen did they look up.

After a sniff at my shoes, Holler bounded over to Dewey, who patted him and stroked his ears. The kind expression on Dewey's face contrasted with the annoyance Clayton always exhibited when Holler tried to greet him.

Warm feelings about Dewey fizzed inside me while Clayton's stock slid lower.

How could I have even a casual beau who didn't like dogs? Impossible.

"There you are, Wallie," Uncle Rory said. "Your friend and I are discussing events in Europe. Now you're here, I'll leave so you two can talk."

"Hi, Wallie." Dewey jumped to his feet. "And, Mr. MacGregor, please stay. I'm sure Wallie won't mind." He looked at me for confirmation.

I sat on a chair near my uncle.

"Catch me up on your discussion of Europe."

Dewey cared about world affairs? Maybe he had hidden depths—Clayton had only shallows.

For the next hour we shared opinions on the economic woes of Germany and President Wilson's failure to move America toward participation in the League of Nations. Holler slept at my feet, and the time whipped along.

When the grandfather clock in the hall chimed five, Dewey took his leave.

"It was a pleasure to meet you, sir." He shook Uncle Rory's hand. To me, Dewey said, "I hope to see you soon."

After the door closed behind Dewey, Uncle Rory spun around to me.

"That's one fine young man. You should snap him up fast."

"B-but what if—" I stammered.

Uncle Rory glowered at me.

"You're no spring chicken, you know."

This was rich. He thought I was almost a spinster while my father and aunt treated me like a child. Maybe I should go to Poppa's alma mater in Austin and study for another degree to ensure being treated like an adult. Independence was calling me.

Before I could protest, someone pounded on the front door. Relishing the reprieve, I rushed to see who it was. Two male cousins from nearby Cuero stood on the porch.

The taller one said, "We've come to see Rory."

News sure traveled fast in small towns.

The next twenty-four hours were a blur. Our cousins Hank and Doug stayed for supper—and ended up staying the night too. They occupied Uncle Rory's time completely. At first I had dreams of gleaning interesting tidbits from their talk, but after countless stories of deer hunts and turkey shoots, I lost all hope. The one time Doug asked Uncle Rory what he'd been doing the last many years, my uncle changed the subject and that was that.

I was sure I could do better, if only I could get him alone.

On Saturday afternoon the cousins finally left. By that time, however, I had to dress for the dance. I hustled into my Mary Janes and new blue dress, still aiming for time alone with Uncle Rory before Clayton arrived. At five thirty, when I had cornered my uncle in the parlor and shut the door, I heard Poppa come out of his study.

"What's for supper, Athalia?" he called. "How soon will we eat?"

"Be ready in a few minutes, Mister Walter," she answered from the kitchen.

Uncle Rory and I emerged from the parlor and joined Poppa in the dining room. During supper I fumed inside, but I told myself to be patient. On Sunday I would dig my uncle's life story out of him. I didn't want to wait, but it looked like I had to.

Or maybe he'd still be awake when I came back from the dance. Perhaps I could make it back early.

Clayton arrived right on the dot at six-thirty.

"Think you'll be back by midnight?" Poppa said.

"If you wait up for me," I said, looking pointedly at Uncle Rory, "I'll tell you about the shenanigans of the high school students."

"Wait up if you want," Poppa said to Uncle Rory, "but I'll be in bed long before then."

My soul bubbled with joy.

This could work. With Poppa out of the way, I could grill Uncle Rory to my heart's content. I rubbed my hands in glee and pictured a long list of his exploits all lined up on sheets of paper. I'd take notes before going to sleep so I wouldn't forget anything.

Clayton was watching me.

"I see you're excited to go to the dance. Let's go."

Silly man. Did he really think I was happy about spending the evening with him?

"Sure, I'm ready. See you in a few hours, *Uncle Rory*."

Clayton helped me with my jacket, blue to go with my dress, and escorted me out to his father's Cadillac. I looked back at the house to see Uncle Rory watching from the porch. He waved and grinned broadly, looking self-confident and handsome. When I was his age, maybe I'd be able to look back on many adventures and grin about them too.

I returned his wave and settled into the front seat of the big motorcar.

"Isn't our new car a honey?" Clayton said. "Biggest and best in this part of Texas."

I didn't like it when he showed off. So what if his father owned the largest bank in the county?

"Its top speed is sixty-five miles an hour, so fast it's hard to find a road that can accommodate it. After the dance, I'll show you a country road that's just right for, uh, for high speeds. That'll be fun, won't it?"

He winked at me.

Good gracious, I did not like the sound of that. Clayton was always trying to get me alone in some dark spot, and evidently tonight would be no exception.

Maybe I could come up with an excuse to go home early.

CHAPTER TEN

CLAYTON AND I were first to arrive at the high school. Despite my worries about his character, I had to confess he was a big help preparing the gymnasium for the dance.

Soon students began filing in, and within the hour the dance was in full swing. Fifty students whooped it up, dancing to the best fiddle player in the county. He played polkas, ragtime tunes, and two-steps.

Clayton acted like the perfect gentleman, offering to bring me punch and cookies every half hour. He also separated couples when I pointed out that their ardor was dangerously close to unseemly.

I was, after all, Aunt Ida's niece. I knew the standards to uphold, and the students needed to hew to them. Some, like the Jackson brothers, needed more reminding than others.

After Clayton and I danced three polkas in a row, I was ready to get off my feet. Even more so when I caught him staring at my bosom. My heaving bosom.

"Let's sit this out, shall we?" I said.

He positioned two chairs so that I could keep a close eye on the crowd. Just because they'd behaved well so far didn't mean their good manners would continue as the night wore on. What a relief there seemed to be no beer or liquor onsite. The Volstead Act might not be popular in some quarters, but it made my job as chaperone easier. Not to mention giving Uncle Rory a new occupation as a rumrunner.

I plopped onto the chair Clayton had arranged for me and was fanning my over-heated face when I noticed Dewey Brandon threading his way across the dance floor, dodging students along the way.

Oh, fudge. I sensed trouble ahead.

Dewey stopped in the middle of the energetic dancers, ran a hand through his hair, and gazed around the gym. When he noticed me, he pivoted and rushed to my side.

Clayton, arms folded across his chest, stepped in front of my chair, attempting to keep Dewey from talking to me.

"Wallie is with me, so you just go right on back home, Dewey."

"No, sir, I won't. I only want to talk to her."

I stood.

"It'll be all right, Clayton. Give us just a minute."

Clayton scowled.

"Well, if you're sure. I don't want to make a scene, but I've got my eye on you."

His attempt at fierceness was comic.

I motioned to Dewey.

"Let's step over there where it's quieter."

In the tranquil corner, I leaned against a chair and took off one shoe.

"I prefer cowboy boots." I flexed my toes. "What're you doing here, Dewey? You knew I'd be with Clayton."

"After seeing you yesterday, I got to thinking. You knew I wanted to bring you to the dance, but you didn't give me an answer until it was too late for me to make other plans."

Dewey might want to make "other plans?" With someone else? The face of Mr. Brown's new clerk in the shoe store came to mind. Hadn't Dewey mentioned her recently? A small shock tingled through my body.

"And you know I'm sweet on you," Dewey continued. "Still, I've got to say this. I don't like how you're treating me."

I was embarrassed. What he said seemed right, once he pointed out how my thoughtlessness looked from his side.

I hung my head.

"I see your point. Maybe I did behave rather badly, but in my defense I have to say that a lot's been happening at my house, so your invitation slipped my mind. I didn't mean to be rude, Dewey, and I'm sorry."

His expression softened a little.

"Thank you. That's good of you to apologize, but I need to know if I have a chance. I have plans to make and I need—"

He broke off, looking uncomfortable and rattled.

My heart jumped into my throat. I wasn't ready to talk in this manner to Dewey—or to anyone, for that matter. I didn't want to pursue the topic any further, but when I started to change the subject, Dewey squeezed my hand.

"Look, we can talk tomorrow. Then we'll have time to figure everything out." Dewey looked over my shoulder. "Hello, sir."

I turned around.

A small, wiry man materialized unexpectedly beside us. Behind his glasses, his eyes were wild.

"Excuse me, Miss Walter. Hello there, Dewey. I'm sorry to interrupt."

My state of mind was such that I hardly recognized my neighbor, Mr. Carson. Why was he here? He didn't have school-age children. Besides, he was a staunch Baptist and didn't believe anyone should dance.

What possible reason brought him to this place of sin?

Ordinarily a reserved man, he occasionally railed at the depravities of the modern world.

Oh dear. What if he came to shut down the dance?

"Mr. Carson, I'm surprised to see you," I said, keeping a lid on my suspicions.

"I came to fetch you, Miss Walter. You must come home right away. Right away."

He held out his hand to me.

I didn't budge.

"But why?"

Clayton joined us, pushing Dewey aside.

"What's going on? Is something wrong?"

Mr. Carson ignored Clayton and moved closer to me.

"Your father sent me because he couldn't come himself. We need to leave right quick. Please come now."

"Is Poppa all right, Mr. Carson? You're scaring me."

"He's fine. Now, will you please hurry up? I need to get you home."

"Hold it," Clayton said. "I'll bring her."

Mr. Carson pushed toward him, an impressive glare on his face, and Clayton inched back a step.

"Follow along if you like, boy, but we're leaving now."

He captured my hand and began to tug me across the dance floor.

Every so often, Mr. Carson's heritage showed. He could be fierce when strength was called for. His grandparents were the famous scout and frontiersman Kit Carson and his wife, a full-blooded Cheyenne woman.

Clayton stepped back again, holding his hands up in front of himself as if to guard against attack.

Dauntless, Dewey never moved an inch, calling to me, "I'll see you tomorrow."

Students stopped dancing and gaped as we passed. Noticing them, I realized I couldn't leave the adult overseers one person short. Someone had to take my place as chaperone.

"Wait, Mr. Carson. Give me a second."

I wheeled around and rushed back to Clayton.

"Can you stay? I promised I would supervise, but I must see what's wrong at home."

Clayton rolled his eyes and grimaced. He never liked to be told what to do.

"Oh, all right. I'll stay. You go on, but I'll come to your house after the dance ends."

Before he finished speaking, I was already rushing away and back to my neighbor. As soon as Mr. Carson and I were outside, I stopped to confront him.

"Now tell me what's wrong. I won't go another step until you do."

"It's your uncle."

He lowered his head and muttered something indistinct.

"What about my uncle?"

"He's had an accident with your father's motorcar."

"He had a wreck? But Poppa said he wasn't to drive it."

"He wasn't driving. He was working on the car, and he, uh, well, he——"

I yanked on his arm.

"What? Tell me."

"The Model T fell on him and squashed, uh, squashed him like a bug."

A wail escaped my lips, and I staggered against Mr. Carson.

"You're saying he's done for." A sob caught in my throat, and I clutched Mr. Carson's hand. "Uncle Rory is dead, right?"

"Yes, I'm afraid your uncle has passed on. I'm sorry, very sorry indeed."

The air suddenly felt cold and clammy. I wanted to draw my jacket closer around me, but I couldn't move. Earth stopping spinning. Nothing was as it had been only minutes before.

Poppa was all right, but Uncle Rory was gone.

Something buzzed around my head. Eventually I figured out Mr. Carson was trying to get my attention, and his words broke though.

"I must get you home to your father."

I nodded jerkily, the only thing I was able to do.

He helped me into his Studebaker, and we drove into the night. All I could think about was the way Uncle Rory had waved goodbye to me earlier in the evening.

He had looked so happy.

CHAPTER ELEVEN

THE DISTANCE TO my house was short.

The drive took an eternity.

Mr. Carson approached each corner cautiously and slowly. So slowly. His caution made me crazy. At least my anxiety snapped me out of my near catatonic state and thrust my mind into gear.

Why didn't he rush through the night? I wanted to pound my fists on the dashboard. But of course I didn't. I wasn't raised to behave that way. But I did muster up my civilized voice to ask him to drive a little faster.

Eyes trained straight ahead, Mr. Carson said, "This speed is safe. We can't have a second death by motorcar this evening."

A meek reply seemed in order, and maybe he wanted praise for his driving, or for his car, a recently acquired Studebaker. But I could only manage to grind my teeth and fidget.

More years seemed to pass until we turned onto Orth Street. Along the block, neighbors stood at the edge of their lawns, pointing or gesticulating wildly. All in the direction of my home. The lights were ablaze, and I thought of the touring carnival that had left only weeks before.

How bizarre. Gunmetal was a typical small town where inhabitants lamented that the sidewalks were rolled up by eight each evening.

This night might be an exciting occasion for some folks, but not for me. Not for Poppa.

Mr. Carson stopped in front of his house and turned off the Studebaker's motor. I threw open my door and jumped out. Poppa's hunting dogs howled in their outdoor kennel. They weren't used to throngs of people milling around our yard. Small wonder the pointers were agitated.

My feet flew across the grass, carrying me back to the carriage house. Noticing moisture on my cheeks, I stopped and wiped my eyes with the back of my hand, then looked around for Poppa. In the dim light he was difficult to pick out from the others.

The Model T loomed ominously inside the wide-open carriage door. I feared to look at it, but steeled myself and did so. And there he was—Poppa stood over a mound lying perpendicular to his car.

Thank the Lord a blanket covered the lump. I froze in place and gawked.

Uncle Rory lay underneath that blanket. A dead Uncle Rory.

Someone yelled, "Mr. MacGregor, your daughter's here."

Poppa strode out to where I stood and wrapped me in his arms.

"You shouldn't be here."

I braced myself against his concern and tenderness.

"Then why send Mr. Carson to get me? I am *not* going inside. I will stay right here. With you."

"Now, Wallie, sweetheart, listen to reason and—" Poppa began.

My tears started up again. Everything was unreal, and I was not myself. My usual composure deserted me. Too many emotions overwhelmed my ability to maintain self-control.

I had never seen a dead human before. Sure, on our ranch I saw plenty of dead animals, both wild and domesticated. I was no stranger to death, disease, or even dismemberment.

But this was different.

That lump on the ground was my uncle.

I hadn't known him long, true. Yet I felt attached to him in a way that was beyond comprehension.

Now I would never get to know him better. Would never understand him. Would never learn his secrets.

If only I'd had the opportunity, I might have helped straighten out his life, at least a little bit. Such an arrogant delusion. I recognized that I'd been developing a secret plan. I'd intended to be a good influence, and now that would never come to pass. He was beyond my reach.

A man stepped out from the shadows. Dr. Dillenbeck, our family physician, had taken care of our family for decades. Poppa must have called him.

Before Dr. Dillenbeck had a chance to speak, I started questioning him.

"What killed my uncle? Are you sure this was an accident?"

Poppa grabbed my arm.

"That's enough, Walter."

But I couldn't help myself. I could not be quiet. Just couldn't.

"Dr. Dillenbeck, did you know there was someone who wanted to kill my uncle? His life was in danger. *Did you know that?* Well, did you?"

The town sheriff and his deputy joined us.

In a booming voice, Sheriff Finch said, "What's this about a death threat? Is that correct, Judge?"

Poppa dropped my arm and faced Sheriff Finch.

"Pay no attention to my daughter. She's overexcited, even fancies herself a female Sherlock Holmes. She reads too much."

"Imagine that, a girl detective. That'll be the day."

I recognized Deputy Misak's voice. Anger sparked through me. I refused to be silenced or made fun of by anyone. Even by my own father.

I glared at the group of men surrounding me.

"The timing of this so-called accident is suspicious. Two days ago my uncle came from Galveston, escaping a man who had pledged to kill him. Tonight he is dead."

"You don't say?" Sheriff Finch looked at Poppa, who nodded glumly.

"So this odd coincidence needs to be explained." Feeling bolder, I raised my voice. "There's a definite possibility that Uncle Rory was murdered."

"Come over here, Miss Walter," Dr. Dillenbeck said.

He reached for my hand and drew me toward the motorcar.

I hesitated, but I did follow. He led me carefully around the mound lying on the dirt floor and stopped at the front of the vehicle.

"See this jack? It looks like Rory had placed it under the car so he could see the undercarriage. He was lying beneath the car, no doubt inspecting some, uh, thingamabobs he told your father needed fixing. Then the jack gave way. No one was here to help him, although perhaps no one could have. The accident didn't happen too long ago either. Less than three hours."

My stammer embarrassed me, but I had to ask.

"How do you, uh, how do you know that for sure?"

Dr. Dillenbeck looked at my father.

"Shall I answer her?"

Poppa hesitated, then nodded.

"Go ahead. She'll keep at you until you tell her."

Pointing to the body, Dr. Dillenbeck said, "The deceased is

still warm, and there is no rigor mortis yet. That leads me to conclude that the accident happened less than two or three hours ago."

Bile rose in my throat, and I almost gagged.

"I see. But this is no accident. My uncle was murdered." I whirled around to face the sheriff. "You need to find the killer. That's your job."

Dr. Dillenbeck seized my shoulders and turned me back around so he could look into my eyes.

"Surely you're mistaken. There is no mystery here; it was an accident. No doubt tragic, as any death is, but nevertheless an accident. I see no reason to suspect any kind of foul play whatsoever."

The men who had joined us at the front of the motorcar murmured positive sounds. Evidently they agreed with the doctor.

My pulse pounded in my ears. Rage threatened to boil out of me like an overfull pot on the stove. I surveyed the ring of men and tried to hold my temper. Poppa stood near the back, his head hanging down. He was upset with me and wanted me to be quiet. For once I wasn't motivated to please him.

"I am *not* some foolish female like you all seem to think I am." I looked at each man in turn. "I am quite certain that I'm correct. Uncle Rory's death deserves to be investigated fully."

"But there is nothing to *investigate*," Sheriff Finch said.

My voice was loaded with fury.

"Then why are you here?"

"Now, now, calm down, little missy." The sheriff adjusted his gun belt and thrust out his chest. "When I got word of a sudden death, I just reckoned comin' over here was the right thing to do just in case. So I checked things out, and there ain't nothin' to do. It's a danged accident—that's all it is. And that's final."

My rage finally boiled over. Instead of yelling, I responded in a low voice that I hoped emphasized how much I seethed inside.

"Don't patronize me." I hissed when I pronounced the word *patronize*.

I intended to sound like a snake, I was that angry.

Someone yelled, "Stop right now."

I recognized Poppa's voice a second before he burst out from the pack of men. When he reached my side, he was breathing hard.

"All right, gentlemen, the show's over. Why don't you all head on home? Sheriff Finch, I'll be right back, just as soon as I get my daughter into the house and settled down."

What happened next shocked me. My very own father manhandled me toward the house. However, when we reached the back steps, I couldn't take it anymore. I balked, jerked my arm away from him, and attempted to run back to the carriage house.

"Stop it, Walter."

Poppa grabbed my arms and frog-marched me up the steps and into the kitchen. Once we were inside, he released me.

Holler rushed over, ready for a loving pat or a treat. I ignored him. He whined and pranced around my feet.

"Go away, shoo. Not now."

If I hadn't loved him so much, I might have kicked out at him, so great was my distress. I rubbed one arm where Poppa had clutched me and pictured rubbing my bruised ego as well.

"Why're you treating me this way, Poppa?"

"You shouldn't behave like this."

"Like what? I have reasonable suspicions. If I were male, you'd listen to me. The sheriff would too. But instead, y'all treat me like a child."

"You're behaving like one."

My answering wail pierced the air, and Holler let out a deafening howl in empathy.

77

Poppa raised his voice over the din.

"I demand that you calm yourself."

With hands on hips, he glared at me.

I didn't respond, only stared back. My chin quivered, and even though I couldn't make it stop, I refused to cry. Evidently my silence satisfied Poppa.

"Now then," he said, "I know you're upset. Believe me, I'm mighty upset too. But I have to go back and tend to, tend to—"

He bit his lip, and his eyes filled, but he paused only briefly before continuing.

"Will you solemnly promise to stay in the house while I return to Rory's, uh"—he gulped—"his body? There are sad duties I must fulfill, so you've got to help me, Wallie. I can't be forever worrying about what you're going to do next."

Part of me took offence at his last statement, although Poppa's personal torment registered on me for the first time. The loss of his only brother must have made him feel even more wretched than I felt. Shame flooded over me, and I finally gave in to my tears.

"Sorry, Poppa, sorry." I sobbed and gulped and stuttered. "I'll stay inside. You can trust me."

He exhaled heavily, planted a kiss on my forehead, and hurried out the back door.

A chair beside the kitchen table beckoned me, so I staggered to it and plopped down. Holler followed me, and I cradled him in my arms. For a long time I rubbed his ears and crooned to him. In the end I calmed him and soothed myself as well.

Through the kitchen window I saw that three men still stood with Poppa—Sheriff Finch, Dr. Dillenbeck, and Mr. Carson. Watching them with rapt interest, I pondered the scene out back, drank a glass of water, and wondered what to do.

The house was so still, so quiet. I heard only the snuffling sounds my puppy made and an occasional sharp word or two from outside. The house was mine for a little while. All mine.

Here was a fine opportunity, one too good to forgo. My promise to Poppa was to stay inside, but I hadn't said I'd stay put in the kitchen. That line of reasoning easily squelched any guilt that struggled to bloom in my mind.

Leaving Holler buttoned up in the kitchen as an early warning system, I raced up the stairs and flew into the bedroom Uncle Rory had used. He had taken very few possessions when he'd fled Galveston. It wouldn't take long to go through them all.

My craving to learn more about him hadn't stopped with his death. I wanted to know—had to know—about his past. Besides, I wasn't merely going to *snoop*. I intended to find a valuable clue that would ultimately lead to his killer. I remained absolutely convinced that Uncle Rory's death was no accident.

Proving my gut feeling was another matter altogether.

On the bed lay several items of clothing. I tossed them quickly but found nothing of interest hidden in them. On the floor lay a second pair of boots I had never seen him wear. Feeling silly, I nonetheless turned them upside down to see if anything had been stashed inside.

Darn it. Nothing there either.

His wallet lay on the dresser. Pushing aside a growing sense of despair that I would come up emptyhanded, I took everything out of the wallet and laid the objects across the dresser. Several five-dollar bills and a handful of change comprised his walk-around money. Would he have a bank account somewhere? Why was there so little money when he had boasted about his job that paid well?

There were a few handwritten receipts for purchases made in Galveston. Names of shops he had frequented could help me discover people who had known him in his role of bootlegger— and one receipt was noteworthy. A signature by a Susanna

Weston noted my uncle's payment for a week's worth of room and board at her house. I underlined the street address, then folded that receipt in with the others and made a tidy little packet.

My party dress lacked pockets, so I stuffed the receipts down the front of my bodice.

I pulled a small cardboard folder from the wallet. Inside were three old photographs, creased and torn in a few places. They gave every indication they had been in his keeping for a good long time. I pushed torn edges back together and peered at each photograph closely.

In the first I recognized Grandfather MacGregor. He wore his conductor's uniform and stood in front of the house I lived in now. The picture made me sad. I suspected Uncle Rory had missed his family, even though he had chosen to stay away for many years.

The second photograph showed Poppa as a younger man. He posed beside a body of water and held up a string of fish. Here was a lovely slice of frozen time. My guess was this snapshot was made on a fishing trip right before Uncle Rory had fled town.

The third photograph set the nerves jangling up and down my arms. A young woman with long, pale hair posed before a house similar in style to our own. Although her face wasn't at all familiar, the house poked at my memory.

I contemplated the picture for several minutes, but I couldn't place the house. Holler barked downstairs, so Poppa must have come in. I couldn't let him catch me in Uncle Rory's bedroom.

But why should I feel guilty? I wasn't doing anything bad. Still, who needed another altercation tonight? Not me. Not poor Poppa.

In a flurry of activity, I put everything back into the wallet and made sure all the items I'd inspected were left as I had found them. As I snuck out of the bedroom, I decided to return for something I needed besides the Galveston receipts.

The folder that held and protected the photo of the girl.

CHAPTER TWELVE

I FOUND POPPA in the dining room pouring from the decanter of Kentucky sour mash—the same one he had shared with Uncle Rory. That memory gave me a pang, but I pushed down my anguish, burying it as deep as I could.

My duty was to help my father bear his grief, not to think about my own. Well, yes, and perhaps to get a sense of how he felt about the so-called accident. How could Poppa possibly believe it wasn't murder? I would have to tread carefully.

"How're you holding up, Poppa?"

The look on his face nearly broke my heart.

"As well as can be expected under the circumstances." He set the decanter down, then picked it up again and thrust it in my direction. "Would you like a drop or two of this?"

Some other time I would've been pleased at recognition of my adult status, but not on this night.

"Yes, please," I said simply.

We moved into the parlor with glasses in hand. I placed mine on a side table.

"If I don't bust Holler loose from the kitchen, he'll start

chewing the baseboards. I'll be right back."

Holler greeted me with leaps of joy, ecstatic as usual to be released from his kitchen prison. He ran straight to Poppa in the parlor, jumped onto his lap, and licked his face. Poppa gave a wan smile and fondled Holler's head.

Canine companionship can be a great comfort—that's a basic tenet of the MacGregor household. Beagles are canny dogs, and mine seemed to sense that his human family was grief-stricken.

I settled in an armchair and picked up my glass of whiskey.

"How do things stand now?"

Poppa placed Holler gently on the floor and folded his arms across his stomach. His face and general countenance suggested he had aged ten years in only one evening. I promised myself I would stop bumping up against him. I shouldn't cause him any more distress than was his to deal with already.

He cleared his throat before saying, "Sheriff Finch and Dr. Dillenbeck oversaw getting Rory's body to the morgue. There'll be formalities for me to handle, but those can wait until Monday morning. Under ordinary circumstances, I would attempt to contact his employer in Galveston, but that's not something I choose to do." He shook his head. "I ain't gonna kick that particular hornet's nest, no, sir."

Good grief. Ordinarily Poppa's grammar was impeccable. I'd never heard him speak in such a colloquial manner before. Either he was beyond exhaustion, or his brother's speech pattern had infected him. Maybe a combination of both. In any event, I suspected that his sense of safety was crumbling.

We sat in silence for a while. Holler propped his little chin on Poppa's boot and gazed dolefully up at him.

When Poppa closed his eyes, I thought at first he was going to doze off, but instead he began to speak.

"It's hard to think that only two days ago my brother appeared on our doorstep to, um, grace us with his presence.

Now he's gone, and I must accustom myself to his absence all over again. Over the years I'd gotten used to the idea that I would never see him again, so finding him and then losing him yet another time is doubly hard."

He opened his eyes and gazed at me with such sorrow that I wanted to throw my arms around him. But of course I didn't.

Poppa wouldn't appreciate such a display of unseemly emotion. While that was true in ordinary times, this was decidedly not one of those. Still, I kept my seat, just to be safe. I didn't want to be accused of being maudlin.

"Did I ever tell you the story about how Rory and I got charged by a javelina while we were out hunting?" he said.

"You didn't. Please tell me."

"We were out at the ranch and were fixin' to—"

Footsteps sounded on the front porch. When the doorbell rang, Holler barked and rushed to the door.

"Damn it all. Who in tarnation can that be at this hour?" Poppa pushed to his feet and dragged himself to the door.

"Good evening, Mr. MacGregor."

"What are you doing here, Clayton?" Poppa said.

I slumped forward, remembering Clayton's promise to swing by after the dance had ended. To say the least, his presence was not welcome. Why did he feel the need to check up on me? He was so infuriating. I was a grown woman.

Levering myself up, I joined Poppa and Clayton in the front hall, where my self-styled beau was expounding on why he'd stopped by to see me.

"And I hope you don't think I was derelict in my duty to bring your daughter safely home, but Mr. Carson forcefully insisted that he had to follow your orders. So now I'm making sure she's safe."

Clayton surveyed the quiet house, looking puzzled.

"But excuse me, sir. Nothing seems to be wrong around here, so I'm confused."

Oh, Clayton, why don't you just go away and leave me alone?

Poppa and I sighed simultaneously. I opened my mouth—to tell Clayton to come back another time and that I was too tired to talk—when Poppa intervened.

"Come into the parlor, Clayton, and we'll explain."

I trailed after them, tripping over Holler as he lunged to greet Clayton.

Once we were seated, Poppa described briefly what had happened in the carriage house. Clayton expressed his horror, and his condolences, and after that there seemed nothing else to say without descending into reams of details that Clayton didn't need to hear.

The telephone rang. Its sharp peal bruised my frayed nerves, and I leapt to answer it.

"I heard about Rory's death." Aunt Ida started without preliminaries. "Should I come over and help you with something? Let me speak to your father."

"It's Aunt Ida," I whispered to Poppa with my hand over the receiver.

He shook his head vehemently.

"He'll call you tomorrow, Aunt Ida."

I ended the conversation as quickly as was seemly and rejoined the men.

Poppa said, "What were you just saying, Clayton?"

"Well, sir," he said, "I was about to tell you about the stranger I saw when I parked out front a few minutes ago."

My head snapped up. "What did he look like?"

Clayton rubbed his chin, then said, "In the dark, all I could see was an outline. Tall man, reed thin. Wore a cowboy hat. Seemed odd he was loitering at this hour. Standing out in the open, just smoking and staring at your house. Nothing seemed wrong when I drove up, so I couldn't for the life of me figure out why you needed to leave the dance in such a rush. Much as I could tell, that guy was no one I'd ever seen before, so I thought

85

I'd ask about him."

I glanced at Poppa to see if this news had caught his interest.

In a bland tone, however, as he stared into his whiskey glass, he merely said, "Probably just a fellow waiting to see if the commotion was finished for the night."

As for me, I was suddenly pleased that Clayton had come to visit. Otherwise, I might never have known that the man from the Show Me State had returned.

A shiver ran through me when another possibility came to mind.

Perhaps the man had never left.

CHAPTER THIRTEEN

AFTER A RESTLESS sleep, I awoke earlier than usual. When I switched on the bedside lamp, the clock on the table showed it was only five. I tried to go back to sleep. I failed.

After the previous evening's astonishing events, that was no surprise.

Once my mind began to spin, it would not stop.

A tall stranger, death threats, bootleggers, Galveston, a blanket-covered mound—these grim considerations and more jostled for attention in my head. I needed to write down my thoughts, needed to put some order to them.

I took my journal out of the drawer in my bedside table. Writing down my thoughts would usually slow my teeming brain.

This time as I wrote, my thinking only picked up speed.

There'd been nothing ordinary, nothing usual about my life since Uncle Rory had returned home. Even with him gone, I suspected our home would not return to normal anytime soon. Would it ever do that? Or would my understanding of normal have to change?

I realized that I knew little about how Uncle Rory came to be crushed under a motorcar. I needed to learn the details of the event itself, gruesome as that might be.

Before I began snooping in earnest—going off half-cocked, to borrow a frequent expression of dearly departed Aunt Hazel—I needed to be sure that a determined person could have murdered my uncle and contrived to make it look like an accident.

I'd scarcely begun to ponder how to attack this problem when Holler stirred in his little basket at the foot of my bed. I rushed to pick him up, not wanting him to wake Poppa. I kept him quiet as I threw on clothes, then tiptoed down the stairs with him in my arms.

In the kitchen I listened for sounds from upstairs that indicated Poppa was awake.

Hearing none, I whispered to Holler, "We did it. Now if we're lucky, we'll have fifteen minutes to nose around before Poppa gets out of bed."

We slipped out the backdoor and once we were in the yard, I set him free. Smart puppy that he was, Holler seemed to understand me—yapping, leaping in joyous loops, and then dashing after a squirrel trying to bury a pecan. When he treed the poor critter, I rushed to retrieve Holler before he climbed up after it. His beagle heritage taught him how to do that. He was forever astonishing me at the heights he could reach in a tree. I carted him to the carriage house, where I found the large main door wedged shut with a board. I managed to open it—no easy task with a dog squirming in my arms and licking my face.

Once inside, I shut the door behind me and placed Holler on the ground. He ran immediately to sniff at a red splotch on the dirt floor beside the Model T. Seeing Uncle Rory's death spot made my stomach lurch. My imagination was often too vivid for my own sanity. I brushed my nerves away and crept closer to where Uncle Rory must have been lying when the motorcar fell on him. This was not the same place where I'd seen the blanket-covered body last night.

Someone had moved him, probably Poppa or Dr. Dillenbeck. I would ask Poppa about this later.

I studied the vehicle for several minutes, trying to work out what had happened. I was so focused that I didn't hear the door open. When Poppa asked what I was doing, I jumped sky-high.

"Golly, you scared me." My heart raced triple time, and I clutched my neck. "I'm just, just trying to—"

His tone was dry, but I heard no disapproval in his voice.

"You're trying to figure out what happened here last night."

What a relief. Slowly my heart returned to its usual number of beats per minute.

"Have you reached a conclusion?" he asked.

I couldn't decide if he was teasing me or being sincere—or perhaps snide. I chose to answer seriously.

"All right, here's what I think. I saw the tire and patching material over there." I pointed near the right front side of the car. "Uncle Rory used the screw jack to prop up the car so he could take off the tire. So far, so good. Then he must have decided to go under the car for some reason. The screw jack gave way, and the car fell on him."

I kicked at the screw jack that lay on its side, useless.

"Is that about right?"

"You're correct, as far as you went." Poppa's lips actually turned up for a second before they pressed down again in a grim line. "After supper last night, Rory asked if he could work on the car, and I agreed. The time got away from me, and when I realized it was dark outside, I came out to see what was going on. That's when I found him here, with his upper body underneath the car, with the full weight of it on top of him. All twelve hundred pounds."

He coughed into his hand, struggling for composure.

"Did you move him?"

Poppa coughed again.

"When I found him lying there, I tried, but the Model T was too heavy for me. Once Dr. Dillenbeck got here, together we lifted the auto. We already knew that Rory was, was...hopeless."

"But why was he under the car? Fixing a tire doesn't require that."

Poppa squatted on his heels and pointed.

"See this wrench and empty container? Looks like he was changing the oil while the car was up on the jack. He probably was on his back, loosening the drain plug, ready to drain the oil from the oil pan into that empty container. That's when the screw jack gave way. The Model T fell on him, and he never had a chance."

He pushed himself to a standing position, sighing.

"I hope he went quick. I don't want to think that he suffered a long time." He passed a hand over his eyes and grimaced. "And there I was, in the house reading about my upcoming court cases while he lay dying."

Together we contemplated the front of the motorcar in silence.

Finally I spoke.

"So someone could have crept in here and dislodged the screw jack, couldn't they? It sounds entirely possible to me."

In the distance I heard a neighbor's dog bark. My head jerked around to Poppa.

"Wait, Poppa. Did our dogs make a ruckus last night—you know, when you were in the house and Uncle Rory was out here?"

He shut his eyes, furrowed his brow.

"Can't be sure. Last night is a blur. It's possible the dogs barked, but that's not unusual. So even if they did, they wouldn't necessarily have caught my attention. Nor would their disquiet necessarily have been caused by a prowler."

He placed a hand on my arm. His shoulders sagged, and he shook his head sadly.

"You won't let this go, will you?"

"I'm sorry, Poppa, but none of this feels right to me."

"Of course it doesn't. This is an unnecessary tragedy, but that doesn't mean it was murder."

Holler whined. I turned and saw him sticking his snout into a corner past the front of the Model T. I had forgotten about him as I'd focused all my attention on the car and the calamity— I was loathe to call it an accident at this point.

Holler had something in his mouth and was gumming it.

"Hey, what have you got? Give me that."

I took the thing out of his mouth.

"Look at this, Poppa. Just look."

I thrust the cigarette toward him.

"A cigarette. How unremarkable."

"But that's just the point. It *is* remarkable. No one smokes in our house. Not even Uncle Rory with all his, hmm...vices. I remember you two talked about that, how you got sick when your dad demanded you both had to smoke too many cigarettes as a punishment."

I waited to see if Poppa would say anything.

When he didn't, I said, "So who came into the carriage house last night? Did you see anyone smoke? You were the first one here. I bet you shut the door when you went into the house to call Dr. Dillenbeck, didn't you?"

Poppa looked at me with a steady gaze.

"May I see that please?" he said.

When I handed him the cigarette, he studied it, unblinking, for a long time, turning it side to side. "This hasn't been out here long. It's not dirty enough."

"It's a clue, Poppa. A clue."

I felt so triumphant, I was crowing.

"If someone presented this as evidence in my courtroom, I wouldn't think it was significant. There are too many ways this cigarette butt could have gotten in here."

"I didn't say it was *evidence*. It's suggestive. It's a *clue*." I crossed my arms over my chest and glared at him. "And what about the strange man from Missouri I talked to Friday morning—probably the same guy Clayton noticed hanging around last night? Both of us saw him smoking. That's interesting—even suggestive—don't you think? You should tell Sheriff Finch about the stranger that Clayton and I saw at different times. You should call the sheriff right now."

I waited for Poppa to answer, and his continued silence infuriated me.

"Isn't Uncle Rory's death worth investigating? Your only brother, for Pete's sake."

CHAPTER FOURTEEN

PERHAPS I GOT carried away. Certainly Poppa thought so.

He turned on his heel and marched out of the carriage house. Holler rushed to follow him, but Poppa closed the door with a loud bang.

Holler jumped back and whimpered. He didn't like being shut inside.

"Yes, I know, boy. I irritated him. I took a cheap shot and had better apologize."

But before I left the carriage house, I picked up the cigarette butt where Poppa had left it, wrapped it in my handkerchief, and placed it carefully in my pocket.

After we tramped into the house, Holler and I, we found Athalia in the kitchen fixing one of her usual hearty breakfasts. That at least was normal. And *that* was a comfort. Without speaking, she wrapped her arms around me and squeezed.

"You heard?"

Of course she had. Half the town had probably badgered her for details on her walk to the house.

"I'm so sorry, Miss Walter. Such an evil, bad thing." She

stepped back. "You want to talk some about it?"

"Later. I need to see Poppa."

"In the dining room. Told him eggs be about ready."

Filled with contrition, I slithered into the dining room and sat in my accustomed place, kitty-corner to Poppa.

"I'm sorry. I didn't mean to upset you."

He looked at me with sorrow in his gaze.

"I'm not upset. You disappointed me by saying something a well-mannered young woman would never say."

His words were a punch to my mid-section, but I felt them in my heart and stifled a gasp. Never disappointing him was one of my main goals in life.

Hanging my head, I mumbled again.

"I'm so sorry."

Athalia bustled in with platters of food.

As she placed them on the table, she said, "Y'all eat hearty. You need strength to get through today. Reckon folks'll come visit."

Poppa groaned.

"I suppose they will." He helped himself to scrambled eggs and passed the platter to me. "Thank you, Athalia. Your food will fix us up if anything can."

We ate in silence until the first of our visitors arrived.

Bang. Bang. Bang.

I rose to my feet.

"Aunt Ida is up early today. I'll get the door."

The grandfather clock in the hall chimed eight when I ushered her into the dining room. She took off her ever-present white gloves and seated herself opposite me at the table. Peering over her spectacles, she eyed Poppa and then me.

"I'm glad to see neither of you seems too much the worse for wear. I was sorry to hear the news of your brother's death, Walter. Can you please bring me up to date on the events of last night and the funeral arrangements?"

Poppa began his sad litany of events and then dutifully answered all Aunt Ida's questions. Her grilling—for grilling him she surely did—left nothing else to ask. My attention stayed focused on Poppa's words because I wanted to ensure that his story stayed consistent. I was almost disappointed that what he had told me tallied with what he told her.

If there had been any wiggle room, I would have exploited it, trying to dig up more information.

Poppa must have satisfied my aunt's curiosity, because after two cups of Athalia's excellent coffee and thirty minutes of constant conversation, she stood.

"I'll help with the funeral if you wish me to do so; just let me know what I can do. But now I must leave to prepare for church." She cocked her head at me. "I presume you will stay here to receive people who wish to express their condolences?"

My heavens, attending church was the farthest thing from my mind.

"Yes, ma'am. I can't leave Poppa alone to face everyone."

When she and I were saying our goodbyes on the front porch, two motorcars stopped in front of our house. The procession of visitors had begun.

For an interminable stretch of time, Poppa and I received both the sincere and the curious. Some of our friends and neighbors appeared genuine in their condolences while others were downright intrusive in their questioning. I was amazed at how quickly so many people heard about Uncle Rory's death. Good grief, he had only arrived in Gunmetal two days before. The grapevine was working overtime.

Right before eleven o'clock, the last family of visitors departed, babbling about their need to leave for church services. When the house emptied, I collapsed on the sofa in the parlor and was about to catch my breath when the telephone rang. I punched the cushioned seat and groaned. This Sunday was proving to be a long and crowded one.

Athalia answered the telephone, then called out, "Mister Dewey for you, Miss Walter."

My immediate response was to slump down and wish to stay huddled on the lovely, velvety sofa for hours and hours. But duty and manners called, and I dragged myself to the phone in the hallway. I even smiled as I said hello, trying to infuse my words with a modicum of cheer. Or at the least, politeness.

"How are you holding up?" Dewey asked.

His concern for my feelings pleased me. Here was someone who didn't immediately launch into an inquisition about the deadly event. What a blessed novelty.

"We've had quite a shock," I said. "My uncle wasn't here long, and I was just getting to know him. Actually, Dewey, your conversation with him yesterday showed a side of his character that offset some of his peculiarities."

Dewey hummed a low, happy sound in my ear.

"I'm sorry for your loss, Wallie. I enjoyed talking to him and was surprised at how much he knew about world affairs. Now, is there anything I can do for you and your father? I can come over to keep you company and help you receive visitors, or if you'd rather, I'll take you for a drive once your father releases you from family duties. You just say the word, and I'll do whatever you think is useful."

Dewey's thoughtfulness surprised me. He continued to show more depth than I'd thought possible for him. Remembering Uncle Rory's praise for him caused me to sniffle.

"Don't cry, darling Wallie."

I straightened my shoulders and took a deep breath.

"I'm bearing up, Dewey, and thank you for your kind offer of help. Let me see how the afternoon goes. Earlier the house was full of people here to pay their respects. I expect once church concludes and families have had their Sunday suppers, then more visitors will descend on us. Maybe toward the late afternoon a drive would be restful."

"Let's say I'll drop by around four, then. How's that?"

We agreed, and when I hung up the receiver, I realized that I too was humming. I looked up to see Athalia watching me.

"Hmm. So it be like that, then."

She returned to the kitchen singing one of her more joyful gospel songs. I think it was "Go Tell It on the Mountain."

The first visitor of the afternoon was Mrs. Carson from next door.

"I skipped church this morning so I could bake something for you and your father." Still standing on the front porch, she thrust a chocolate sheet cake toward me. "No, I won't come in. I've seen all the visitors you've already had. I just wanted to help."

Dumbfounded, I stared at her as she skittered down the front steps. A memory bubbled up from my childhood. Back then, my friends and I had often wondered about the quiet Mr. Carson. If he had been more forthcoming, we could have asked him questions about his famous grandfather, Kit Carson. We all wanted to know how many Indians he had killed during his exploits. According to our textbooks, he went after "evil redskins" with great zeal. Yet none of us dared ask him or go near his house since both he and Mrs. Carson were fanatic about their privacy.

Still, one boy said he'd peeked in their windows once when they weren't home. The boy swore he'd seen Indian scalps hanging from a bookcase. I said that was nonsense. The boy said, "Prove it," and so I set out to do that.

I chose a dark and rainy Saturday afternoon to slip next door. My target was a screened-in porch attached to the back of the Carsons' house. When I thought the coast was clear—no one inside—I entered that porch and peered in the kitchen window. Despite all the precautions I took to spy safely, my luck was bad that day.

The window I chose was located over the kitchen sink. I

looked in, and Mrs. Carson looked right back out at me. She shrieked. I shrieked and ran. She charged out of her house and caught me halfway across her yard, close to landing on my own property.

I couldn't recall what she yelled at me. Her fiery words were lost to time; her combative demand to stay off her land stuck. I never returned.

That had been my only encounter with her until Holler entered my life in recent months. My new puppy started to wander into her yard. Whenever that happened, she admonished me. Given our few encounters, the cake Mrs. Carson baked and delivered to my hands seemed like a peace offering. Her kindness surprised and pleased me.

I clutched the cake and marveled at what an odd woman Mrs. Carson was. As I watched, she followed the sidewalks to her own house, and her feet never did touch our lawn. My gaze stayed glued to her until she disappeared inside her house. At least she followed her own rules since she insisted everyone stay off her land. As far as I could recall, she had never set foot on our porch before.

Behind me, Holler uttered a low growl. Placing the cake on a hall table, I bent low to pat his head.

"Don't worry. For once she wasn't scolding you."

In the kitchen I found Athalia preparing a lunch of cold fried chicken for Poppa and me. We knew there would be no time for a big Sunday meal.

I put the cake on the kitchen table.

"Mrs. Carson brought this."

Athalia looked at it and sniffed. "No need for that. I take care of y'all just fine."

"Of course you do. She was only being neighborly. Say, what do you know about her and her husband? They're both so reserved and quiet. They don't seem at all happy. The Carsons have been our neighbors ever since I can remember. Seems odd I know nothing about them."

Drying her hands on her apron, Athalia considered my question.

"I hear tell she lost all her babies. That's hard on a lady, sure enough."

She returned to filling a plate with chicken pieces.

I was musing on the tragedies in some folks' lives when Aunt Ida announced her return with her customary *bang, bang, bang*.

When I opened the front door, she sailed right in.

"Just dropping by for a bite of lunch, and I want to discuss a trip we can make together."

"Really?"

Road trips were the cat's pajamas and all too rare. I swear my ears quivered in anticipation.

Aunt Ida stripped off her gloves, then turned to me.

"My cousin Lucy in Houston needs my help caring for her ailing husband. If I leave after Rory's funeral, you can join me on the drive over. It'll do you good to get away."

Curses. How could I leave at such a bad time?

"But Poppa needs me."

She rubbed her hands together briskly.

"Not to worry. Your grieving father has an important court case to keep him busy. So what do you think of my plan?"

What did I think about going to Houston? My heart trilled a resounding yes. After all, Houston was only a short train ride from Galveston, and I had lots to investigate in that sinful port city.

CHAPTER FIFTEEN

THE NEXT FEW days involved a blur of mind-numbing activity. Countless friends stopped by to offer condolences and inquire about Uncle Rory's death. While Poppa and Aunt Ida tended to funeral matters, I kept our household running steadily despite the steady flow of visitors—with an enormous assist from Athalia and her luscious baked goods.

Even Holler helped entertain the guests, not that I wanted his assistance. He just couldn't help himself.

When visitors heard him whine from the kitchen, they'd invariably say, "Do let him out. We love dogs."

And then, once liberated, that rascally pup would gallop into the parlor and beg for cookies.

On Wednesday morning our minister, Reverend Smoot, performed the funeral service, and Uncle Rory's body was interred in the MacGregor family plot later that day. Few people attended. Cousins Hank and Doug drove over from Cuero, but Poppa had discouraged other kin, far-flung across Texas, from journeying to Gunmetal for the service.

At the cemetery, I stood beside Poppa as he contemplated

his brother's grave. My father had been unusually quiet since the death. I had tried to bring him out of himself—and failed miserably. He refused to discuss everyday matters, skipped meals, and ignored Holler—and the rest of us too, for that matter.

Now Aunt Ida lowered her head to whisper in my ear.

"Let him be. A man should be allowed to mourn in his own way."

I nodded and walked away from the gravesite and back to Poppa's new car. Just the day before he had traded in his old motorcar for a new one. Also a Ford Model T, the new one had four doors instead of two. That, of course, was not the reason Poppa had made the change. I myself had no desire to see the ominous death vehicle ever again.

Aunt Ida joined me in the roomier interior. We waited a long time for Poppa to join us.

She sat in the front passenger seat. From my place in the back, I leaned forward and tapped her shoulder.

"Are you absolutely certain I shouldn't stay home? Somehow it feels wrong to go gallivanting off to Houston. Look at Poppa." I pointed out my open window toward the grave. "He seems so forlorn."

Guilt lay on my shoulders like a shroud.

"Your concern does you credit, Walter," she said, "but your father needs to settle his feelings about his brother by himself. I doubt there's much you can do to help him. In fact, he may prefer to be alone. His big case starts next week. Didn't I tell you it'll provide a good diversion?"

"I hope you're right."

Hope and guilt warred in me.

At the crunch of footsteps, I looked up to see Poppa slogging up to us. His sad expression shattered my heart into little pieces.

The mood during the drive back from the cemetery was

somber, and we spoke little. Poppa dropped Aunt Ida off at her home, and when we reached our house, he retired immediately to his study. Athalia had made sandwiches, and I plodded upstairs to my bedroom with one on my plate. Holler came with me, and what a lucky dog he was. He got more leftover bits than usual because I was too distressed to do the sandwich justice.

Later that evening I sat at my writing desk, bringing my journal entries up to date. I wrote down all the events that had taken place after Uncle Rory's passing, the dealings I'd had with different people, and the emotions I'd felt. As I reviewed those jottings, I realized that I'd gained no new insights into possible foul play. Even though I was no less curious than I had been, I'd been too overwhelmed with taking care of other people's needs to look after my own wants.

Well, horse feathers. I decided to make up for lost time, silently pledging to begin the very next day. Then the day after that I would escape Gunmetal with Aunt Ida. Usually during my visits to Houston I called on other relatives. Not this time, though.

Although I'd planned to quiz relatives about Uncle Rory's past and then finagle a way to take the interurban down to Galveston, that plan wasn't workable. With time running short, I simply had to shift my focus from family duties to stealthy sleuthing. My itch to explore my uncle's old haunts simply had to be scratched.

The receipts of purchases Uncle Rory made in Galveston lay in my desk drawer, next to the cigarette butt Holler had discovered. I took out the receipts and read through the clutch of them, probably for the tenth time.

On a clean sheet of paper I wrote down the names of the stores where the purchases were made. Those included a dry goods store called Haberlein's, a barber shop on Mechanics Street, and something called the Chop Suey Club located on Twenty-First Street. There were three receipts from the club, and those raised my curiosity most. Not that I suspected the place engaged in anything illegal, but rather I hoped the club and other businesses could connect me with folks who had known my uncle.

Perhaps they could tell me more about his habits, even about his friends and foes.

Perhaps one of my relatives in Houston would recognize some of those places. If not, I could consult the telephone directory for Galveston. There was a large one for Houston, and although Gunmetal was too small to have its own directory, I figured that Galveston would since it was twenty times larger than my hometown.

Even though I'd learned nothing new about Uncle Rory in the last few days, there was actually another area where fresh perceptions had bloomed. Dewey Brandon had stepped forth as a stalwart and kind supporter of me and my family.

How had I missed his shining qualities before? He was dependable, intelligent, and devoted to me. In truth I'd always recognized his devotion but had cavalierly dismissed it. Now I conceded how wrong I'd been to dismiss Dewey's affection so quickly.

During the last few dreary days, even Poppa had taken to perking up whenever Dewey appeared. He helped take care of guests and ran whatever errands needed doing. I gazed out my bedroom window, recalling one particular incident.

Tuesday evening, when Dewey had gone out to feed the hunting dogs in the backyard, Poppa watched him leave with a slight smile on his lips.

"That is one fine young man," he said.

To my absolute surprise, I had to agree.

Athalia, handing Poppa a plate of his favorite pecan pralines, took the opportunity to add her own two cents' worth.

"Yes, sir, Mister Walter. That Dewey Brandon be one perfect gentleman." She left singing the words to "I'm Just Wild about Harry," but substituting the name Dewey.

I couldn't help but smile.

And why hadn't I noticed before that Athalia was entirely in Dewey's corner? Now I realized she always burst into song whenever she knew he was coming to visit.

In marked contrast, Clayton had been a perfectly useless pest. He arrived with condolences on Sunday afternoon but hadn't been able to sit still long before he invited everyone out front to admire his father's new Cadillac. When some of the male visitors accepted his offer, I was relieved to hear him take his leave.

As Clayton had walked out of the parlor, Holler nipped at his ankle. Clayton pushed my puppy away with his foot. Holler wasn't hurt, but his feelings must have been. He yapped and slunk over to me, cowering behind my legs.

Clayton halted midstep, sneering down at Holler.

"Dogs don't belong in the house. Why isn't he outside with the others?"

Yes, I was glad to see the back of Clayton, and his words sealed his fate. If there'd been any doubt in my mind about him before, it vanished in that instant. I had picked up Holler and carried him into the kitchen for a nibble, convinced that he needed cheering up.

Now I closed my journal and replaced it in the drawer. The hour had grown late, nearly midnight, and I was weary. I picked up a new book borrowed from our town's Carnegie Library and snuggled into bed with it. *The Mysterious Affair at Styles* by Agatha Christie had been recommended by Miss Bolger, the librarian. Knowing I relished the stories of Arthur Conan Doyle, Miss Bolger said I'd enjoy Christie's new mystery. It was an ingenious tale of a Belgian police officer who became a famous detective in London. When I asked how he ended up in England, she explained he had moved there after the German invasion of his country during the Great War.

Miss Bolger had laughed and said, "To be sure, Hercule Poirot is a very odd character, notable for his egg-shaped head and magnificent moustache."

Well, Monsieur Poirot would have a hard time living up to my great esteem for Sherlock Holmes, he of the ever-present pipe. Whether or not Sherlock himself had a moustache, I couldn't recall.

After reading through the first twenty pages of the new mystery, however, I saw that the little Belgian just might have staying power.

Early on Friday morning, Aunt Ida swung by to pick me up for our journey to Houston. Poppa and Athalia stood on the front porch and watched us pull away from the curb in my aunt's two-month-old Buick.

"We're on our way." Aunt Ida's voice held uncharacteristic gaiety. "Just one hundred thirty more miles to go."

I patted the Thermos filled by Athalia with coffee for our trip.

"This should come in handy. Plus all the sandwiches and cookies we have in the hamper in back."

Once we hit the open road, I started daydreaming of Galveston. Although I'd visited Houston once or twice a year for what seemed like forever, Galveston was a different proposition. I'd been there only one time, when I was eight. All I remembered was the construction of a massive seawall along its sandy beaches. Poppa had been dismayed at the mess, and we had never returned for a holiday.

"Aunt Ida, what do you know about Galveston?"

"Why are you asking about it?" she said.

Oh dear. Should I confess that I planned a side trip to Galveston? What if Aunt Ida didn't want me to go? She was sure to smash my plan to smithereens. I decided to fudge my story— just a little bit, that was all.

"I only went to Galveston once," I said, "but I was young

and don't remember much. I thought about Galveston since it's so close to Houston. I know Houston, but not Galveston."

Aunt Ida took her gloved right hand off the steering wheel and rubbed her forehead.

"Such a shame what happened to Galveston. I remember the town back before the great storm—back when it was the most exciting, prosperous place in all of Texas. Then the hurricane came and almost wiped it off the map. The city leaders are trying to bring the town back, but they haven't made much headway yet." She shook her head. "Such a shame, really a shame."

"When was the storm? I know it was huge and tragic but not much else."

"The hurricane hit in September of 1900. They say eight thousand people died, and thirty thousand were left homeless."

"My heavens."

"The storm swept across the whole island where Galveston is located. Most buildings were destroyed, and vegetation died because of being overrun with salty seawater. My friend Amanda was staying at the Hotel Galvez during the hurricane."

"What happened to your friend?"

At first, Aunt Ida didn't answer, and when she did finally speak, her voice was low.

"Amanda died in the storm, but that wasn't known for weeks. She was declared missing. The island's communications were cut off from the mainland—all telephone lines were down. Later we heard that dead bodies were stacked in layers and hauled out to sea, but those corpses washed back up on shore. Amanda's was among them."

I shuddered.

"How awful. I'm so sorry."

Aunt Ida cleared her throat.

"After the bodies washed back to shore, the city began to burn bodies instead. The fires went on for weeks and weeks."

I made no reply. What else was there to say?

We motored in silence for miles, past grazing cattle and fields of cotton. One time the motorcar hit a deep rut, jostling us so hard that our heads flopped. Aunt Ida uttered something that sounded suspiciously like a swear word, but I figured I must have imagined it.

Still, despite plenty of distractions, I couldn't stop thinking about Galveston.

"So," I said to Aunt Ida, "I reckon you've been back to Galveston since the storm, right?"

Aunt Ida looked sideways at me and nodded.

"What's it like now?"

She snorted.

"It certainly isn't the Wall Street of the South any longer. That's what the *Houston Post* used to call Galveston. These days local businesses struggle to survive, and Houston has taken the shipping business that used to go through Galveston."

We hit another bump, and our heads rolled.

I laughed.

"Whew. This is fun, isn't it?"

"You bet," Aunt Ida said. "Hope we don't have a blowout. That would delay us for hours. In a pinch, I can change a tire, but I don't want to in my good clothes. And I especially don't want to ruin these new driving gloves." She waggled her leather-clad fingers at me.

I thought about commenting on her great love for gloves, but I feared Aunt Ida would think I was making fun of her.

Instead I said, "Our pioneer foremothers would be proud of us, taking this trip by ourselves."

"Speaking of pioneers," she said, "that reminds me of immigrants. Did you know that Galveston is also called the Ellis Island of the West?"

"Really? Why's that?"

With scorn dripping in every word, she said, "*What* did

they teach you in school?"

Aunt Ida had taught high school for many years. No wonder she was up-to-date on the hurricane that devastated Galveston. She must adore details like that.

"Ever since the War Between the States ended," she said, "thousands upon thousands of people from Europe have come to America through the port of Galveston. At first it was mostly Germans and Moravians, and then many Jews flooded in from the Russian Empire. In the last decade it's been Italians. Now I hear tell it's these Italians who are heavily involved in the bootlegging run out of Galveston."

She turned her head and gave me a hard look.

"Speaking of bootlegging—"

"Yes?"

"Are you hoping to get down to Galveston while you're in Houston?"

"Umm, well. I'd like to."

"I bet you want to find out more about your uncle's life. Come on now. Fess up, or I will make sure we head right back to Gunmetal before you have a chance to nose around."

CHAPTER SIXTEEN

HOW SHOULD I answer Aunt Ida's question? What were the odds she would approve of my traveling to Galveston from Houston—even if only for a day?

There'd been times in the past few days when she'd stated surprisingly progressive opinions. She was nosy, just like me, so perhaps she'd also like to discover what Uncle Rory had been up to in Galveston.

Telling her the truth held a downside, of course. She might put her foot down, hard, then telephone Poppa and send me back to him fast.

So...enough dithering. Mentally I dusted off my hands. As Aunt Hazel had always advised when she sensed I was being timid—nothing ventured, nothing gained.

I said, "You're perceptive, Aunt Ida." A little flattery never hurt to sweeten the way out of an argument. "I'm dying to go to Galveston to try to find anything that relates to Uncle Rory's death. By the way, I think it was murder, not an accident."

She tossed a grin my way.

"I guessed as much, especially after your father told me—even though you didn't—about your wild theory that someone killed Rory."

A flash of lightning went off in my head.

"Is that why you asked me along on this trip? Were you trying to *facilitate* my getting to Galveston?"

I could scarcely breathe as I waited for her answer.

In a confident tone she said, "Might could be, my dear. Might could be."

Then another thought hit me. Good lord, was it possible that she wanted to accompany me to Galveston?

So I asked her.

"You're so headstrong," she said. "I was afraid you'd sneak off to Galveston all by yourself. That sounds reckless—possibly dangerous. I know the place, and you don't." She shared a self-satisfied smirk and puffed out her chest. "So I concluded I was ready for a little adventure, and I *will* keep you out of trouble. You may be assured of that."

Surprised by the wave of relief washing over me, I blurted out, "Sounds like a useful instinct to me."

Maybe I had fooled myself into thinking I could venture into Galveston alone.

During the next little while, until we made a rest stop about halfway to Houston—around Wallis—I recounted my conversations with Uncle Rory about his past. I also described the incidents that led me to believe that he'd been murdered.

"What sticks in my mind is how nervous Uncle Rory was when he landed on our front porch eight days ago. When I opened the door to find him standing there, he was so agitated and in a real hurry to get inside. He kept looking back at the street, as if afraid someone had followed him. He was scared, Aunt Ida. Really scared."

She nodded thoughtfully.

"I see."

"He did settle down after that, once Poppa said he could stay at our house." I swallowed the lump that arose in my throat. "Uncle Rory seemed to feel safe with us. Alas, he was mistaken. He wasn't safe at all."

Tears welled in my eyes, and I blinked them back.

"And you say the sheriff refused to take your ideas seriously?"

"Sheriff Finch dismissed everything I had to say. I was made fun of—even played for laughs in front of a group of men."

Aunt Ida's face twisted into a scowl.

"I'm not surprised, but I am disgusted. Many's the time men have laughed at my views. Then later some *man* said the same thing and he was taken seriously."

She tossed her head and snorted.

"Believe me, Walter, you must get used to that kind of treatment. Keep leading your life the way you see fit. A long time will pass before most men even *begin* to think women can make serious contributions to any areas other than rearing children, cooking meals, and keeping house."

"But now we have the right to vote, so I bet progress for women will speed up."

"Oh my dear, I hope you're right, but mark my words—it won't be so easy."

Surely Aunt Ida would prove to be wrong in the years ahead. Civilized human beings would realize how much women could offer society in so many fields. Not wanting to contradict her, I turned my head away—hiding my proud smile and watching the scenery slide by.

More and more miles piled up until, up ahead, tall white silos appeared. These held the substance that gave the company town of Sugar Land its name. Aunt Ida directed the Buick down a road that paralleled a railroad line, and we followed it into the town.

At a stop sign across from a dry goods store, she slowed the automobile.

"Remember what I told you about immigration funneling through Galveston? Isaac Kempner owns all this, and his parents were Jewish immigrants from Poland and Germany. The land was part of a sugar cane plantation worked with slave labor before the Civil War. Kempner bought it all twenty years ago and named it Imperial Sugar."

I pointed at the sugar stacks.

"This belongs to one man?"

"Kempner's family owns it. He made great improvements and runs one of the few company towns in America that's actually good for its workers."

"You surprise me. Have you been reading socialist tracts in secret at home?"

Aunt Ida chuckled and revved the vehicle's engine as we moved along the street lined with prosperous stores.

"Merely trying to further your education, Wallie. If you like travel, you might as well use it to broaden your horizons and learn something in the process."

"I hope to travel more and meet interesting people—someone from Germany or Poland, or maybe even a Jewish man like Mr. Kempner. Talking to foreigners sounds exotic to me. I know second-generation Germans, but somehow they don't seem exotic. They just talk kind of funny."

Peals of laughter filled the car.

"My dear, you must get out more. Who knows—perhaps Galveston will help open your eyes."

"Then here's to Galveston and captivating experiences."

Soon we left the orderly town behind, and the road noise increased.

"We're now only twenty miles from our destination," Aunt Ida said. "It's the worst part of the journey from Gunmetal to Houston."

"I remember this stretch of road from my trips with

Poppa." I rotated my shoulders to get the kinks out. "Riding over all these crushed shells and the noise they make get on my nerves."

For the next hour the Buick rocked and swayed, the sounds of crunching shells incessant. The paved streets of Houston were a relief.

My aunt's cousin, Lucy, lived in Houston Heights. It wasn't an area of the city I'd visited. I was curious about the name since the whole city was on flat land as far as the eye could see.

We drove north of downtown to Heights Boulevard. A street car line ran down the esplanade, and I marveled at the stately homes we passed on either side. Then we turned right onto Eighteenth Street, and a block later, at the Harvard intersection, we arrived at Cousin Lucy's house. It was a three-story Queen Anne with elaborate gingerbread decorations, several gables, and even a turret.

Aunt Ida stopped the car at the curb and honked the horn.

A white-haired woman in a wicker chair on the porch waved at us, then she rose, straightened her old-fashioned, ankle-length skirt, and moved at a cautious pace down the steps.

"Ida, darling," she warbled, "here at last."

They exchanged quick pecks on their cheeks. Next Lucy grabbed my hands in hers and swung them.

"And you must be Miss Walter. My gracious, you are a tall young lady."

She had to tilt her head back to look me in the eye. She herself was so tiny that I judged she didn't reach a height of five feet. This woman and I were strangers. Lucy was a cousin on Aunt Ida's father's side, and I knew only her mother's family.

In no time at all, her maid whisked our belongings into the house, and we were ensconced in a mauve-painted parlor, one that sported every frill and frippery known to mankind—lavender ceramic roses, pink fans with feathers and lace, and a fringed purple shawl draped over a grand piano. How could Poppa and I possibly live another week without buying a few such objects? Our home was desperately stark by comparison.

While the cousins exchanged their news, we drank coffee from delicate china cups and nibbled on dainty cookies. Cousin Lucy explained that her husband lay in bed upstairs, that she checked on him at least once an hour, and that she was delighted we had come to keep her company.

"The doctor saw Howard this morning and deems him fair to middlin'. That's an improvement, I assure you." She spoke with her hands pressed together primly in her lap. "Yet I am oh so thankful you two have come."

She turned to me.

"And now, as for you, young lady, what would you like to do while you're here? I'm afraid our company will bore you. Ida and I do love to reminisce about our girlhood days." She clapped her hands in delight, as a young child might. "But I have an idea. The Heights has a new library, just opened last year. Do you like to read?"

Without letting me reply, she started up again.

"The library is in a temporary location, but you can walk there, only two blocks. When it's completed, the new facility *will* be splendid. Do come for another visit when it opens."

"Thank you, ma'am, and—"

"Wallie loves to read," Aunt Ida said, "and if your new library has British mysteries, she can hole up there for hours on end."

I beamed at my aunt.

"That's a swell idea, and—"

"Don't say *swell*. You sound uncouth."

It had been days and days since Aunt Ida last admonished me, and her sharp tone brought me up short.

"Beg your pardon." I ducked my head, partly to hide my mortification and partly to hide my sudden flare of anger.

I decided to change the subject.

"Cousin Lucy, why's this part of town called the Heights? I sure don't see any hills."

She set aside her coffee cup and picked up a cookie.

"We lie some twenty feet above downtown Houston. You could say someone was clutching at straws when he named this the Heights."

Her laugh was like a tinkling bell, a joy to hear.

The maid entered the room and handed her mistress a newspaper. When Cousin Lucy held it up and scanned the headlines, she laughed again. This time the sound was less pleasant and held a hard edge.

"Have a look-see." She held the front page up to Aunt Ida. "A few days ago the Coast Guard stopped a schooner off Galveston Island and confiscated a thousand cases of liquor." She folded the newspaper and, shaking her head sadly, placed it on a table. "I don't know what's going to become of that place. Maybe Galveston will sink into the Gulf of Mexico from the weight of its own iniquities."

Aunt Ida and I exchanged glances.

"Wallie and I are hoping to spend a day in Galveston before we make our journey back home to Gunmetal."

Cousin Lucy's head jerked toward Aunt Ida.

"Why on earth would you want to go to Galveston? It's still a mess and very depressing to see."

Aunt Ida ran a hand over her hair, and I watched her take a breath so deep that her bosom moved up and down. Was that a sign of her agitation? Would she confess why we wanted to drive there?

I underestimated my aunt's self-control.

In a calm voice, she said, "I want to see how the new seawall is progressing and how much the city has rebuilt since my last visit two years ago."

"Ida, that's *not* a good idea." Cousin Lucy sounded grim. "I can tell you what it's like and save you a trip. Since your last visit, Galveston filled up with rumrunners and gamblers and, um, ladies of the evening. Prohibition has made the port area more depraved than ever. Hardly the place to take your precious niece, don't you agree?"

Aunt Ida tilted her head toward me.

"Perhaps we shouldn't go after all."

My heart sank to my very toes.

To come within striking distance of Galveston—only fifty miles away—and then not be allowed to visit? That would definitely kill me.

Even if I had to walk, I would get to Galveston.

Come what may.

CHAPTER SEVENTEEN

OUR DINNER LATER that night was interrupted by a telephone call.

The maid announced, "You have a call from a gentleman, Miss Walter."

All three of us gasped—Cousin Lucy, Aunt Ida, and I.

"This is most unusual," Lucy said.

I rose from the table and looked at her.

"Excuse me, please. I must see who this is."

I hurried into the hall and picked up the receiver. My hand was shaking. I feared that something else had happened to someone back home. What about Poppa?

"Hello. This is Walter MacGregor."

A loud voice boomed in my ear.

"Always such a shock when I hear your name like that. It's funny, actually."

My temper flared.

"Clayton. Why are you telephoning me here? My cousin was unnerved that I would get a call."

"I didn't know you were leaving town. Athalia told me you

went to Houston, and you've no idea how long it took me to dig up this number."

"Well, you shouldn't have. I don't like being pestered. I will be gone for several days. Whatever you have to say, we can talk when I get back home. I must return to the dinner table. Goodbye."

That may have been the rudest thing I'd ever allowed myself to do in my entire life, but I had had enough of Clayton. When I returned to Gunmetal, I would make it clear that his attention was no longer welcome.

For the rest of the long and tedious evening, I sought a word alone with Aunt Ida, desperate to ensure Galveston was still part of our plans. But Cousin Lucy made that impossible. She hovered around my aunt like a bothersome housefly, even dragging her upstairs to help check on her husband.

Eventually I gave up and went to bed, taking along a *Photoplay* magazine borrowed from Cousin Lucy. The cover story profiled Lillian Gish, darling of the silver screen. I learned about her preferred foods, vacation places, and pets. A picture of Miss Gish with her dog made me think of home.

Huddled in bed under the pink quilt—Cousin Lucy's preference for shades of purple and pink was obvious—I wondered how Holler was doing without me. Poppa was usually too busy to spend much time with him. I hoped that Athalia was keeping my beagle puppy with her in the kitchen. Poor Holler, now bedded down and alone for the night, must be missing his own little basket upstairs in my room. I wouldn't say I was homesick, but I did think of home with fondness.

And then there was Dewey. I smiled and slipped farther under the quilt while my toes curled in delight. What a lovely surprise he turned out to be. I wondered what he would say if I went back home and told him of my exploits in Houston—and in Galveston too, should I be lucky enough to travel there.

Ah yes, Galveston.

A scheme sprang into my head. What if I went to the library tomorrow and, instead of reading British mysteries, I thumbed through Galveston newspapers and its directory?

I could search the locations of Uncle Rory's haunts ahead of time. Once we got to Galveston, I'd lose less time seeking addresses—and no doubt running in circles—and thus be able to spend more time asking people about him. Even if Aunt Ida accompanied me, preparation was still a good idea.

At breakfast the next morning, I managed to speak to Aunt Ida alone.

However, she was so rushed that when I asked about Galveston, she merely flapped her hand and said, "Not now. We'll talk later."

Then she rushed upstairs to help Cousin Lucy nurse her ailing husband.

When I stepped out on the front porch to check the weather, I noticed heavy storm clouds looming in the south. After retrieving from my room the umbrella that I had luckily brought along, I walked the two blocks to Heights Boulevard and found the library's temporary location. After a helpful librarian pointed out a collection of materials about the great storm and its aftermath, I settled in for a slog of reading about Galveston

I wanted to burrow into the *Galveston Daily News* and devour accounts of the famous hurricane from the year of my birth. Instead, I began with November 1918. The armistice ended the Great War on the eleventh, about the time the Spanish flu epidemic hit Galveston. The worldwide disaster forced the city to shut its schools for two weeks. I temporarily forgot my primary purpose—looking for places noted in Uncle Rory's receipts—so engrossed was I in learning about Galveston's death, disease, and rebuilding.

Finally I worked my way up to issues of the current year, 1923, and found a short article about two brothers from Sicily who had bought the Chop Suey Club. I brought out my list of receipts and read my notes. Yes indeed, there it was—the Chop Suey Club. The newspaper stated that it was located on Seawall Boulevard at Twenty-First Street.

Uncle Rory had three receipts from the place, all signed by *S. Maceo*.

That sounded familiar. Going back through older newspapers, I saw small weekly advertisements for a barbershop on Mechanic Street. Its proprietors were Sam and Rosario Maceo.

I read the Galveston paper until I ran out of issues. Within those pages I found one more mention of the Maceo brothers' club. A reporter described how they had "prettied up the traditional Balinese décor" and were serving more customers than the previous owners had.

Hot diggity. The Chop Suey Club sounded like a fine restaurant. That was where I wanted to start my sleuthing.

A gentleman with a long silver beard sat near me reading the current issue of the *Houston Post*. When he laid it aside and shuffled to the library's exit, I retrieved the paper and searched for any mention of rum-running in the Galveston area. I found an article on the second page that detailed the incident that had incensed Cousin Lucy. Only a few days earlier, the Coast Guard seized a thousand cases of illegal liquor offshore from Galveston Island.

Jeepers. What if some of that liquor was destined for a small Balinese-style restaurant? The mere idea gave me a chill. Still, wouldn't it be the bees' knees if it had been?

Walking back to Cousin Lucy's house, I scarcely noticed the heat and humidity of Houston, always so much more pronounced than in Gunmetal, even in the normally mild weather of November. My head was too full of sinister possibilities to dwell on the weather.

Herschel, the cuckolded husband who had threatened to

kill Uncle Rory, might not be the only fellow who had wanted him dead. It would be too easy if Herschel did turn out to be the killer—almost boring when I thought more about it. What if my uncle had gotten crosswise with Galveston's criminal elements—with the leading bootleggers? The possibility of uncovering that connection thrilled me.

When I came to the intersection of Eighteenth Street and Harvard, with my destination straight ahead, a warm rain began to fall on me. That was when I realized I'd left my umbrella behind in the library. I hotfooted it up to Cousin Lucy's front porch and shook myself the way a wet dog does.

Once inside, I tried to slink upstairs to change my clothes before anyone noticed me.

Alas, I was unsuccessful. Aunt Ida's voice sang out from the direction of the parlor.

"Come here please."

"I'm drenched," I called out.

She sailed into the front hall, glanced at me, and recoiled in horror at the damp mess I'd become. Her mouth fell open, but no words emerged.

She finally squeezed out a few, saying, "What's on your face? Have you been down in a coal mine?"

I made my way to a hall mirror, my damp shoes squishing with each step. Dark gray streaks decorated my cheeks and forehead. I held my palms up and saw matching gray splotches there.

Without pausing to think, I blurted out the truth.

"I was reading back issues of the Galveston newspaper for hours. Didn't realize my hands were dirty."

"I *told you* we would talk about Galveston later." Aunt Ida raised her eyes to the ceiling, as if hoping for divine help. "You should go upstairs and clean up right now."

Oh mercy. Aunt Ida and her lengthy list of *should*s.

"But I found out so much today that I think—"

She pointed up the stairs.

"Go. Now."

Why did she persist in treating me like a schoolgirl? Heavens to Betsy, at twenty-three years old I was a woman. And high time I stood up for myself.

I flung my hands to my hips and squared off with Aunt Ida.

"I have to explore what Uncle Rory was up to in Galveston. The reason for his murder ties back to that place. I'm sure of it."

"But it's *not*—"

I kept talking, for the first time ever running over my aunt's words.

"And I'm *really* sure it was murder. If no one else believes that, I simply don't care. Despite Cousin Lucy's warnings, I *will* go to Galveston. She's just a nervous Nellie. You've been there before and nothing happened to you. Aunt Ida, we *can* take care of ourselves."

Her shoulders sagged, and for a second I felt a pinch of sympathy for her. It wasn't like me to talk back to her.

"All right. Let me give this some more thought."

Even though her tone was grudging, her words were the right ones—the very ones I needed to hear.

When Aunt Ida withdrew to the parlor, I took that as a sign of retreat. Why, it might even amount to something huge, like Napoleon's withdrawal from Russia.

Was that Tchaikovsky's "1812 Overture" I heard?

I dared to hope that I had won this battle.

Later that evening, Cousin Lucy showed me books on Galveston's catastrophic storm. If she thought photographs of destruction would discourage me, she was mistaken. Such drama only spurred me on.

Aunt Ida would never have made a mistake like that. She knew me too well.

"The devastation was widespread and the city became a breeding ground for sin and corruption." She paused, as if considering her declaration. "Not that it was a center of holy behavior before, but the city grew worse. Much, much worse. That's why I think it's terribly unsafe, unwise, for you two to travel there by yourselves."

Cousin Lucy's stare raked my face. When she turned to Aunt Ida—doubtless hoping to see agreement on her face—my aunt sat up straighter in her chair and visibly bristled.

"I take umbrage at that, cousin," she said. "You *know* I would never let my niece wander into a dangerous situation. I am surprised—even shocked—that you think that of me."

Hallelujah. Maybe Cousin Lucy's well-meaning advice would backfire. I knew how stubborn Aunt Ida was once someone challenged her and said she could not do something.

I waited, scarcely allowing myself to breathe, as the two older women faced off across the dining room table. After what seemed like an eternity of tension, Aunt Ida folded her napkin and placed it beside her plate.

In a voice that reminded me of the sweetest Texas Hill Country peach jam, she said, "Now that your husband's health has turned the corner, I fear Wallie and I must leave. We will depart the day after tomorrow."

I froze every muscle in my face, trying not to give any emotion away. But inside I was begging her, pleading with her, to say that we would be motoring off to Galveston.

Cousin Lucy stared at her plate, then lifted her head and spoke in an icy tone.

"And will you be driving straight back to Gunmetal from here?"

Aunt Ida's chin jutted out, reminding me of the bold bald eagles featured on American patriotic banners. "No, we will not."

And that is how I got my way.

Two days later, on Monday, Aunt Ida and I set off again in her Buick.

Destination: Galveston, Texas. Population 44,000.
Erstwhile Wall Street of the South.
Current hub of illegal booze and sin on the Gulf Coast.

CHAPTER EIGHTEEN

THE TERRAIN WE covered between Houston and Galveston looked as if Athalia had laid it out on her ironing board and pressed it flat with her trusty iron.

Rice fields stretched out, smooth and level, for endless miles on either side of the road. As we drew nearer to the Gulf of Mexico, mighty clouds scuttled across the sky.

From the driver's seat, Aunt Ida nudged my arm lightly, interrupting my thoughts.

"Do you have any idea where to go once we reach Galveston? I'd rather not spend the night unless we have to, so we need a plan."

"I have a few ideas."

Aunt Ida emitted a most ladylike snort.

"We could begin at Uncle Rory's boarding house but—"

Her head jerked in my direction.

"How do you know where he stayed?"

I tried but couldn't suppress my grin.

"I went through his belongings after his death. Receipts indicated three places where we can start our, hmm, *investigations."*

"My goodness, Walter. Oh, Walter." She shook her head. "What am I going to do with you?"

She drove in silence for a few minutes, and I let her simmer.

Eventually she said, "Although I admit you are a clever girl, your ideas—and even sometimes your behavior—are hardly what I would call proper or ladylike."

I spoke out much more boldly than I felt, and even had the temerity to giggle.

"How can I disagree with that assessment?"

"As I live and breathe, Wallie, I don't know how you turned out this way."

She pulled a face and drove on again in silence.

When Aunt Ida called me Wallie, rather than Walter, it was often a good sign. Now I hoped she was softening toward my strange predilections.

I pressed on.

"Receipts from two other places also caught my attention, but I didn't know what to make of them. That is until—lo and behold—I dug up news of those places in old copies of the Galveston newspapers in the library."

Aunt Ida merely sniffed and kept her eyes on the road. However, I fancied her right ear bent my way.

I confess that I wasn't above teasing her a little.

"Want to know what the receipts were?"

"Go ahead and tell me. I know you will anyway."

"Uncle Rory frequented a certain barbershop and also a place called the Chop Suey Club. I wrote down both their addresses."

"Anything named *club* sounds like a den of iniquity. You can chop that off your list right now, young lady."

I took a quick peek at Aunt Ida to see if she had tried to make a joke. Alas, I couldn't tell.

126

In a booming voice, she exclaimed, "I certainly hope that barbershop isn't in a shady part of town. Port cities are often quite rough. We must pull on our gloves, stand up straight, and act very proper. Most men, when faced with two women like ourselves, will behave in a mannerly fashion. And if they fail to act like gentlemen, then we shall leave at once." She twisted to look at me before returning her steely gaze to the road. "Do you understand me, Walter? Do I make myself clear?"

There she went again, calling me Walter.

"Yes, ma'am, perfectly clear."

In a flash I recognized that my most difficult task would be to stretch Aunt Ida's principles—and tolerance of my nosy instincts—as far as they could go. My job was cut out for me.

Having her along as a mature guide did have its advantages since she knew her way around Galveston Island, but whoa, Bessie! Her principles and standards boded ill, threatening to trip me up in pursuit of clues.

Angling my face away from Aunt Ida, I cast my determined gaze on the passing landscape. If Uncle Rory's killer was out there somewhere, I would find his trail. I was up to the task of sleuthing. I just knew it in my bones. All I had to do was hunker down and prove it.

A picture of Poppa alone in our large home flitted through my mind. What if he was in danger? I caught my breath and sat up a tad straighter.

Surely Poppa would be safe. If a criminal had been sent to bump off my uncle, then that task was finished. Why would anyone linger any longer in Gunmetal, risking being caught? With a smile on my face, satisfied all would be well back home, I shut my eyes.

Fifteen minutes later we drove onto a roadway that went over water and stretched as far as I could see.

"How amazing." I leaned forward trying to see farther. "This is the longest bridge I've ever seen. Why, it must go for

127

miles and miles. It takes my breath away."

"I must correct you." Aunt Ida used her stuffiest schoolmarm voice. "This is not a bridge but a causeway. It spans the two miles from the mainland across West Bay and on to Galveston Island itself."

On our left a train passed us, going the opposite direction, heading north to the mainland.

"Bridge, causeway? What does it matter?"

"Don't be ignorant. It's a matter of engineering. A causeway is constructed of tamped-down material. It's supported from underneath, unlike a bridge."

"All right, thank you. I learned something today." I looked out at the small boats that dotted the gulf waters. Pelicans flew overhead, occasionally diving down to snare their seafood dinners. Sprinkled along the piers were men with fishing poles.

Once the causeway reached the island, it turned into an avenue lined with oleanders.

Every few blocks Aunt Ida muttered something to herself, but when I asked what she said, she only said, "Nothing, dear. It's nothing. I just recall what used to be here before the storm, and it hurts me to recognize the absences."

Our outlooks were so different. She was reminiscing about a town in its heyday before the great storm of twenty-three years ago, and I was eager to rush into all parts of the city as it existed today, right this minute. Aunt Ida's emotions and desires didn't harmonize with mine. Patience was a virtue I lacked at the best of times, and this was not even one of those.

Besides, I still fumed over the way she'd berated me for being ignorant. I doubted she'd agree, but I made the suggestion anyway.

"Let's go to the barbershop first, if that's all right with you?"

"Not yet."

Her tone was so determined that my objections withered in

my throat.

"We will see the seawall first," she continued, "and drive by the Hotel Galvez. You won't remember much from your visit here as a child, so a short tour will get you oriented. Then, at that point, we'll drive by the barbershop. You said you have the address?"

"Yes, on Mechanic Street at Kempner." I slapped my forehead. "Kempner? Is the street named for——?"

"That's right. The German immigrant who came to America through Galveston and made good."

I clapped my hands.

"That's great. The street is historic. I must see it. Oh my, we have so much to do."

"Slow down and have some patience. You're not the only person who has made this trip, you know."

"Yes, ma'am."

I loathed coming to heel, but what else could I say to her after all that?

Aunt Ida turned right off Broadway, drove several blocks along Twenty-Fifth Street, and then went left along Seawall Boulevard. After two blocks she pulled to the side of the road.

"See that pier up ahead? Once upon a time, when I was young, it used to include two pavilions shaped like plump pagodas. They disappeared in the big storm. The pier was rebuilt but the pagodas weren't." She let out a big sigh. "I still mourn their absence." She sighed again, even more heavily. "Everything is fleeting, like my youth. Well, never mind. Let's get out and walk."

And so we did.

During an ordinary visit I might have been interested in the engineering feat that constructed the long, high seawall—but of course this was no ordinary visit. Turbulent emotions tossed my thoughts. I chewed on a snagged cuticle, trying to keep myself from blurting out my frustration.

How ironic. The elevated seawall was designed to keep future storms from lashing Galveston with heavy floodwaters; however, walking along it created a stormy effect on me. Seagulls flew overhead, calling to each other and swooping down to snare anything edible.

We walked closer to the pier Aunt Ida had pointed out. Long and made of wood, it jutted out into the Gulf of Mexico. Two foot-ramps led to it from the seawall. Nothing as fanciful as pagodas met my eyes, but the pier did contain several buildings of ordinary boxlike shapes.

Drawing closer, I was able to read the painted signs on the various establishments. First I noticed an ice cream parlor, and then I observed a miracle. The Chop Suey Club stood right in front of me.

My legs couldn't carry me fast enough over the walkway and onto the pier. Aunt Ida called to me, but I ignored her.

When I reached the sign, I stopped and stared at the wooden storefront. It seemed like a miracle because I hadn't even attempted to find it and yet there it was. My heart beat rapidly, but not from the short run.

Was Uncle Rory's killer inside? How could I find out?

My lapel watch told me that it was only ten o'clock in the morning, so it made sense that the club was closed. Peering through its clouded windows, I could make out only shadowy movements.

Someone was inside but so indistinct that I couldn't tell if the person was male or female. I was so intent on snooping that when Aunt Ida approached me and spoke, she startled me, and I shrieked.

"Walter MacGregor, stop it," she said. "*If* you continue to behave badly, then we will leave this island at once. You're already making me question my decision to bring you here."

"You were wrong."

I pressed my hand to my mouth in dismay. Oh dear. Not

the wisest words I had ever voiced to my aunt.

"*Excuse me?*"

I backpedaled as fast as I could.

"What I meant to say was...this doesn't look like a *den of iniquity*, does it? It appears to be an ordinary restaurant that regular people frequent. Maybe we can return when it opens. And I promise that I will behave. Truly I will."

I was not too proud to plead.

Before Aunt Ida had a chance to reply, a slim woman in an astonishingly short dress walked out through the front door.

So that was what a real flapper looked like. I could see every inch of her *knees*.

Her hair was bobbed, and a sparkling band encircled her head. She carried a small beaded purse and wore the most beautiful silk shoes I had ever seen in my life. They were a darker shade of green than her dress. Her lips were painted a bright red. She looked like she belonged at a fancy New Year's Eve dance.

Of course she noticed that I was gaping at her.

"May I help you? What do you want?"

Her speech hurt my ears, sounding odd, not at all refined or southern. She wasn't from Texas or anywhere nearby, I concluded.

Aunt Ida placed a hand on my elbow and tried to tug me away. Again I ignored her.

"May I speak with you a minute please?" I said to the stranger. "I am the niece of Rory MacGregor, and—"

"He's not here now," the flapper said, "and I don't know when he'll be back."

"I know that," I said.

"Beg your pardon?"

"He's never coming back. He can't. Rory MacGregor is dead."

The woman and Aunt Ida gasped in unison.

131

Oh, tarnation, what had I done? This, our first encounter in Galveston, wasn't going the way I had imagined that it would.

The flapper backed up a few steps, located a pillar holding up the club's porch, and clung to it for support.

"I must tell Vivian. She's gonna be very upset."

"Is she here? Will we be able to talk to her?"

Vivian was the name of Uncle Rory's last paramour. If I were lucky enough to speak with her, surely I'd make great headway on my investigation.

Aunt Ida jerked my arm again, hard.

"Come away right now, Walter. I insist."

The woman's eyes opened wide.

"Who's this Walter guy? Now he's gotta talk to Vivian too? She ain't gonna like the sound of this one little bit."

CHAPTER NINETEEN

MY UNUSUAL NAME often confused people. Most of the time I handled those situations well, explaining smoothly that I was named for my father. After that, I always answered whatever peculiar questions someone felt he or she was entitled to ask.

This incident was different.

I felt less than sure-footed. Ill at ease and thus at a disadvantage, I mumbled and stuttered. The stunning vision of femininity made me feel like an oafish fool.

The flapper stared at me, watching me flail, listening to my blathering.

"What's wrong with you?" She turned to my aunt. "Is she simple?"

Aunt Ida plunged right in, working her jaws like an upright snapping turtle.

"I will thank you to mind your manners, young woman. This is my niece, and her name is Walter MacGregor. She wishes to inquire about her recently deceased uncle, Rory MacGregor."

She stopped, seeming to realize this might indicate that she herself was also related to Rory. That was another misunderstanding she would not stand for.

She stood straighter and rushed on.

"I myself am not a MacGregor. I am from the maternal side of my niece's family."

The flapper let go of the pillar and stepped toward us. Her face lit up, and she laughed.

"You two oughta go into vaudeville. You'd make a great team."

That didn't sit right well with Aunt Ida, naturally, and she reared back and thrust out her bosom.

"Young woman, I've never even *seen* a vaudeville show let alone appeared in one. I'll thank you not to cast aspersions on our character. You've called my niece 'simple' and now you think we're suitable for risqué entertainments." To me she said, "Wallie, I have had enough. I told you the Chop Suey Club was not a suitable place to visit. We are going. Now."

"Whoa there, Nellie."

The flapper moved so close to Aunt Ida and me that I could smell her perfume—Yardley's English lavender. I had a bottle of it too since Hollywood actress Lillian Gish loved it. Since this flapper was thoroughly modern, maybe I was too—if only a little.

She flashed a smile, and her dimples appeared. Quite fetching.

"I don't mean no disrespect."

So the flapper possessed some manners, even if her knowledge of grammar was spotty.

She continued, "Me, I say vaudeville is the cat's pajamas, but if you folks here in the sticks don't, well then, that's jake with me."

She eyed me.

"Why don't you bring the lady inside? I'll fix you a cup of

Joe, and we can hash out what we need to. Anyways, I want to hear what happened to poor Rory. He was a prince of a guy. I always liked him. Woulda taken up with him myself if Vivian hadn't gotten to him first."

Oh my, we just might have hit the mother lode.

"Aunt Ida, please."

I rolled my eyes in the direction of the door leading into the establishment and nodded my head in the same direction. I almost got down on my knees and begged. I was prepared to do anything to induce my aunt to agree to entering the club and talking with this sassy female.

"My name is Glenda." She reached up to adjust her headband, then smiled prettily. "Please do come in and have a cup of coffee with me."

I stepped onto the club's porch.

"How kind of you." I turned to Aunt Ida. "Coffee will do us good, right?"

She clutched her handbag to her chest.

"Well, all right. But just for a few minutes."

Her huffy tone undercut her words. Still, she moved onto to the porch.

Glenda opened the front door and ushered us inside. My eyes struggled to adjust to the dimness until she pulled the string on a light hanging from the ceiling. That light and others like it were shaped like Chinese lanterns. They gave the place a vaguely Oriental ambience.

The room was not large but did accommodate about twenty tables with wooden chairs around them. A bar ran along one side of the room, but no bottles of liquor were displayed on it. Only cups, saucers, plates, and bowls.

"Please have a seat," Glenda said, pointing to a table. "I'll go to the kitchen and see if the coffee is ready. Lucky for you folks I've got a pot on the boil. Be right back."

Once she left, Aunt Ida looked around, making sure we

were alone, and then she unleashed her wrath. First, she plopped onto a chair and set her handbag on the floor with a loud thump. Glowering at the floor, she changed her mind, picking up her bag and placing it on her lap. I held my breath as she adjusted her skirt, making sure that her legs were properly covered. Then she let me have it.

"We will have coffee with this, this—this person, and then we shall depart. We shall leave this island and return to Gunmetal. I will give your father a complete rundown of your behavior, and then I—"

Glenda re-entered the room. I may never have been so glad to see anyone in my whole twenty-three years. She picked up a serving tray from the bar, on which she placed cups and saucers.

"How do you take your coffee?"

Her ever-present smile was bright—with those shrieking cherry-red lips—but it did seem sincere. I could have been wrong, but I failed to see why Aunt Ida had taken against this woman so bitterly.

My best guess? Aunt Ida disapproved of her modern and forward style.

"My aunt will take cream and sugar." I returned Glenda's smile. "And I like my coffee black and strong."

Glenda's smile grew wider.

"Me too."

She pulled a third chair up to our table, then fetched the tray and placed it in front of us. She left for the kitchen, returning with a tin pot from which steam was escaping. Unlike ours back home, the pot was dented and greasy. Athalia always kept ours pristine and shiny.

When Aunt Ida noticed the coffee pot, I thought she might faint. Her skin turned ashen, and she gulped visibly. She placed her hand over her cup.

"None for me, thanks."

"Are you sure? There's plenty," Glenda said. "Besides, I do

make the best coffee south of Chicago. That's my hometown, by the way."

Aunt Ida shook her head.

"Thank you, no."

No wonder I hadn't recognized Glenda's accent. I'd never known someone from Chicago before.

A quiet awkwardness fell as Glenda and I blew on our coffee. I waited for Aunt Ida to speak, but she didn't even raise her eyes. I looked at Glenda, and she smiled at me so sweetly that her dimples popped up again. I took heart.

"My uncle's death was a shock. He had returned to visit us, his family, after many years away. I was just getting to know him."

I gulped, realizing I was getting emotional. I took a deep breath before I could continue. "And then, well, then he had an accident working on my father's automobile. I decided to come here with my aunt"—I nodded her way—"to collect his personal effects."

Glenda patted my hand. "I'm so sorry, doll. Rory was such a lively guy. It's hard to think of him as gone. Is there anything I can do to help you?"

"Thank you. There just might be something. I must confess that I'm curious about his time in Galveston. He told me that he'd been working here for at least a year and mentioned Vivian. He also—"

"Did he mention her husband too? Hate to bring this up, but Rory left in such a gosh-awful hurry last week that I figured he was runnin' from him. Herschel, Viv's guy, is one huge son of a gun, even though it turned out Rory had no cause at all to be afraid of him."

What? Here was news.

Glancing at my aunt, seeing her gaze still fixed to the table top, I felt compelled to continue the conversation. Let her stay scandalized. I was on a mission and simply couldn't afford to care much about her sense of propriety.

In for a penny, in for a pound. Wasn't that the old saying?

"Uncle Rory did mention the absent husband," I said, "but he also said he wanted to return to Galveston. He told me he hadn't known that Vivian was married."

Glenda's laughter rang out through the empty room.

"She don't act like she's married, that's for darned sure. But you know what?"

Aunt Ida began to drum her fingers on the tabletop.

Glenda lowered her voice to a conspiratorial whisper. "Vivian's husband didn't stay long after Rory left town, and I can tell you why that was."

"Do you think he could have followed my uncle?"

"Golly, I never thought of that. Might could be, but I wouldn't bet money on it. Nope." She shook her bobbed curls hard. "Vivian told me he had to return to Houston, had to go back to his job. But she confided in me he had come all the way down here to tell her he was gonna divorce her. Said he had another gal back in Houston he wanted to marry."

Glenda giggled and tossed her hair. She leaned closer to me.

"I'm here to tell you our Vivian was mighty relieved to hear that from Herschel. She was crazy about your uncle, and that's a fact."

Now Aunt Ida raised her head and looked directly at Glenda.

"Are you certain that the husband wasn't after Rory?"

"Sure am. I'd swear on a stack of Bibles."

Aunt Ida's tone was dry.

"That isn't necessary."

"But hold on, Glenda," I said. "That version doesn't tally with what Uncle Rory told me. He said a pal told him that Vivian's husband was out to kill him."

"Nope, don't think so. That's not what Viv told me. Maybe

Rory left Galveston before he learned the truth about Herschel. What a damned shame that would be."

Aunt Ida sniffed. She loathed swear words.

Glenda swung her way.

"Beg pardon. I forgot my manners."

Aunt Ida nodded and folded her hands in her lap.

Glenda said, "Who was this so-called pal of Rory's, anyways? You know, the guy who said Herschel wanted to do Rory in? Maybe he's the one who had it in for Rory."

The plot wasn't just thickening. It was downright curdling.

I rubbed my forehead. All of a sudden my head hurt. My preconceptions were jumbled, and untangling them would be difficult. I needed to hear more from Glenda, but I wasn't sure what to ask.

"I've no idea who my uncle's friends were here in Galveston. The only person he mentioned by name was Vivian. Who did Rory hang around with, besides her? And what did he do in his spare time? I understand he was often on the move— making deliveries around the state."

Glenda sat back in her chair and gazed at me steadily. I had the impression she was deciding how much she could afford to tell me.

"It's all right," I said. "I know he was working for rumrunners." I stopped and flapped my hands uselessly. "Or bootleggers. Whatever you call them. But I don't care about all that. I only want to learn more about my uncle and his life."

"What good'll that do you?" Glenda spread her hands and shrugged. "The guy is dead."

I let out a small gasp. "Just trying to make sense of things."

A tear rolled down my cheek.

Glenda's mouth, perpetually smiling since we had met, turned down. Even when she frowned, however, she was still gorgeous.

"I'm sorry," she said. "That came out all wrong—harsh-like—and I didn't mean it to, believe me. In this place"—she gestured around the club—"I've gotten used to figuring out who I can trust and who is out to get us. Galveston is a pretty wide-open city, but my bosses always tell us to be careful. We can't go blabbing to strangers. You know, because of the business we're in. I'm sorry, but really, you two popped up out of God knows where. I've got to wonder if you truly are related to Rory."

Aunt Ida's head snapped up, her mouth open to respond. Before she could say anything to condemn Glenda, however, I put a restraining hand on her arm.

"I see your point, Glenda. Guess we did drop in out of the blue and start asking you questions. So let me set your mind at ease. Is there anything you want to ask me? What can I tell you? I only just began getting to know this uncle I'd never met before. I liked him a whole lot, though, and then—bam. He was taken from us. The finality of it was brutal."

Another tear trickled from my eye.

Glenda reached into her pocket and brought out a lace-edged handkerchief. She passed it to me, and I smelled her Yardley's English lavender again. I wiped my eyes and kept hold of the handkerchief.

A crash sounded from the kitchen. All three of us twitched, startled by the loud noise. Glenda glanced at the clock on the wall behind the bar and slumped in her chair.

"Jumpin' Jehoshaphat. I bet that's my boss. I forgot all about him. Damn it."

Aunt Ida raised her eyebrows, and I expected her to chastise Glenda, but she didn't say a word, only drummed her fingers more briskly than ever. Her foot began to swing back and forth too. Since she was clearly impatient but controlling her temper, maybe she was getting used to Glenda.

No, probably not. Only wishful thinking.

Aunt Ida wanted to avoid prolonging our visit. I bet she

wondered why she should bother to argue with this young woman that she immediately judged to be a hussy.

The door to the kitchen banged open, and a short, dark man entered. He had thick and oily black hair and a heavy black mustache to match. In his surprisingly broad hands was a large soup kettle topped by a lid. When he noticed all of us seated at the table, he jolted to a stop.

"What the hell's goin' on? Who're these broads, huh, Glenda?"

She jumped up from her chair and ran to his side.

"Mr. Maceo, please. These ladies came to talk about Rory. They say—"

His voice roared through the narrow room.

"You know the rules."

Glenda stood next to him, her mouth agape. He pushed her aside, nudging her with the kettle, and walked to the bar, where the kettle landed with a thud. A small amount of pale liquid slopped out from under the lid onto the top of the bar. I was close enough to smell the rum.

If this man was Glenda's boss, then he could've been Uncle Rory's too. My curiosity turned to horror, though, when the man grabbed Glenda's arm and she cried out.

CHAPTER TWENTY

GLENDA'S BOSS SPOKE even louder this time.

"You know the rules. No one gets in here if the place ain't officially open. Nobody," he said, shouting now.

Glenda bit her lip, dipped her head.

"Right. Got it."

Her dimples went into hiding, forced there by her boss.

He released her arm, pulled a leather pouch out of a pocket, and thrust a pinch of tobacco into his mouth. He chewed a few times, openmouthed, then walked over to us.

"What's this news youse two got about Rory? He shoulda been back by now. He ain't quittin' on me, is he? I pay that bastard more than anybody else. He's that damned good."

Part of what made this man so scary was his voice. Not only was it earsplitting, his accent was peculiar too. Several times I had to guess what he said. He spoke English easily, so I doubted he was foreign-born. This brute was outside my experience.

With thumping heart and wobbling ankles, I rose from my chair and moved closer to Aunt Ida for her emotional strength.

She didn't look scared but nevertheless appeared at a loss for words—perhaps a historic first. Her mouth opened and shut several times, like a fish's, but she never spoke.

"My aunt and I came"—I stopped to gulp a breath—"we came here to collect Uncle Rory's things. You see, uh, I guess you don't know this yet, but, uh, he died in an automobile accident several days ago and—"

"Son of a bitch."

Aunt Ida inhaled sharply.

I carried on.

"We came here because he worked here for—for—you, as you said."

The trauma of making that announcement left me light-headed, and I pressed my hand to the table to steady myself.

The man's brow furrowed, and his dark eyes bored into mine. We stood staring at each other until finally he broke the silence, saying, not unkindly, "My sympathy to youse and your family. It's tough to lose a relative. But I don't know what we can do for you."

He thrust out his big paw to shake my hand, and I took it, too scared not to do so.

"My name is Rosario Maceo. My brother and I liked your uncle. Always a good worker, and dependable, that's what he was. I said that before—even before I knew he kicked the bucket."

I pressed my lips together, hard, stopping myself from blurting out something I'd regret.

"Thank you, sir." I motioned toward my aunt. "This is my Aunt Ida, and I am, uh, and my last name is MacGregor, the same as Uncle Rory's."

"And her first name is Walter." Glenda giggled. "Imagine that."

Mr. Maceo paid no attention to her, and I didn't know if he heard my given name or not. Instead he walked to my aunt and

143

offered her his hand.

"My condolences, madam. You were his mother, I guess?"

Blood rushed to my aunt's face, and she hesitated, then spurned his handshake, placing her right hand in a pocket.

"Good gracious, I am *not* a MacGregor. Rory was no kin of mine. I'm from the other side of my niece's family." She cleared her throat. "I am her chaperone. I couldn't allow her to traipse down here to Galveston alone."

Mr. Maceo nodded. Ostentatiously, I thought.

"Very wise, madam. Youse never know what awful things can happen to a young'un alone."

Aunt Ida breathed out audibly, looking shaken, but somehow found the strength to continue.

"We had not seen Rory for more than twenty years. He was the black sh—"

She stopped, appearing to realize she might insult Mr. Maceo if she professed her usual opinion of Uncle Rory.

Silently I applauded her decision. Annoying Mr. Maceo would be foolhardy. Even in my naivety, I did have at least the good sense to recognize that.

He patted his dark, luxuriant moustache as he watched Aunt Ida.

Then, turning to Glenda, he said, "Come to the kitchen. Gotta talk to youse about today's deliveries."

He spun on his heel and clomped out of the room.

In her haste to follow him, Glenda lost one of her shoes. When she stopped to put it back on, Mr. Maceo bellowed at her from the kitchen. She ran after him, shutting the door behind her.

Exhausted, I sank onto my chair.

"Good grief, Aunt Ida. Mr. Maceo is so confusing. He has polished manners, dresses immaculately, seems like a gentleman. Yet he's got to be a very bad man, doing the job he does and threatening us too."

Pushing back her own chair so vigorously that it squealed along the wooden floor, she stood.

"I told you we shouldn't come here. When will you learn to listen to me?" The words ripped out of her mouth, laden with spite. "We're leaving right now, before those awful people return. I mean it."

"But I want to——"

"Walter MacGregor, I said we are going, and we are going now. Right now."

I stood slowly, my mind gyrating with all the unasked questions that Glenda would never hear. Before I had a chance to lament them properly, she returned from the kitchen.

"Please excuse the interruption." To my surprise, she appeared calm, speaking in silken tones. "Mr. Maceo has other work to do elsewhere, so he left. Now we can talk in peace."

Glenda joined us at our table.

"Please, ladies, take your seats. Walter, you haven't finished your coffee yet. And I'm bettin' you have more questions for me."

After all that had just taken place, how could she appear so composed? Maybe she was used to Mr. Maceo's behavior, but his vulgarity left me unsettled.

Aunt Ida straightened.

"We must leave. I don't want to be driving after dark and——"

"But I telephoned Vivian, and she's rushing here to talk to you."

"That was kind of you. I really would like to ask her about my uncle."

Glenda's delighted grin caused her dimples to come out of hiding.

"Figured you would. Everything'll be all right now. My boss won't bother us again."

Aunt Ida and I exchanged glances. I'm sure I bristled with

defiance and fancied her expression signaled annoyance—I knew her scowl well—but I was not going to kowtow to her. I was not. Talking to Uncle Rory's last girlfriend, Vivian, was too important.

Stubbornly I held Aunt Ida's gaze, until, in an icy voice, she said, "If you insist on staying, then I must move the automobile to a better place. We left it beside a construction site, and I don't want careless workmen to scratch my new auto."

"Why don't you move your flivver to the Hotel Galvez, right across the street?"

Glenda's tone sounded artificial and overly bright to me. She might be calm on the surface, but she seemed more tightly wound ever since she talked to her boss in the kitchen. Her hands were shaking, so Mr. Maceo's behavior bothered her more than she let on.

Sherlock Holmes always observed the details of characters he interrogated, focusing intently to learn as much as he could about a person.

What could I tell about Glenda? She had changed after her boss entered the scene.

What had he said to her? And why had he left so abruptly?

Aunt Ida glared at Glenda.

"In the first place, I know perfectly well where the Hotel Galvez is located, and in the second place, my automobile is *not* a flivver. I'll have you know it is a brand-new Buick. No one has *ever* called it a flivver."

Now Glenda would be in my aunt's bad books until kingdom come. With the Buick as her most cherished possession, she was the only spinster in our whole county who drove her own automobile. Besides, she knew darned good and well that it didn't fit the definition of a flivver—it was neither old nor cheap nor small. She didn't have anything to prove, so why was she so testy?

Aunt Ida placed a firm hand on my shoulder and pushed me

onto my chair.

"You sit right there and wait for me to return. I won't be gone long. To tell the truth, I wouldn't mind talking to this Vivian person either, so don't you dare move."

With that, she huffed her way out the door.

By golly, my aunt must have decided my plan to learn about Uncle Rory's life in Galveston was valid. I wished my arm were long enough to pat myself on the back.

After Aunt Ida scurried from the club, I cocked an eyebrow at Glenda.

"It's always tricky dealing with my aunt. It never helps to get her riled up."

"Evidently not." She tossed her curls and laughed. "But how come you let her treat you like you're ten years old? You're even old enough to vote, for Pete's sake. What gives? You shouldn't let her push you around like that."

I began to reply but faltered when I heard a crash in the kitchen.

Glenda's head jerked in the direction of the noise.

I said, "Didn't you say Mr. Maceo left?"

"I saw him go. That must be his brother and—"

The vision of her boss steaming through the door contradicted her.

Everything happened so fast after that. I only had time to form a thought about how to react, and then Mr. Maceo took charge and changed the whole situation.

He barged over to our table and grabbed Glenda's arm, pulling her out of her chair.

"Go lock up. We're leavin'. Tommy's waitin' for us out on the street."

He shoved her so hard toward the door that she fell to her knees. I watched Glenda pick herself up quickly, and then I felt my arm wrenched upward.

"Get up, youse." Mr. Maceo also yanked so hard that I

147

stumbled when I stood, but he caught me. "You're comin' with me. I'll teach youse to be nosy."

Glenda ran back to us.

"Mr. Maceo, please. She didn't do nothing, honest. She didn't mean any harm and only wants to learn more about Rory and—"

"Don't care what she wants. I know what I want. That's what should matter to you."

He thrust her ahead of him into the kitchen and kept a vice-like grip on my arm as he walked me along. He bullied us through the kitchen and out the side door. It opened onto a walkway running along the pier.

"Lock that." He pointed to the back door out to the pier, and after Glenda obeyed, he issued another command. "Walk up front and see if that old biddy is anywheres around. Don't want her seein' us make our getaway."

Glenda slunk toward the seawall, peeked around the front of the pier, then hurried back to us.

"It's okay. No one is out front but Tommy."

A car waited in front of the pier, its engine running. On an ordinary day I'd be thrilled to ride in a Lincoln with fancy running boards.

Obviously this was no ordinary day.

Mr. Maceo snarled at Glenda, "Get in front beside Tommy." Then he opened the back door and shunted me inside. "All right, Tommy," he yelled. "You know where to go. And make it snappy."

"Yes, sir," came the obedient reply from the driver's seat.

"Where are you taking me? Why are you doing this?"

My voice sounded shrill, and I tried without success to keep it from quavering. I lunged for the opposite door, but he grabbed me and held fast.

I'd upset him. I'd said too much, and now he was going to kill me. Would he shoot me—or maybe put me in cement shoes and throw me in the gulf waters off the pier?

"Quiet." Mr. Maceo had no difficulty in keeping *his* voice firm. "Why do youse broads hafta ask so many questions? You'll see where you're goin' soon enough. Ain't that right, little miss bright eyes?"

He leaned forward and punched Glenda in the back. Even though it wasn't a tough punch, she squeaked anyway. I guess he startled her.

I tried to imagine what Sherlock Holmes would do in a case like this, but I couldn't recall reading a story in which he was kidnapped. Guess I'd just have to go along for the ride. It seemed I had no choice anyway.

I dreamed up a dim hope of being returned to the Chop Suey Club in short order, but however fast this trip went, it would not be fast enough to get me back before Aunt Ida returned and began to look for me. I pictured how frantic she'd be when she couldn't find me at the club.

Well, hell's bells.

That was what my daddy occasionally said when at his most upset. And since he could say it, then I could think it. I didn't even feel bad about thinking it either.

If this wasn't a time for me to swear, then I didn't know when I could.

CHAPTER TWENTY-ONE

THE JOURNEY TO our unknown destination loomed in front of me. Cooped up in the Lincoln's back seat with Mr. Maceo, who smelled strongly of garlic, I was terrified. What if he decided to—

No, I could not let my mind go down a dangerous side road.

I was no fool. I knew not to toy with or sass this man. Seeing his firearm peeking out from his suit jacket underscored the importance of that conclusion.

Back home in Gunmetal I'd always longed for an adventure, almost without my conscious mind realizing it. Now I had stumbled into one, and I wasn't right pleased. I must mind my p's and q's. This could even be a matter of life and death.

Oh no, the very same words Uncle Rory had used.

The driver pressed the heavy Lincoln hard. When it hit a bump, I flew inches off the seat and landed with a thump. I clutched the armrest and sent a silent prayer into the heavens. Prayers were definitely in order.

Glenda turned to look over her shoulder at me, appearing

as calm and pretty as she had before Mr. Maceo yelled at her. Perhaps she was used to shenanigans like this.

"That big place is the Hotel Galvez," she said, "where your aunt went to park her car. The one that's not a *flivver*." When Mr. Maceo turned his head to look out the window, she winked at me, mouthing, "Stay calm."

"Shut up, youse."

Mr. Maceo, still gazing at the passing scenery, sounded perfunctory, not angry. Guess he was used to barking at people.

A few blocks later, we came to a commercial street lined with shops two and three stories high. Tommy pulled up beside a colorful striped barber's pole. A sign above the door announced the name of the establishment—the Maceo Barbershop.

I gripped my purse and thought of the receipts resting within—the ones that helped me discover Uncle Rory's hangouts. A feeling of triumph zinged through me, but that didn't last long. Due to my supposed cleverness, I'd fallen into a danger zone. I stared at the barbershop and feared what awaited me inside. My sense of dread soared.

Uncle Rory had been in cahoots with these men, and look where it got him.

A longing for home seized me. If I got the opportunity again, I'd treasure my boring life, walking my puppy down a too-calm street where nothing exciting ever happened.

I fought to control my thoughts, to remain calm.

Right.

I swallowed hard. I must *appear* calm too, even though my heart beat two hundred times a minute and breaths were hard to take.

"Okay, Tommy."

Mr. Maceo's voice erupted in the enclosed space, making my eardrums quiver.

"Take Glenda into the shop, then come back and wait in

the car. I'll handle Miss MacGregor." He looked at me. "Sit right there, toots. I'll come 'round your side and help you out. I wanna keep you nice and safe."

Nice and safe? Did he mean to imply the opposite?

His tone held a threatening edge. Or perhaps I only imagined that.

While he walked around the vehicle, I breathed deeply, in and out, in and out. With any luck, we'd have a friendly little chat about my interesting uncle and then I'd be sent on my way. With even greater luck, I would discover I was in no danger at all.

This was what some folks called *just whistling Dixie*.

The door beside me screeched open.

"Here's what you wanted, toots. You're gonna meet people who knew Rory MacGregor."

He gazed up and down my long legs. I was thankful my skirt wasn't as short as Glenda's.

"You're a tall one, ain't ya? Whoa there, watch your head. Don't wantcha to go hurtin' yourself now."

He let out a nasty snicker.

If he wanted to intimidate me, he succeeded. However, I refused to give him the satisfaction of showing it. No sirree, I would call on my fighting MacGregor blood. Rob Roy wasn't my ancestor for nothing.

Besides, I was Texas born and bred.

As he handed me out of the Lincoln, Mr. Maceo adopted an air of courtliness and polish.

"Thank you," I said, pretending to be appreciative.

I recalled what Aunt Ida suggested on the drive down from Houston—we should stand up straight, act like ladies, and shame unworthy men into behaving like gentlemen.

So there was my idea. I flung another silent prayer up to the heavens that this plan would work. While I was at it, I also offered up a prayer for the Almighty to care for Aunt Ida. For all

I knew, Maceo henchmen were accosting her right then.

Tommy held the door to the barbershop open, and I walked through ahead of Mr. Maceo. I held my head high and pretended I was Cleopatra sailing on her burnished gold barge.

Glenda waited inside, already seated on one of the three barber chairs. She crossed her legs and swung one back and forth. Her eyes shifted back and forth too, glancing at everyone in the room again and again.

Three others were in the shop when we entered—two men and one woman. The first was an elderly Negro who held a pile of folded white linen towels. The second man wore a beautifully tailored tan suit and spats. Swept straight back from his forehead, his hair was made shiny by brilliantine. With great difficulty I avoided staring at him—his handsomeness was that distracting. He reminded me of Rudolph Valentino, the star of two moving pictures I'd seen in San Antonio—*The Sheik* and *Blood and Sand*.

When I noted the third stranger—a woman—I bet my shock showed on my face. She was no modern woman—not a flapper like Glenda—but an out and out, honest to goodness floozy, a timeless stereotype. If Aunt Ida saw her, she'd flush purple with indignation.

I guessed this was Vivian.

Oh my, Uncle Rory had weird taste in women. Her dyed red hair was long and curly; no bob for her. Although her dress fell to midcalf, it was sexier than Glenda's—so tight it caressed and outlined all her voluptuous curves. The bodice was cut low and displayed her ample bosom. She perched on a counter and chewed gum loudly.

I shook my head, trying to clear my thoughts. No doubt about it—I wasn't in Gunmetal anymore.

The man wearing the spats stepped up to me and made a slight bow.

"Hello, Miss MacGregor. I'm Rosie's brother, Sam

153

Maceo."

I was perplexed. "Rosie?"

Sam Maceo grinned.

"Rosie—short for Rosario. That's unusual here in America, but my brother and I are from Sicily, where it's common. When we were small, we immigrated with our parents to Louisiana. Later Rosie and I moved to Galveston to open this barbershop."

I said, "I see."

And I did see. His unusually long introduction was helpful. The brothers' background explained Rosario's odd speech pattern. The family was Italian. Sam's accent was appealing, though. Like everything else about him. He was also refined, certainly compared to his brother.

Sam Maceo patted his black hair with a light touch.

"Actually, my given name is Salvatore. But everyone just calls me Sam." He winked at me. "I hope you will too."

His polite demeanor offered me a foothold, and I took it. If he followed a soft approach and pretended to be a gentleman, then I would respond in kind. Yet not for a second could I believe his behavior was anything more than a ploy.

But two could play at that game.

"My name is unusual too," I said. "I'm Walter MacGregor in honor of my father Walter. You may call me Wallie if you like."

I tried to sound genteel but not like a complete pushover.

Sam Maceo shook my hand.

"Pleased to meet you. I shall be proper and call you Miss MacGregor. No doubt you're descended from the famous Rob Roy MacGregor, the daring Scottish outlaw. As a matter of fact, that was a running joke between your uncle and myself."

His face fell. He released my hand and placed his on his heart.

"My condolences for his tragic accident."

"Thank you," I murmured.

"I promise not to keep you long," he continued. "We need to ask questions about your uncle's death."

But did you cause his so-called accident? That's why I'm here, but you won't learn that from me.

Stuffing those thoughts behind me, I gave Mr. Maceo a half smile—attempting to appear demure—and kept quiet. Best to let the unctuous brother conduct this meeting, and I would take my lead from him. I was out of my depth and knew it. No use fooling myself and fantasizing otherwise.

"I fear I can only offer you a barber chair, but please have a seat."

Sam Maceo took a white towel from the Negro and flapped unseen dust off the chair. What a shame this man was a gangster; he did have exquisite manners. His brother should emulate him.

I sat.

Sam said, "Come here, Viv."

The woman stepped forward.

"This is Rory's girlfriend, Vivian," he told me. "You gotta help her. She's upset by Rory's tragic end. Go ahead. Tell her about his death."

I nodded in Vivian's direction, not meeting her gaze.

All right, folks, here we go.

I began my spiel, omitting my suspicion that Rory had been murdered. I skipped lightly over the aspects of the car's collapse onto my uncle's body, described in lavish detail how happy Uncle Rory had been to return to his kinfolk and to Athalia's great fried chicken and biscuits.

In the midst of enlightening everyone about Uncle Rory's kindness to me, to my puppy Holler, and to everyone else around—all right, I confess to embroidering a great deal—Sam Maceo stopped me.

"Excuse me," he said. "I apologize for the interruption. I don't understand why Rory went to Gunmetal. It's nowhere near the job we sent him on. Can you please explain?"

This question brought me up short. Despite his silver-tongued manners, this Maceo brother didn't fool me. Given his profession, I knew an inherent toughness lay beneath his polished surface. A few tell-tale signs gave him away too. His eyes watched me like those of a bird of prey. His jaw clenched and unclenched. He balled his hands into tight fists.

I needed to cover up—in truth, to lie about—why Uncle Rory returned to his family home. I couldn't tell this man— rumrunner, bootlegger, gangster. What was he really? Whatever he was, I'd never divulge that Uncle Rory left Galveston running for his life. My story had to be convincing. It couldn't display any rough edges. Its outlines must be as sleek as the man interrogating me.

To give myself time to think, I began to cough, and then I coughed some more.

Waving my hand, I managed to say, "Water, please."

Glenda ran to a sink in the back of the shop—I'd noted it upon entering—and filled a glass from the tap. She hurried the water to me, and I drank, smiling gratefully when I finished. After a few more coughs, I imitated settling down.

"Now, let's see," I said. "You asked about the reason for my uncle's visit. Is that right, Mr. Maceo?"

He nodded. His brother rolled his eyes.

"Get on with it, girlie."

"Now, Rosie," said Sam Maceo. "Let her settle down. She'll get there. Won't you, Miss MacGregor?"

He smiled his encouragement at me.

I took another sip of water and smiled back.

"Here's what I remember. It's kind of complicated because his story kept changing. Uncle Rory's reason to visit got tangled up in family matters. He hadn't been home in years. My father and he had a terrible fight, way back when. But someone in Gunmetal had somehow gotten word to Uncle Rory that his brother was ailing."

I stopped and looked down at my hands, folded primly in my lap.

"Poppa has a heart condition, you see. We don't know how long he'll be able to go on—that is, before he, uh, expires." I wiped an imaginary tear from my eye. "But when Uncle Rory first arrived, he acted as if he breezed into town merely on a whim. He didn't want to confess that he'd come to see his brother one last time. He only admitted that to me later."

"How old is your father?" Sam Maceo asked.

"Fifty," I said.

"And what does he do for a living?"

Oh dear. Now I was wading into deeper, more treacherous waters. I saw no way around admitting that my father was a judge. Maybe the Maceos already knew this detail, and if I left it out, there'd be hell to pay. At least I could fudge a little, downplay his importance in the community and his law-abiding nature.

I exhaled and shrugged my shoulders, indicating the topic bored me in the extreme.

"Poppa was originally a lawyer and dealt mostly in real estate transactions and mineral rights. That kind of thing I don't really understand much."

I flapped my hand in the air, attempting to look like a silly, stupid female. I shuddered a little, as if I was terribly confused. Maybe I should go to Hollywood and perform on the silver screen myself. Under safer conditions, I could have enjoyed my playacting. Surely my performance was convincing—at least I hoped it was. But now came the difficult lines—explaining my father's current position.

I gritted my teeth. *Concentrate. You can do this. Full steam ahead.*

"What Poppa does now is easier to understand. He's a county judge, and I can go watch him in his courtroom if I want to and—"

The two Maceo brothers burst out laughing.

This time my confusion wasn't feigned.

"What's so funny?"

Rosario Maceo said, "Don't have to tell *us* what judges do. We work with lotsa them."

I didn't understand their levity but decided it wasn't a bad sign. At least when they laughed, they weren't shooting me. If they killed me, why, then I'd never be able to marry Dewey.

What?

Where had that thought come from?

I quickly filed the marriage idea away to think about at another time, a safer time. I had to focus on the matters at hand and think about romance later.

Much later.

I stood.

"Can you please have Tommy run me back to the Chop Suey Club? My aunt will worry about me. I promised to wait for her there."

Sam Maceo said, "You haven't asked Vivian what she knows about Rory yet. You said you wanted to do that."

I thought fast and came up with a plausible answer.

"I'd like to, but my aunt is old and easily agitated. She has a heart condition too."

Oh, how she'd grumble if she could hear me now. There—that tallied two cases of heart disease I conjured right on the spot.

I looked at Vivian.

"Could we meet later this afternoon and talk then?"

"That's right kind of you, Miss MacGregor." For the first time, Vivian spoke. She sounded breathy and very southern, as if she had just blown in from Alabama. "I'd be real pleased to do that, thank you."

Rosario Maceo stomped his foot. "This ain't no tea party. What do y'all think you're playing at?"

Sam Maceo made a choking sound.

"Settle down, Rosie. We discussed this. I see no reason why Tommy shouldn't run Miss MacGregor back to the club now. Everything seems on the up and up."

"Maybe to you, but not to me."

Rosario pulled out the gun I saw earlier.

"I got more questions, and they're tougher'n yours."

CHAPTER TWENTY-TWO

RED. THAT WAS what I saw. I saw red.

According to Poppa, Grandfather always said those words to explain why he'd blown his stack, angry as all get out. Grandfather's excuse was that his temper was in his blood. For centuries MacGregor men were known for their terrible tempers. In our ancient land of Scotland, our clan was so ferocious that King James VI outlawed the surname and a person could kill a MacGregor with impunity. This bizarre law lasted from 1603 to 1661 and was reinstated from 1693 to 1784.

When I flew into a temper—rare but nonetheless fierce— Poppa said I reminded him of our ancestors, although he himself was blissfully untouched by this trait.

Now the threat of Rosario Maceo's drawn gun made my anger flash. I lost all reason.

A tiny voice behind my ear urged caution.

"Remember Poppa's lament: your temper will get you in trouble one day."

But I blew past that advice and plopped back down on the barber chair that I had just vacated.

"Questions? *You* want to ask *me* questions? That's rich because *I've* got questions for *you*."

I was yelling but could not tone myself down or stop.

Glenda said, "Don't do this, Wallie. It's not wise."

Trying to get away from the fracas, Vivian backed up so far that she ran into the wall.

Sam Maceo's mouth fell open.

"Now look what you've gone and done, Rosie. Put that gun away. I *told you* how we would play this, and you agreed."

I knew it.

Sam Maceo was not an authentically good person; he only imitated one. He was conning me. I bet he got downright nasty if the occasion called for it.

This ersatz gentleman rushed over to me.

"For such a charming young lady, you have a very fiery temper. Let's make a deal. I'll excuse your lack of manners *just this once*, because I understand what it's like to lose a beloved relative. It must have been a shock to someone as young as you. In return, you'll give me what I want."

He bent down and pushed his face close to mine.

Good golly, the man was wearing cologne. What kind of gangster did that? Well, for all I knew, they were all Dapper Dans. At least it was better than his brother's eau de garlic.

"Miss MacGregor, I'm going to ask you politely."

He waited to let his implied threat hit me, and hit it did. Hard. I heard the unspoken but clearly intended repetition of *just this once*. He straightened up. And in those seconds I thought I would faint from an overload of fear.

He cleared his throat.

"Miss MacGregor, I ask you nicely to control yourself and to calmly state your questions. Are you willing to do this?"

Was it my imagination, or did everyone in the room heave a collective sigh of relief? Everyone, that is, except the brother. The brother—who traded in bullying tactics and brute strength—issued a loud snort.

My head fell forward, and as I stared at my shoes, I tried to organize my thoughts.

Then, as if an unseen hand reached down to shut off a gramophone, my mind ceased to whirl. The title of my minister's recent sermon popped into in my head—"The Truth Shall Set You Free."

Those words from the Gospel of John settled in my mind, and I raised my eyes to Mr. Sam Maceo and blurted out the truth.

"Rory MacGregor's death was no accident. Someone caused my father's Model T to fall on him when he was working on it, lying underneath the chassis."

A communal gasp rose from the people in the room. I looked at each one of them in turn, ending with Rosario Maceo. To him I nodded.

"That's right. I may be the only person who believes that Uncle Rory was murdered, but nevertheless that is my firm opinion. That's why I came to Galveston. I must figure out what he did before coming to Gunmetal that caused someone to murder him. I didn't tell you the truth before, but I am now."

"See. I told you she was up to no good," Rosario shouted at his brother. "She lied to us."

"Let her finish. She's got more to say." Sam Maceo kept his voice calm and steady. "She raised an important point, and the implication may be even more important to us as it is to her."

"Thank you very much."

Assuming an air of righteousness, I burrowed more comfortably into my barber chair. I crossed my arms and tried to look grave and stern. I pretended I was the Hollywood actress Lilian Gish, only I would save *myself* from dire consequences. Some *man* always came along to save her.

Lilian Gish was *not* a Texan.

"Uncle Rory told me he feared for his life." I paused, and

when I saw they were all hanging on my every word, then and only then did I continue.

"And that's why he came home to Gunmetal. Someone in Galveston tipped him off that Vivian's husband threatened to kill him, but Herschel wasn't after him. I'll make a wild guess here," I said, staring at the polite Maceo, "but I don't think that you had a reason to kill my uncle either." I cocked my head. "But maybe you know someone who did. Am I right?"

This time it was Sam Maceo who snorted, an incongruous sound coming from someone so refined looking and stylish.

"For a mere chit of a girl, you got really big ba—er, lots of gumption."

Off in the corner, Vivian tittered.

Sam Maceo still held the floor.

"We thought there was something fishy—you turning up here out of the blue. We wondered what really happened to Rory. So, yes, you're right; we didn't have him killed. Why in the world would we want him dead? He was the perfect employee. We liked him. I give you my word on this."

His brother spoke in a fake whisper.

"Right. Like somebody can take *your word* to the bank."

Then came his usual snort.

"Watch it, Rosie."

Sam twisted around and glared at his brother in a way that made my scalp tingle.

"All right, okay. I'll keep my trap shut for now."

Rosario stepped back a few paces.

Sam turned to check his reflection in the large mirror behind a barber chair and stroked his mustache.

My goodness. He did look satisfied with himself.

Glenda lurched from her chair and ran to Vivian. They hugged and held each other, crying a little.

The tension in the room leaked away, and I felt like crying from relief, yet I couldn't afford to show such feminine weakness. Still, I smiled at Glenda and Vivian. They displayed their emotions freely. And that helped me. Their tears felt like my own, and my body relaxed as a result.

I looked down at my lapel watch.

"I wish we could talk more about this, but I'm still worried about my aunt. I've been gone half an hour. She'll think something awful happened to me. I don't want her to think I was kidnapped. Can we please continue this conversation back at the Chop Suey Club?"

Sam Maceo shot a questioning look at his brother, who shrugged in response.

"I don't care no more. Do what you want now," Rosario said.

Sam said, "Then I think we should—"

"Wait. I got it," Rosario shouted. "Sam, you go back with dese broads. I gotta stay here and do haircuts. Besides, you got lotsa more patience with dese stupid girls than I do."

He returned his gun to its shoulder holster.

Glancing through the front windows of the shop, I noticed several men milling around on the sidewalk. The rum-running gangster brothers appeared not to care what their customers thought.

Well, what did I know? Perhaps in Galveston it was common to see a guy pull his gun and threaten a damsel, putting her in distress. Hadn't I just saved myself by using my very own wits? All I needed to do now was keep doing that.

Why, this was a cakewalk.

Within minutes, however, new events sapped my confidence.

Tommy brought the Lincoln back to the front of the barbershop, and we began to pile inside—Tommy and Glenda got in the front while Sam Maceo and I shared the back seat, as I had earlier with Rosario Maceo.

That was when a Negro boy—looking no more than ten

years old—ran up to the barbershop. He caught hold of the store's doorknob, his chest heaving. Then he turned, noticed the Lincoln, and ran to the driver's door.

Tommy cranked down his window.

"What's goin' on, Leroy?"

The boy gulped for air.

"Gotta talk to Mr. Sam. It be real important."

Mr. Maceo got out of the car and pulled the boy behind the Lincoln. They held an earnest-looking discussion, but I couldn't hear any of it. After several minutes, Mr. Maceo handed the boy some dollar bills, then punched him on the shoulder in a friendly way. Pocketing the cash, the boy loped down the street, whistling. Mr. Maceo rejoined me in the back seat.

Sam Maceo had a habit of touching people. How softly—or roughly, as the case might be—he touched a person indicated how he felt. While Rosario demonstrated his feelings easily, Sam appeared to hide his behind a silky surface. His pokes and punches, however, gave a bit of his true feelings away.

Tommy jammed the big automobile into gear and pulled away from the curb.

"We got trouble, boss?"

"Sure sounds like it. Better get us back to the club, and don't spare the horses. Two associates from Chicago are waiting for us, and Leroy says they're mighty upset. They busted into the kitchen when he was washing dishes. They threatened him, held a knife to his neck, and made him deliver a message to us."

Tommy's head twitched, hinting at his desire to turn to look at his boss, and Glenda's whole body twisted around so that she could face Mr. Maceo. Her eyes grew wide as she watched him take out his gun, spin the cylinder, and mouth the number of bullets it held.

"Don't worry, ladies," he said, noticing our anxious looks. "I'll take care of you. You're safe with me."

Had Aunt Ida seen the two men from Chicago? Was she

done for?

"Did Leroy happen to mention an elderly woman at the Chop Suey Club?" I asked.

Sam Maceo shook his head and laid his gun on his lap.

"No, he did not."

Collapsing against the back of the seat, I wondered who would win out in a struggle between Aunt Ida and two goons from Chicago.

CHAPTER TWENTY-THREE

THE LINCOLN HURTLED down Twenty-First Street toward the Gulf Coast. Bumps and sharp turns unnerved me, and here I was jostled left and right and already worried about the gun that Mr. Maceo held at the ready. As we drew near the giant pier and the Chop Suey Club, I peered anxiously through the front windshield. Up ahead, several people stood on the seawall in front of the pier.

One was Aunt Ida. Talking to her was a uniformed policeman. The scene took my breath away. My heart began fluttering. My aunt had called a policeman about my disappearance. Now I was in real trouble.

Still staring, trying to control my palpitations and nerves, I noted two men who lurked a few feet away from my aunt. They wore dark suits and fedoras, and their flashy style of dress set them apart from other people I'd seen out and about in Galveston that day.

Could these men be the fellows sent down from Chicago?

As the Lincoln drew closer, I noticed how the two men kept their eyes trained on the policeman. At the same time, they inched backwards away from him.

"Hey, boss, we got problems," Tommy said. "A cop's outside of your club."

Sam Maceo bent forward and peered across Tommy's shoulder, scrutinizing the scene on the seawall. Then he chuckled and sank back into his seat.

"Nothing to worry about, Tommy. That's Sergeant Wilson. *He* won't give us any trouble. At least he never has before."

Mr. Maceo threw a dazzling smile my way.

"That gentleman is fond of a specialized product or two we bring in from the Caribbean Islands. As it so happens, the chief of police enjoys the same products."

Poor Aunt Ida. She probably thought she'd called in the cavalry. Instead, she'd summoned the Maceos' goons.

I tucked away in my mind this fascinating revelation—law enforcement officers in Galveston knew the Maceos brought in illegal liquor from the Caribbean and looked the other way.

No wonder the Maceo brothers were so brash. Perhaps my knowing that the Galveston police were in the gangsters' pockets would come in hand on a later occasion.

Still, I needed to address my own special concern.

"Mr. Maceo, you may feel fine now," I said, feeling my stomach flip, "but my aunt will make nothing but trouble for you. You whisked me away without so much as a word of warning to her. Believe me when I say this: you've never tangled with anyone like her."

He replaced his gun in his shoulder holster and smirked.

"Care to place a small wager? Five bucks says your aunt gives *me* no trouble at all."

"If I had money to spare, then I'd take your bet. But alas, I don't." I clasped my purse more tightly in my hands. "What about the men from Chicago? Aren't they a potential problem too?"

He shook his head. "On reflection, I believe Leroy overstated that situation. He is terrorized easily, even when there's no real danger. Nevertheless, we will prepare for all eventualities."

He tapped Tommy's shoulder.

"Keep your gun at the ready, just in case."

"Right, Mr. Sam." Tommy pulled up to the pier and put the car in park. "I'll keep the engine running too, just in case."

"Good man," his boss said.

And then all four of us prepared to face the music. Or at least I assumed that was the case since I couldn't read the others' minds—although I certainly wished that I could.

Glenda and Mr. Maceo got out of the car. Tommy remained, as assigned, and I stayed seated too. I had lost my desire to learn more about Uncle Rory's associates for the time being.

Or was I simply afraid of Aunt Ida's wrath?

Glenda went into the club, and Mr. Maceo walked right over to Aunt Ida, addressing her in a cordial fashion and gesturing to where I sat in the back seat. Instead of looking pleased that I had returned in one healthy piece, she frowned and adopted her most belligerent look—one I knew all too well. Her hands were on her hips. Her lips were pressed so tightly together that they disappeared. Her eyes were narrowed into slits.

Of course, I would have preferred a show of delight for my reappearance. But that faint hope withered and died pretty quickly right there on the spot.

I climbed slowly out of the car. I bet I looked like Holler when he realized he'd done something bad. If I'd had a tail, I would've tucked it between my legs and skittered away. But I couldn't leave. I had to face the consequences of disappointing—perhaps even scaring—my aunt.

At my approach, Sam Maceo grabbed my hand and drew

me into the conversation. "I apologized to your aunt," he said, "for insisting you speak to your uncle's good friend Vivian. I assured your aunt that you remembered your promise to remain at the club until her return." He grinned at her. "However, she has no idea how persuasive I can be. And so here you are, Miss MacGregor, back safe and sound."

My hands clenched, and I chewed on the inside of my cheek. Who cared what he said—*I* knew I was still in jeopardy. The thought of driving all the way back to Gunmetal, alone in an automobile with a furious and judgmental virago, gave me palpitations.

The policeman and the two goons from Chicago—even though they were well dressed, I still thought of them as such—scared me. However, Aunt Ida scared me more. Perhaps Mr. Maceo could take care of the goons. Yet try as hard as he might, turning all his considerable magnetism and charm on Aunt Ida, I doubted he could calm her sufficiently to protect me from her wrath.

The dreadful consequences of my disappearance might not emerge at once, but they were nevertheless inevitable. Somewhere down the line, in the not too distant future, my aunt would make me pay. And pay big.

I kept my head down, unable to look Aunt Ida in the eye. Although Mr. Maceo kept right on talking, his words scarcely registered on me, consumed as I was by anxiety.

Later I could explain to Aunt Ida how the bad brother, Rosario, coerced me to leave the club with him. I hoped she'd believe me when I said I had no choice in the matter. Yet if I explained that, then she was sure to bring up another sin of mine—my desire to come to Galveston and meet these gangsters in the first place.

I no longer thought of them as simple rumrunners or bootleggers. No, once Rosario threw his weight and temper around—once both brothers pulled out their guns—they'd become gangsters in my book.

And shame on Uncle Rory for getting involved with these bad guys. A double shame too, because my fondness for him brought me here to confront these awful men. Surrounded by the odors of fish and fuel, I stood among gangsters, a crooked cop, and my judgmental aunt.

And yet...and yet....

An unexpected thrill of excitement raced through me, head to toes. Why, I was having a bona fide adventure. Nothing like this ever happened to me in Gunmetal, never in all my born days.

In a surge of confidence, I lifted my head and looked straight at Aunt Ida.

To my shock, her expression was soft.

She was not, however, looking at me.

She focused all her attention on Sam Maceo. And that attention was so strong that I swear my body could burst into flames and she would not notice.

What on earth was going on?

When I focused on their conversation, I was surprised to hear them discussing the differences between their automobiles, her Buick versus his Lincoln.

Meanwhile, the police sergeant tapped his foot and sneered. I suspected he had better ways to occupy himself than to watch the town's pet bootlegger charm yet another hapless female. How could that cop have any idea what a supreme accomplishment Sam Maceo had achieved?

No one ever charmed my aunt.

Mr. Maceo must have noticed the policeman's restlessness because he quickly tucked Aunt Ida's hand into his left arm and shook the policeman's hand with his right.

"Thank you for coming to this fine lady's aid when she was in distress. I tell everyone that the town of Galveston has the nation's most outstanding police force, and you, Sergeant

Wilson, certainly are one of its most dedicated members."

The police officer and my aunt both beamed. Off to the side, the two men from Chicago smirked. They seemed not to care if participants in our tableau noticed their disdain. Luckily for them, Mr. Maceo had eyes only for Aunt Ida.

Sergeant Wilson took his leave and crossed the street to the Hotel Galvez. His gait was so jaunty that he almost skipped. When he put something in his pants pocket, I recalled the cash Sam Maceo had given young Leroy only minutes earlier.

Why was I surprised? Corruption required payoffs. Tales from Poppa's courtroom had taught me that.

Logic aside, I felt like Alice through the looking glass. This world was a topsy-turvy version of the one I inhabited. In my home and in my small town, only virtue and hard work were rewarded. And even those values were not lavishly recompensed. All the money the Maceos made from selling illegal liquor must have given them plenty left over to shower bribes on Galveston and its citizens.

Before I could ponder this notion further, Glenda exited the Chop Suey Club and ran across the walkway from the pier and onto the seawall. She had stuck an ostrich feather into her headband, and it wobbled gaily in the wind.

"I'm rustling up some eats and put a pot of coffee on. Come into the club, folks."

Aunt Ida unhooked her hand from Mr. Maceo's arm and opened her mouth, ready to make a pronouncement. I guessed what she would say next, and I proved to be correct.

"We are behind schedule." Aunt Ida leveled a stern gaze at Mr. Maceo. "We've stayed in Galveston too long already. Although I've enjoyed discussing the various attributes of our automobiles, we mustn't keep you from your work any longer. Now come along, Walter. My Buick is parked right across the street."

I stiffened my backbone—and my resolve—and prepared

to take on my aunt's fury.

Please, Lord, give me strength.

I tried to speak, but Aunt Ida beat me to the starting line.

"No, Walter, I want nothing to eat. Neither do I need coffee. What I want is to hit the road and to do so immediately. Do you hear me?"

Glenda watched me closely with a sidelong gaze. I recalled how she had challenged me to stand up to my aunt, and I agreed with the thoughts she seemed to beam my way.

Now would be a good time to begin.

But how?

I looked at Sam Maceo.

"Isn't Vivian on her way to talk to us?"

He nodded.

"Aunt Ida, surely we need to wait for her," I said. "Talking to Vivian is a main purpose of our visit."

I rushed on, talking over Aunt Ida when she tried to voice her opinion. That was something new—and an unexpected pleasure.

"One more hour won't hurt," I said. "What's more, Glenda was considerate to prepare food and drink. A bit of lunch will set us up for our long drive back home."

I moved closer to Glenda, all the better to absorb her positive encouragement.

"Do you need any help in the kitchen?"

I tried to convey that I was taking her good advice to challenge my aunt's hold over me.

Glenda flashed a look my way that I fancied held comprehension.

She managed to gesture a thumbs-up without my aunt noticing, then she grinned and said, "No, thanks, but I'll keep your offer in mind."

I remained by her side and stared back at Aunt Ida.

"Are you coming?"

I had thrown down the gauntlet. My aunt's eyes narrowed into slits again, and I imagined she was considering whether to pitch a fit in front of company or to maintain her ladylike dignity, an attribute she valued as highly as breathing.

Even if she let me win now, she would chastise me later.

She let out a loud breath.

"Very well. A cup of tea would help soothe my nerves after such a harrowing morning."

Glenda's dimples popped into view.

"Then please follow me, folks."

Only four of us walked across the gangway—Aunt Ida, Glenda, Mr. Maceo, and me. The men from Chicago had disappeared. I wondered where they'd gone, but they weren't my concern as I suddenly realized that the morning's drama had left me both hungry and thirsty.

"Here, let me help you." Sam Maceo took Aunt Ida's arm with exaggerated care. "Some of these boards on the walkway are loose. I don't want you to fall."

I quickened my step to follow them more closely, all the better to eavesdrop.

He pointed toward the end of the pier that jutted into the Gulf.

"I understand there were pagoda-shaped buildings out there before the Great Storm. How I wish I'd seen them. That's why our club has Oriental decorations, in honor of those defunct buildings."

My aunt gazed up at him, and I swear she batted her eyes. Her face softened so much that I expected her to swoon with delight.

Holy moly. How could this male charmer be a sibling to the rough and nasty Rosario Maceo? Watching Sam Maceo operate successfully on Aunt Ida suggested that I should change my approach to her. I suspected, however, I lacked the innate ability to cajole her or play to her softer emotions. She'd kept them well hidden until she was subjected to his skilled flattery.

Once we were inside the club, in short order Sam Maceo settled Aunt Ida and me into chairs at a table near the long bar. He played the genial host while Glenda bustled around, bringing coffee and sandwiches. They both made a big fuss over tea prepared to Aunt Ida's exact specifications—hot and strong with plenty of sugar ready on the side.

In the middle of our repast, someone knocked on the door. Because the club wasn't yet open, Sam Maceo had relocked the door after we entered.

Glenda hopped out of her chair.

"There's Vivian. I'll get the door."

In fact, it wasn't Vivian who entered the dining room.

The two men from Chicago had returned, and this time I got a better look at them. Their fancy, uptown suits were navy pinstripes and double-breasted. Also, like Sam Maceo, their hair was pomaded with brilliantine, but unlike him, they didn't doff their hats when they came inside.

Clothes make the man, as the saying goes. Or, to quote from my college Shakespeare course, "The apparel oft proclaims the man." And the Chicago men's clothes were yelling at us— demanding we pay them the respect they figured they so richly deserved.

If their individual styles attempted to imitate that of Sam Maceo, then they had failed and failed miserably. While his style was elegant, theirs were merely flashy. No true gentleman would layer on heavy gold rings and watches. What was even worse, their manners—or lack thereof—resembled those of the thuggish brother, Rosario Maceo.

They brushed past Glenda without acknowledging her and clomped over to our table, swinging muscle-bound arms. Truth to tell, they seemed like apes dressed in suits.

Sam Maceo stood to greet them, holding out his hand. "Hey, great to see you guys, but can't you come back this evening? These ladies need my attention now. Why don't you get yourselves over to my barbershop? Rosie will get both of you all fixed up, and then we'll have a good time tonight, and get all our business taken care of too. How's that sound?"

One man merely grunted, and the second offered another suggestion.

"Our business can't wait. If you're too busy for us now, then tell us where to find Rory. We'll talk to him instead."

My uncle knew these men, had dealings with them? After years hanging around with louts like these, no wonder he was dead. My stomach tightened, and I choked on my coffee.

Sam Maceo drew his words out slowly.

"About that, Frankie. Here's the thing..." He spread his hands wide. "There's a prob—"

"We stopped by his boarding house to see him, but no one knew where he was. We heard he's been gone more than a week."

"Listen, fellas," Sam said, pulling Frankie by his elbow away from our table, "I got a delicate situation going on here. Let's talk about your business tonight. I'll bring you up to date on everything then. Besides, I'm sure you're tired from the long train ride down from Chicago and—"

"Naw, it weren't so bad," Frankie said. "Just tell us where Rory's at and we'll scram."

"Right," the second man said. "Quit givin' us the runaround. We're here to do business. Al told us to find out if you're ready to make the deal or not."

I wanted to say something—to scream out that Uncle Rory was dead. But there were now as many gangsters in the room as there were normal people. Three to three—with the good side made up of females, and all of us without guns.

I knew what the bulging jackets of both Chicago guys indicated. They carried guns just like the Maceo brothers did. If I knew what was good for me, I'd keep my mouth shut.

I cast a sideways glance at Aunt Ida, but she was sipping her tea intently. A placid look on her face gave nothing away. Taking my cue from her, I picked up my coffee cup again and drank.

After a few swallows, however, I was ready to gag. I had to do something and do it soon or I would explode. But when I slid my chair back, Aunt Ida's hand clamped onto my wrist.

"Stay put." She spoke softly so that only I could hear. "Don't you dare move. Let those men take care of their business their own way. Keep quiet and we'll get out of here as soon as we can."

Every nerve in my body tightened. I was now so tense that when someone else pounded on the door, I gasped. Aunt Ida hissed at me softly.

"Get ahold of yourself," she said.

Glenda, still standing near the bar, rushed to the door.

Vivian pushed her way into the room in a breathless flurry. The bracelets stacked on her arms jangled, and her high-heeled shoes clattered across the wooden floor. I could smell her perfume from yards away.

Two pairs of male eyes swiveled her way and stayed glued on her curves.

Oh, heavens. She was going to blab the news about Uncle Rory's death.

CHAPTER TWENTY-FOUR

VIVIAN TOOK ONE look at the men from Chicago and sashayed over to them. She moved so close to Frankie that I thought she might kiss him.

"When did you blow into town? Didn't know you fellas were coming down to visit."

She stepped back and hiked up the neckline of her dress. It had slipped, displaying even more of her magnificent bosom than before. Then she shook her head slightly and appeared to change her mind, because she pushed the dress down to its original location.

I felt my eyes bug wide.

I barely heard Sam Maceo murmur, "Excuse me, ladies," as he turned his back to us.

Good heavens.

I'd never seen a woman behave in such a fashion. I snuck a peek at Aunt Ida, but she was focused on the street outside the window—rather pointedly, I thought. I was too curious to do the same. I felt compelled to watch Vivian.

The goons licked their lips—doubtless to keep from

drooling—and their eyes followed Vivian's every motion. Maceo stepped forward and gestured at the tables, but neither man moved to sit down.

Frankie's partner poked him.

"Aren't ya gonna answer the dame's question?"

Frankie stood straighter, puffed out his chest, and tugged at his tie.

"Guess my mind wandered. Our boss, Al, sent us down to talk to Rory, but we can't find him and—"

Vivian whimpered and pressed a hand to her forehead.

"You haven't heard the sad news yet? My Rory got smoked." She drew a handkerchief out of her sleeve and wiped her eyes with it daintily. "My heart is crushed. Rory was the best fella there ever was. He took real good care of me." She gave Glenda a sly look. "If you know what I mean."

Frankie and his partner reeled to confront Maceo, talking at the same time. Frankie drowned out the other man, who retreated into silence.

Frankie yelled into Maceo's face.

"Rory's dead? When were you gonna tell us?"

For a fraction of a second, our host's expression registered surprise, then the look vanished. His air of polished assurance returned. He lowered his voice, but I managed to make out his words.

"Take care what you say." He pointed at Aunt Ida and me. "This dear lady and her niece are Rory's relatives, and they've come to claim his personal effects. Naturally they are grief-stricken and easily upset. I'm sure you understand now why I didn't tell you before about the death. There's no need to talk about Rory in their presence."

Without lowering his voice, Frankie issued swear words I'd only heard on the rougher playgrounds of Gunmetal.

"So who did him in, huh? Johnny Jack Nounes? I betcha it was him. Yeah, or one of his men." He shook his finger at Mr.

Maceo. "I *warned you* his Downtown Gang was gonna go after your gang. But *no*, you wouldn't listen to *me*."

A flash of real annoyance crossed Sam Maceo's face, and temper flared into his speech.

"Rory died in a tragic accident, an automobile accident. Nothing more. Now shut up or you're going to make me angry."

"Mark my word, that Nounes guy is a menace. Before we left Chicago, Al told us—"

Sam grabbed Frankie by one arm and pushed him toward the kitchen.

"Shut up, shut the hell up. We'll talk about this elsewhere."

Frankie's quieter partner looked less angry and more worried as he followed dutifully into the kitchen. They hurled the swinging door shut so hard, it bounced off the wall with a horrendous bang.

Vivian and I exchanged stares. Was her heart pounding as hard as mine?

To my surprise, Glenda appeared unfazed. She held up her hand and admired the ruby-red fingernails. Even Aunt Ida merely stirred her tea and peered into its depths.

I figured Glenda, given her job, might be used to men behaving like this, but my aunt?

I never suspected she was skilled at hiding her feelings. No doubt she was also taking everything in and criticizing it. I'd hear all about it later.

Vivian walked to our table.

"Gosh darn it, didn't I kick up a good ole fuss?"

She plopped onto a chair in a most unladylike manner. She wiped her face with her handkerchief and stuffed it into the neckline of her dress.

Aunt Ida's raised eyebrows conveyed that she'd registered Vivian's tacky manners, but otherwise her expression remained placid. I knew good and well what her real thoughts were about

Vivian. Inside my aunt's head, the word *trollop* was circling.

I bent toward Vivian's ear and whispered, "Who's this Al in Chicago? And what about that Johnny Jack somebody here in Galveston? Maybe they could be—"

Aunt Ida clamped a hand on my wrist.

"Shh. Be quiet."

If she kept doing that, I'd get a bruise.

Vivian wiped her eyes, cocked her head, and looked at me.

"So whaddya think? Was my sweetheart murdered or not?"

I needed to soft-pedal what I really believed. A tenuous version of the truth—my truth anyway—sprang to my mind. I began in a wishy-washy fashion.

"It could go either way, accident or murder. We may never know. My hometown sheriff seems satisfied it was an accident."

I felt myself babbling and stopped the nervous flow of words. Vivian frowned.

"But I'm asking what *you* think. What's your opinion?" She swiveled to look at my aunt. "Or yours."

Aunt Ida placed her spoon on her saucer with deliberate care. Then she raised her chin a fraction of an inch and eyed Vivian.

In a voice so calm that it seemed embalmed, she said, "Perhaps the better question to ask is about your own guess. You knew Rory best. I hadn't seen him in years. Do you think someone was out to kill him? Is it plausible he could make a foolish mistake while working on an automobile? Could he have been so careless that the thing fell on him and crushed him?"

Keeping an eye on the kitchen door, Aunt Ida lowered her voice. "What about Johnny Jack Nounes, that man Frankie mentioned? I presume Nounes lives on the island. Sounds as if he could've had reason to kill Rory."

Vivian sucked in a deep breath, then coughed.

"I only know that Rory was a careful man, but even careful men die in accidents." She rolled her head from side to side.

After another deep breath, she said, "In fact, accidents happen all the time."

Was she implying the accident was real or a deliberate event?

Why was she remaining so tough? Because she was a tough broad, I supposed. Oops, I mustn't use—or even *think*—that word. The darned gangsters were burrowing into my mind.

"Stop it, Viv. Stop with the games." Glenda said. "Rory don't need protecting no more, and these ladies ain't gonna spill what you say to 'em. I know you loved him, so quit pretending. We all know you've got to be hurting."

Vivian's face crumpled. She laid her arms on the table, put her face down, and wept loudly. She didn't react when her handkerchief slipped from her bodice and fell to the floor.

In my judgment, her tears were real. Despite her hardened exterior, this woman cared deeply for my uncle. Whether or not she was a tramp, I felt sorry for her. After all, despite what Aunt Ida might think, I supposed even fallen women had feelings. After revealing her emotions, Vivian showed she was not as tough as leather but rather a tender-hearted girlfriend.

"I did love him. I did." Vivian's wail was heartbreaking. "And he was nuts about me. But now I'm so scared, I don't know what to do. Rory acted real odd before he left Galveston. When I asked him what was wrong, he said it was nothing. That I shouldn't worry."

Now we *might* be getting somewhere.

I moved forward in my chair to ask Vivian a question, but when shouts erupted in the kitchen, the words froze in my mouth. My hammering heart jumped from fear to anticipation in a flash. I'd never seen a real fight before and must confess I was a little disappointed when the shouting soon subsided into a dull murmur.

I began to explain to Vivian who I was and what I was doing in Galveston. But before I could proceed to lay my questions out on the table, she stopped me.

"I'll gladly tell you all I know. I'll tell you how Rory acted during his last weeks here and what he said." She looked over her shoulder at the closed door to the kitchen. "I just don't wanna talk around Mr. Maceo and those other guys. I don't know what they'd make of my information. But I'm not afraid of *you*. I can tell you have sympathy for what's in a woman's heart—and in a man's too, for that matter."

"All right. I'll hold off on my questions. I appreciate your cooperation."

I was running out of time, however. Aunt Ida looked ready to flee.

"But I warn you my aunt and I must get on the road soon. It's a long drive back to Gunmetal, where we live. We don't want to—"

Aunt Ida cut me off.

"Two women should never drive alone on country roads in the dark. We cannot stay much longer." She took a sip of her tea. "On the other hand, I do agree with my niece. I'd like to hear what you have to say."

Well, I'll be.

Maybe Aunt Ida was as keen to hear Vivian's words as I was.

Glenda flashed her dimples and thumbed in the direction of the kitchen.

"Mr. Maceo will settle those guys down right quick. My guess is they'll be gone within ten minutes."

Sure enough, the words were scarcely uttered before the door from the kitchen opened, and all three men returned to the dining room. Mr. Maceo had slung his arm over Frankie's shoulders and was talking in an animated, friendly fashion to the other man. Whatever their issues had been, they seemed to have been resolved—at least for the time being.

"Okay, gals," Mr. Maceo sang out. "Us guys are going to

the barbershop. You hold the fort here, Glenda. I'll be back in plenty of time to open up tonight. Don't you worry your pretty little self about that."

"Sure thing, Mr. Maceo." Glenda gave him a little salute, looking pert. "That's jake with me."

Mr. Maceo walked over to Aunt Ida, and a grave look settled over his face.

"I'm truly sorry for the loss of your relative. A fine lady like yourself, well, it pains me to think of your grief. Here's my card." He offered it to her with a flourish and caressed her hand when she reached for it. "If there is anything that I can do for you—ever, at any time—then please do let me know."

When Aunt Ida murmured something and shook her head, he said, "Now, now, dear lady, I'll have none of that. Do not hesitate to contact me. Rory was a fine man. Yes, a very fine man indeed."

Aunt Ida ran a finger over the face of the card. I waited for her typical cutting words to flow from her mouth, but they never came.

Instead she said, "I appreciate your concern." She gave the card one last look, then placed it in her handbag. "Goodbye, Mr. Maceo. Goodbye."

Her eyes followed him as he exited the room.

Their farewell scene was unbelievable. A gangster had conquered my stern aunt. Still, my befuddlement warred with another strong feeling that swirled inside me—excitement. I was excited to think that as soon as the men left, Vivian would divulge secrets about Uncle Rory. Surely she would say at least one thing to astonish me.

Heavens to Betsy, what a day this had been. Had there ever been another like it?

Not in my short life.

CHAPTER TWENTY-FIVE

VIVIAN'S HIGH-HEELED SHOES made sharp, clopping sounds as she walked back and forth across the Chop Suey Club's wooden floor.

I wished I'd thought to bring my journal with me; I didn't want to forget one thing she did or said. How did Sherlock Holmes remember all the details he caught inside his enormous brain?

Vivian clasped her hands in front of her, as if she were about to pray. And then she spoke.

"First time I worried about Rory was when he couldn't sleep good at night."

Vivian looked out the window and toward the Gulf of Mexico.

"Always before that he slept like a champ. I used to say you could stand Rory in a corner, on his head even, and by gosh, he'd go to sleep just like that. He coulda slept straight through a hurricane too."

Glenda giggled, thought better of it, and clapped her hand over her mouth.

"Did he tell you what was wrong, Vivian?"

She sniffled and shook her head again sadly.

"He wouldn't say, not right away anyhow. When I asked him about his—what do you call it, *insomlia?*—he said work was a worry; shipments had slowed down. He kept making pitiful excuses like that, but the change in his habits seemed mighty odd. This went on for a while until early one morning he woke up screaming. He'd never done that before.

"Got a cigarette?" she asked Glenda. "I sure could use one."

Glenda pulled a gold case from her purse and handed it to Vivian, who grabbed a cigarette and lit up. Vivian inhaled deeply a few times, then seated herself at our table.

"That's better. Well now, let me tell you, I'd never seen nightmares like Rory's, and I've been with a few men who had real wild ones."

I pointedly turned to Aunt Ida to see how Vivian's euphemism for having lovers sat with her. Aunt Ida's face registered no change.

Her nonresponse surprised me. I knew she would consider Vivian and Glenda to be fallen women. No doubt she'd have plenty to say about them on the ride home.

"Men who soldiered saw awful things," Vivian said, "and they always had the worst nightmares."

Heat rushed to my face. Vivian had slept with soldiers *plural.* And it appeared that she didn't marry any of them. And where did her husband, Herschel, come in? I angled my head so no one could see my flushed face.

Vivian swiveled to Glenda, confiding, "Why, I remember how one guy—name of Ralph, I think it was—told me about fighting in Cuba and—"

Aunt Ida whimpered.

What the heck? What was wrong with her?

Glenda said, "Are you all right?"

"Excuse me," Aunt Ida said. "A spot of indigestion. I must

have eaten my lunch too quickly."

Needing to pump as much information out of Vivian as I could while I had the opportunity, I ignored my aunt and said, "But Rory was never a soldier, at least as far as we know, so I don't understand."

"That's right." She nodded so vigorously that her long red hair bounced. "I even asked Rory if he had bad memories of some war, but he said no. After that I got downright worried."

Vivian stood and went to the bar. She bent to open a low cupboard and pulled out a bottle full of a clear liquid.

"You ladies want any of this?" she asked. "I need to refresh my courage with a shot of hooch."

Aunt Ida, Glenda, and I declined.

"I hate to drink alone," Vivian said.

"Oh, for heaven's sake, Viv," Glenda said. "Give me some too."

Vivian poured two glasses and brought them to our table. The smell of cheap gin was strong.

There was plenty of that smell wafting around these days. Even in tiny out-of-the-way Gunmetal.

Vivian took a few noisy sips and returned to her story.

"After weeks and weeks of lousy sleep, Rory was pretty ragged and worn out, as you can imagine. I nagged until he finally gave me the lowdown. Even though he pretended he was tough as old boots, Rory didn't want to admit that anything bothered him. But he was truly spooked."

Steel crept into Aunt Ida's tone, and her gaze bored into Vivian's.

"What about?"

Aunt Ida continued to surprise me. Nothing she'd done since we re-entered the Chop Suey Club fit my usual sense of her. Later I might even drum up enough gumption to ask about her behavior.

"Give me a minute."

Vivian fumbled another cigarette out of Glenda's gold case and lit up. She inhaled deeply, then exhaled and watched the smoke swirl into the air. The silence was punctuated only by the sound of waves lapping against the pier.

Finally my uncle's last girlfriend went on with her tale.

"Rory admitted he was afraid to nod off, afraid that he'd have nightmares again. The morning he woke up screaming, that's when he decided to unburden himself to me. Rory said he wanted to try to get his thoughts out so's they'd quit circling inside his head."

She took a long drag on the cigarette.

"His dreams weren't exactly the same, night after night, but some things repeated. There was dead babies, women in torn nightgowns, and men carrying guns coming at him down a long hallway."

A quiver ran through my body. I felt Vivian's experiences as if I were living them. I didn't know what those dreams meant for Uncle Rory.

I asked, "Did he think some other, uh, guy in his line of work—shall we say—was out to get him? Did he fear for his life?"

That was the best I could do to keep from making my uncle sound like a thug.

"Yes and no," Vivian said. "Rory finally admitted he thought something or somebody was after him, but he wasn't sure who or *what*. The first time he talked about ghosts, I laughed in his face. That hurt his feelings, and I felt so bad. He clammed up for a while and left me alone in his room for hours. When he came back, he was drunk and raving out of his head. Said he'd been warned someone was out to kill him and sensed that was true. Said he had to leave Galveston."

All my senses snapped to attention. Now we were getting somewhere. The reason Uncle Rory told me he left Galveston differed only a little from what his girlfriend said.

I twisted toward Vivian. "Who was the man?"

"Can't help much there, I'm afraid. Here's all I know. A long time ago Rory had done something really bad, something that haunted him, made him feel guilty. Rory figured his dreams meant a man connected to that sin was out to punish him, so Rory thought he should try to make amends."

I tried to stay calm, but I feared my words came out like a shriek.

"What bad thing did he do?"

Vivian shook her head.

"Rory never would say. He was too ashamed to talk about it. Then I asked why, after such a long time, this *sin*, as he called it, bothered him again."

She shut her eyes and sat still as a garden statue. Why didn't she finish? The suspense was strangling my breathing.

She opened her eyes.

"Rory said comin' home to Texas, he felt worse. Said he could cover up his guilt before, but it grew so strong it haunted him here in Galveston all the time."

I broke in, no longer able to hold my peace.

"Then it seems like the *sin* occurred right here in Texas."

"Might could be," Vivian said.

Aunt Ida cleared her throat.

"So did Rory leave Galveston to get away from the man, or did he leave to go off somewhere and make amends?"

"Damn it," Glenda said. "I hate to think of Rory being so upset and in such pain. He was always a real gentleman to me."

Aunt Ida's hand flew up to cover her mouth. No doubt she had to stop herself from chastising Glenda for swearing.

A tear trickled down Vivian's cheek.

"I know, doll, I know." She threw a glance at Aunt Ida. "And about your question, well, it's a good one. Rory actually said both things were true. He fled to escape the man *and* he had to leave in order to apologize to someone."

"Did he mention going back to his old home in Gunmetal?" This time Aunt Ida was the one who spoke too loudly.

The room's atmosphere felt thick with tension, lying heavy on us like the molasses Poppa poured over Athalia's cornmeal mush at breakfast.

Vivian put her head in her hands and mumbled something we couldn't hear.

"What was that?" Glenda said.

Vivian's head jerked up. Tears poured down her face. Aunt Ida offered a handkerchief from her purse, but Vivian waved it away.

"I tried to keep him here," she said. "I figured he'd be safer in Galveston, what with the Maceos for protection, but Rory wouldn't admit to anyone but me how scared he was."

I *had* to interrupt.

"Did he tell you where he was going?"

"He never did. One morning I woke up and he was gone, just gone."

Her voice broke on the word *gone*. Tears continued to dribble down her cheeks.

"He left a short note, and all it said was that I shouldn't worry. That he would be careful and that he'd come back to me as soon as he could. That was it."

Glenda reached out to hug Vivian, but she shook her off.

"I should have told someone, asked for help, done more. If only I'd done *something*, then he wouldn't be dead. Now the love of my life is dead. Now that he's gone, what am I going to do now?"

Her wail of anguish pierced my heart. I had thought Cupid shot only love arrows. I had no idea that he could be so cruel.

Aunt Ida passed her handkerchief to Vivian again, and this time she grasped it like a life preserver. She didn't dry her eyes with it, however. Instead, she twisted the hanky back and forth in her hands.

That poor girl. Floozy or not, she had feelings and a compassionate heart, and it was hurting now. One look at her hands was enough to tell me.

Glancing down at my own hands, I saw that I also was twisting fabric—a bunched up handful of my skirt. My nerves were running as high as Vivian's. I bet mine would have given hers a run for their money.

Uncle Rory, after you've gone, now what?

"I'm afraid I made your handkerchief a crumpled mess."

Vivian held it out to Aunt Ida.

"That's all right. Please keep it." Aunt Ida rose from her chair. "We really cannot stay any longer. Home by nightfall, Wallie. Remember?" She looked pointedly at the clock on the wall behind the bar.

The information we had gained was all well and good, but I'd be hard-pressed to get to the bottom of Uncle Rory's death with only those new facts. I simply couldn't bear to leave just yet.

"All right, Aunt Ida. I'm *almost* ready. Just a few more questions for Vivian."

My aunt crossed her arms and looked down at me.

"Walter."

Her tone was sharp.

In the face of her impatience, it took all the pluck I could muster to oppose her.

"Besides, we still have to stop by Uncle Rory's boarding house and collect his things."

Before Aunt Ida could reply, I turned to Vivian and spoke rapidly.

"Is there anything else you can remember about my uncle, some small detail that might point to why he was killed? Anything at all? Even if it seems to have no relation to his death, that detail might be the key to unlock everything. Please think hard. Maybe something about that Nounes fellow."

The answering frown on Vivian's face assured me she was trying to come up with a useful bit of information. I waited impatiently, tapping my foot but doing it quietly so I wouldn't disturb her thoughts.

Aunt Ida glowered at me and then pointedly twisted her head to watch the wall clock's hands *chink chink* through two minutes' worth of time. Those minutes crawled by, measuring an eternity. Glenda toyed with sandwich crumbs on her plate while I willed Vivian to come up with just one more important memory.

Vivian clasped and unclasped her hands. Just watching her made me nervous.

"Only one thing comes to mind," she said at last, "and I doubt if it'll help."

My foot ceased tapping, and I leaned forward.

"Great. Let's hear it."

"Rory and I were together for half a year or so. During those months we had such fun together, lots of good times, just good times. Only twice did he ever say anything scary or sad. Compared to what you've already heard, this other bit seems very small."

"Anything may help. Please don't feel bad."

She squirmed in her chair, adjusted her tight skirt.

"I do feel bad, like I'm breaking a confidence, but I guess it doesn't matter now."

"Rory would want you to help us."

"Okay then," Vivian said. "He told me that a long time ago he had a sweetheart who he loved very much. He always regretted that he had lost her. A light had gone out of his life. This was before our relationship got, uh, really serious and intimate. I like to think that I brought light back into his life."

She angled her head toward me, dejection showing in every movement.

"I'm sorry. That's all I've got."

My shoulders sagged. Vivian was correct. That memory didn't sound like much at all.

"Do you know when their love affair took place?" I asked. "How old he was?"

I ignored Aunt Ida's sudden intake of breath. I guessed my prissy aunt disliked my even knowing what a love affair was.

Vivian began to shake her head before I finished speaking.

"No, nothing else. Nothing. I told you it wasn't much."

Her words, all of them, sank into me deeper and deeper.

But wait a minute.

What if the two sad things Uncle Rory shared with Vivian were *connected*?

What if the sin he had committed had been with this young woman?

So I asked Vivian that question, and her reply was succinct.

"I have no idea," she said, her eyes downcast. "I can't help you anymore."

As her head drooped, Aunt Ida motioned to me. The time had come to take our leave.

I pushed back from the table and picked up my purse.

"Thank you for your patience dealing with all my questions. I am so sorry we brought such sad news."

Both Vivian and Glenda jumped up and rushed to throw their arms around me. Their eager friendliness gave me pause. I couldn't help liking them. That feeling intensified when they began fretting aloud about the long drive to Gunmetal we were about to undertake.

"Are you *sure* you'll be safe?" Glenda asked. "Would you like Mr. Maceo to send Tommy to follow you home?"

"That won't be necessary." Aunt Ida spoke slowly, appearing to choose her words with care.

If she tried to keep a scornful tone from her voice, she didn't succeed.

"Wait." A new thought horrified me. "What if the Nounes

fellow tells his gang to follow us and hurt us? Were you hinting at that, Glenda?"

"Of course not," she replied. "You have a vivid imagination. The Downtown Gang wouldn't come after civilians like you."

I persisted.

"Even if Nounes finds out we're Rory's relatives?"

Glenda and Vivian rolled their eyes.

"You've nothing to worry about from them. They never bother us." Vivian pointed at Glenda and then herself. "Johnny Jack Nounes is a fancy gentleman, like Mr. Sam. People call Nounes the Beau Brummel of Galveston."

"She's right. Sometimes he even puts up with a little bit of competition for his booze business," Glenda chimed in, "but he clamps down when the rivalry gets too stiff. We are never bored around here, that's for sure. Say, come to think of it, aren't you bored living in a small town? Bet you'd like to stay a while longer in Galveston, right?"

I considered her question and realized I would in fact be glad to return home.

"Maybe I'd like to travel more, but my father is the best man in the world and I have a wonderful beau and my puppy will be glad to see me again."

Glenda squealed.

"Oh, I love puppies. You are *so* lucky."

Even bereaved Vivian was able to muster up a faint smile.

Their enthusiasm for dogs helped me realize that they and I were more alike than I ever dreamed possible. In different circumstances, I might have turned out like one of them. I would think of that the next time I was tempted to look down my nose at someone. Now I recognized I'd been doing that very thing ever since I had met Glenda and Vivian.

Aunt Ida broke into my reflections, grabbing my arm and pushing me toward the door. Glenda and Vivian hurried to catch up, and they walked with us all the way down the pier and out to the street. A flurry of farewells followed before Aunt Ida executed a forced march across Seawall Boulevard to the parking lot of the Hotel Galvez.

In less time than it takes to cook a soft-boiled egg, I found myself seated in my aunt's Buick. The cast of gangsters who had pulled us into their world had vanished.

Thugs, gangsters, goons, dolls, guns. Good grief.

Only Aunt Ida remained, a constant in my life. She sat to my left, stolid as usual.

Snap out of it.

Maybe I spoke aloud, because she said, "What's that you said, Walter?"

"Nothing, ma'am. Just thinking aloud."

I handed her a scrap of paper that held the address of Uncle Rory's boarding house. She frowned, gave an almost imperceptible nod, and drove us several blocks inland. Her ability to locate the building impressed me. I hoped to achieve her overall air of competence as I matured.

All my friends back home pushed against the strictures of their mothers. I lacked a mother. Instead I had Aunt Ida. Probably amounted to the same thing.

I would think on this further. My fingers itched to write in my journal.

Aunt Ida parked in front of a seedy three-story building that needed new paint. She pointed a finger at me.

"You stay right here. And I mean it."

"Yes, ma'am."

"Getting Rory's belongings shouldn't take long."

"Wait. The woman's name on the receipt for one week's rent was Susanna Weston. I wanted to talk to her, so maybe—"

"Absolutely not. Stay put."

Aunt Ida slipped out of the driver's seat and slammed the car door behind her. When she hadn't returned in ten minutes, I was surprised. Finally, after an additional ten minutes, she returned with two bulging paper sacks.

"Did the landlord give you any trouble?" I asked.

"Of course not. Not after I paid another week's rent."

"How generous of you. Poppa will pay you back."

"Don't be such a simpleton, Walter."

I bit back a sharp remark. I didn't care if she was my elder and good manners dictated that I owed her politeness; I wished she would stop calling me names.

I took a deep breath and said, "Is there anything interesting in those sacks?"

Aunt Ida shot me a doleful look.

"No."

Guessing her patience with me had ended and knowing that my patience with her was frayed, I decided to stop questioning her. I could rummage through the sacks later in the safety and tranquility of my own home.

Walter, you must have patience, I told myself.

Aunt Ida settled into the driver's seat and drew on her driving gloves.

"I did something for you. When I spoke with Miss Weston, I asked her what kind of boarder Rory was. Clearly she was charmed by him."

"That doesn't surprise me."

"Right. But I also asked her if there was anything his family should know, especially since we hadn't seen him in such a long time."

My head snapped up.

"Really? Did she say anything interesting?"

"Indeed. She explained they'd had only one conversation that amounted to anything, but during that chat he had told her that the only woman he ever wanted to marry had lived right here in Texas. He confessed it was hard to return to Texas knowing he wouldn't see her. He sounded so sad that her heart went out to him."

"And what else did she say?"

"That was all, Walter. No other details. I thought you'd be pleased with what I found out."

Oh, dear. In my eagerness to learn more, I'd upset her.

"Yes, your news is quite helpful. Thank you."

Aunt Ida pressed the starter, but the engine sputtered and failed to turn over. After two more failures, she got out of the car, lifted the hood, and tinkered with something. She returned to the car and tried the starter again, muttering under her breath. The car roared to life, and she shifted the car into gear with great vigor—such vigor that she seemed almost angry.

I was so amazed by her mechanical ability that I nearly asked where she learned it.

I restrained my impulse, expecting her to chew my ear off, to berate me for one thing and another, mile after weary mile. My anxiety silenced me, and I dared not look at or address her.

We were on the causeway heading off the island, when— astonished at her silence—I began casting sideways glances at her. Despite looking every few minutes, I saw nothing to indicate anger or disappointment. Instead, her face stayed expressionless, and she kept her eyes fixed on the road.

Still, her reticence felt ominous—perhaps even threatening. Soon she would start to admonish me. I just knew she would.

My lapel watch announced the time was two o'clock. Now how could that be? The incidents that unfurled so relentlessly that morning amounted to a lifetime's worth of drama. At a minimum, that handful of hours felt like a week. I was exhausted by the unaccustomed excitement.

I must have dozed for a while. When the Buick hit an unexpected bump in the road, I awoke. Another peek at my watch showed it was two-thirty.

Aunt Ida remained as before, expressionless. With that

blank face, she should have been playing poker. Poppa had taught me how to play as a little girl, and I had trouble learning to keep a straight face.

Darn it, I couldn't bite my tongue any longer. I had to ask what she thought about our day's exploits.

I began slowly.

"What a day. I've never spent another one quite like it."

She gave me a fleeting look but said nothing.

"Have you?" I asked.

"Have I done what?"

"Ever had a day like this before?"

She laughed harshly.

"What a stupid question. Of course I haven't."

Stupid? If she kept on like that, she might hurt my feelings. I chose to ignore her insult.

"So what's your opinion of this morning's events?"

"I doubt if we learned anything that would indicate that Rory was murdered."

"I disagree completely."

"I thought you might say that. Go ahead and explain your point of view. I know you will anyway."

So far, so good. Aunt Ida hadn't bitten my head off yet. Still, I thought it best to proceed cautiously.

"Something Mr. Maceo said—"

She raised her eyebrows.

"Which one?"

"Sam."

Luckily I was looking at her and was able to watch her demeanor change. Her head tilted, her lips turned up, and her shoulders relaxed. The transformation made my aunt look a good ten years younger. I wondered what she had looked like at my age. I'd never seen photographs of her as a young woman, only those taken recently.

How did Sam Maceo succeed in charming my inflexible

aunt? He had achieved that herculean task effortlessly. If I hadn't seen her reaction for myself, I would never have believed it to be possible.

Athalia's repeated warnings whispered in my ear—*curiosity killed the cat.*

I answered that piece of my brain with *Shush and never you mind.* I simply had to ferret out the answer.

I baited the trap by adopting a deceptively casual tone to say, "Rosario Maceo wasn't someone I'd like to see ever again. Such a rough and mean man. I don't understand how he and his brother could be so different. Don't you agree?"

"Yes."

Darn it. That certainly didn't get me anywhere.

"Of course, you and Aunt Hazel were very different too."

"True."

Aunt Ida was never one to mince words; direct and to the point was her style. Still, I'd never known her to be laconic. The mystery grew in my mind, driving me crazier by the minute.

"How did you feel returning to Galveston?" I wouldn't give in until she offered up her opinion. "Did it bring back old memories? Had the place changed much since your last visit?"

She smiled wryly, but her eyes stayed on the road ahead.

"You ask so many questions, Walter. Which one do you want me to answer?"

Okay, if I got to pick only one, I'd choose the one that burned brightest in my mind.

"All right then. What did you think of Sam Maceo?"

She let out a small but audible gasp. Then to my horror, she raised a gloved hand and brushed away a tear.

Oh Lord, what had I done? Confusion and contrition washed over me. When I mentioned Sam Maceo earlier, she had looked happy. I hadn't expected to distress her merely by asking her opinion of him. Quite the contrary.

For several more miles we drove in silence.

Finally Aunt Ida coughed and then sighed loudly.

"Rory was not the only one who lost a sweetheart. I did also, and Sam Maceo reminded me strongly of him. The physical resemblance is uncanny. I suppose that's why I took to Mr. Maceo right away. I hope I didn't upset you."

When I didn't reply, she said, "Well? Did I?"

My mouth was hanging open. I shut it, then opened it again.

"Of course not. You behaved like a lady throughout the day. Your manners were perfect, as always."

She let out a puff of breath and chuckled.

"That's a relief. There were points during our unusual visit when I hardly knew what I was doing."

Sensing some kind of reply was necessary, I said, "Yes, ma'am, I understand."

In fact, that was not true, not true at all. I had no idea what she was talking about. This entirely new version of my aunt unnerved me.

Lines from a new poem by Yeats popped into my mind. *Things fall apart; the center cannot hold.* I hadn't understood the poem before, but now I grasped its meaning.

Nothing was fixed. Nothing was certain. You had to find your own center and not depend on anything outside of yourself.

Did I know how to do that?

Aunt Ida nudged my shoulder.

"What's the matter? Are you feeling carsick?"

I jerked out of my reverie.

"Not at all. I'm fine."

To my utter amazement—even consternation—she smiled at me fondly.

"Why aren't you peppering me with questions? The Walter I know wouldn't let such an opportunity pass. Don't you want to hear about my old boyfriend? You'd be wise to catch me when I'm in a mood to reminisce."

Who was this woman? Either some woman was pretending to be my aunt or a spirit from another world was inhabiting her body.

I stammered, "Of course I-I want to-to hear your story about how you met and what…what happened to him."

CHAPTER TWENTY-SIX

AUNT IDA'S EYES crinkled, and she offered a faint smile.

"Once upon a time, when this chapter in my life began, I was about the age you are now. Remember how you loved it when I read you fairy tales?"

Memories brought an answering smile to my lips. "Of course, and you always began with those words. Always."

"So then, once upon a time I became engaged to a handsome young rancher. It was at Christmastime in 1897. Our wedding was fixed for the following October, and the preparations sent the household into a tizzy. My younger sisters—Hazel and your mama—helped me gather my trousseau and plan the wedding."

She clamped her hands more firmly on the steering wheel. Her doeskin gloves were stretched taut, looking as if they would split from the force.

I hesitated to ask, but our safety was more important than her feelings or pride.

"Should you pull over while you tell your story?"

"No, I can be brief. After all, the engagement itself was short."

Her hollow gaze shifted briefly to me, perhaps checking to see I if I was paying attention. She need not have worried.

"When we were courting," she continued, "I didn't see my beau frequently, only when he rode into town on horseback for supplies. However, once we were engaged, he made that journey more often, riding in every weekend. My parents approved of him because of his impeccable manners. We were very much in love. A wonderful life stretched out in front of us."

She seemed unaware that she had slowed the car's speed. Even though her attention was diverted, the lazy tempo didn't seem dangerous, so I held my tongue.

"My fiancé's hair was dark and wavy, and oh my goodness, he was a fine-looking, virile man, so much like Mr. Maceo."

She pushed a stray lock of her own hair back from her forehead.

"Then one weekend he didn't come to town." She flicked her gaze my way. "Mind you, there were few phones back then, but his absence didn't worry me. I assumed something unexpected had detained him—a sick calf, for example. The following weekend he turned up as usual, and when he explained his absence, I had an unpleasant surprise."

Aunt Ida broke off, and I moved to the edge of my seat and clutched the dashboard. What unpleasant surprise? I wanted to urge her to continue, but her face held such sorrow.

I waited while she gazed out the windshield in silence. Finally I could stand the suspense no longer.

"Can you tell me the rest, or do you need to stop?" I asked softly.

"I will proceed. My memories overcame me."

I waited what seemed like five years before she continued.

"My fiancé heard that Theodore Roosevelt was in San Antonio rounding up volunteers for the army to fight Spain.

Roosevelt wasn't president, only the assistant secretary of the navy then. He was holding meetings at the Menger Hotel, persuading men to join the First United States Volunteer Cavalry. My fiancé rode the train to San Antonio and signed up, along with other recruits from the other western states. The army thought that men from the West would need less training since they knew about horses."

"Was that what we now call the Rough Riders? I remember them from my history class."

"Yes." She sniffed, and for a second I feared she would cry. "To make a long, sad story short, I'll jump to the climax. My fiancé fought in Cuba at the famous Battle of San Juan Hill. He died there. And that was that. My fairy-tale happy ending went up in a puff of Gatling gun smoke."

Aunt Ida's shoulders started to shake, and the car swerved to the right and hit a large pothole. When she jammed on the brakes, the car jolted to a stop, throwing us to and fro. Aunt Ida sat very still, breathing heavily.

My heart was beating triple time. I wasn't scared, just startled. Thank heaven our speed had been so slow.

"Are you all right?" I asked.

Aunt Ida's shaking body swiveled in my direction.

"Over and over in my diary I wrote the name I would acquire when I became his wife—Ida Lancaster. I even ordered fancy engraved stationery from back East. Mrs. Samuel S. Lancaster for that. Everyone called him"—her breath hitched—"Sam."

She laid her head on the steering wheel and began to sob.

Not knowing what to do, I patted her shoulder. When that didn't seem to be sufficient, my pats turned into small rubs. Aunt Ida stopped crying. She dried her eyes with the back of her hand.

"Are you hurt?" I asked.

Her short laugh sounded bitter.

"No, dear, but it's unfortunate that Vivian kept my handkerchief."

We were both unhurt, thank heaven. Since I wanted to hear the rest of her story too, I pushed on.

"So maybe you understand Vivian's emotions, how overcome she is by her boyfriend's death."

"Of course I understand. You see, when *my* Sam's death became known, I didn't earn everyone's full sympathy. I lacked the standing of a real widow. And poor Vivian is in a similar situation. People can be cruel, withholding their support and being judgmental."

"But that's unfair."

"Oh, Wallie, you are *so* young. All too soon you will learn the ways of the world. I really must prepare you better."

What else could I say?

"I had no idea you were engaged, and your story breaks my heart."

"There's a little more to tell. I was fortunate that my parents and Sam's understood the depth of my feelings. They helped me get through that painful period."

An armadillo lumbered across the road in front of our vehicle. Aunt Ida followed its passing.

"Those creatures can't see well," she said. "Did you know that?"

Guess she had kept more of her wits about her—even in her grief and after the mishap with the Buick—than I suspected.

"I didn't know that about armadillos. They're so common that I don't think much about them—other than to keep Holler away from them."

"Armadillos are survivors from at least the Cenozoic Era."

Just as you are a hardy survivor too.

"You know an amazing amount about a lot of subjects, Aunt Ida."

I purposely filled my voice with admiration. I reckoned she

could use a healthy dose of it about now.

"Thank you, Wallie. After Sam's death, I buried myself in books. That's how I came to spend my life teaching. Who knows what my life could have been if I had married him."

She lapsed into silence, and I feared her talking streak had ended. However, she wasn't finished quite yet.

After clearing her throat, she said, "I always thought it was ironic. The Battle of San Juan Hill ruined my life. The future I had anticipated evaporated. Yet that same battle made Roosevelt revered and famous. He was elected vice president of the United States and then became president after McKinley's assassination. During his term as president, the army dedicated a monument in Arlington National Cemetery to the Rough Riders who died in the Spanish-American War. The army invited Sam's parents to attend the ceremony, and they asked me to accompany them."

She winced and rubbed her temples with her gloved hands.

"Are you sure you are all right? Would you like me to drive now?"

Aunt Ida glared at me and frowned.

I wondered if I should urge her to finish her story but decided it was better to let her proceed at her own pace. I recognized a growing ache—or perhaps merely tension—in my neck and rolled my head to alleviate it.

Aunt Ida's question was so abrupt and loud that I jumped.

"What's wrong?"

"Just a cramp in my shoulder." Since she had broken the silence, I felt free to ask, "Did you attend the ceremony at Arlington?"

"I did not, and that decision is one of my biggest regrets." She emitted a low snort, most uncharacteristic of her. "That— plus my failure to convince Sam *not* to accompany Roosevelt and the Rough Riders to Cuba."

"Did you try to change his mind?"

"Not really. I figured his mind was made up and that he

would go regardless of how much I argued my case with him. Still, I should have tried harder. I will regret that until my dying day. Sam's luck was terrible. Less than two-hundred Rough Riders were killed in action, in that or any other battle."

A farm truck passed us, headed west as we were, then slowed and turned around. The driver stopped on the side of the road across from us. He honked the horn and waved, but when he didn't receive an answering wave, he approached the Buick. Aunt Ida cranked her window down.

"Yes? What do you want?"

Her posture was erect. Her words were clipped and precise, unwelcoming. All signs of grief had disappeared in an instant, and the woman who remained was the one I was accustomed to.

At the force of her words, the farmer backed up. He touched his straw hat.

"Beg pardon, ladies. I only wanted to see if y'all need help."

"Thank you, no."

I flinched to hear Aunt Ida's sternest voice.

"I appreciate your offer, but we only stopped to eat our sandwiches."

But we had no sandwiches. My aunt had not told the truth.

The farmer scratched his nose.

"Well, all right then. I reckon I'll get on my way. Just not used to seeing two ladies like yourselves alone out on a country road. Y'all better get home by nightfall."

My aunt's tone became icy.

"That's our plan."

The farmer beat a hasty retreat, and I felt sorry for him. He had only wanted to do a good deed. How could he have known that my aunt would be so prickly?

Her quick, slick lie about sandwiches churned in my mind. I couldn't expect her to confess she had almost had a wreck, hitting a pothole—or to tell the farmer she was grieving the death of a long-lost fiancé. Her untruth was inconsequential, but that lie had flown from her mouth as if she were accustomed to cooking up fish stories right on the spot. If it had done nothing else, this journey had acquainted me with the fullness of her character in all its facets.

She cranked up her window.

"To finish my story, here is the final irony. Sam and I had planned to spend our honeymoon at the Menger Hotel. To this very day I cannot set foot in that grand old place despite many invitations to fancy events there."

Overcome by the sadness of her fate, I touched her arm. She grabbed my hand and held it in her own.

"Sam's death ended my dreams of marriage. What's even worse, it also ended my sister's chances of getting married. Hazel and I were close in age and great pals. Because she was younger, she said she wouldn't marry until I did. So neither of us did. When your dear mama married and then had a daughter, Hazel and I rejoiced at becoming aunts. For each of us, *you* were the offspring we never could have."

A lump grew in my throat and hurt so much that I couldn't speak. I managed to squeeze her hand again. When she saw that I shed a few tears, her demeanor changed.

"That's enough of that. No need to be maudlin. But to conclude, I have a suggestion. I hope that from all the things you've seen today, you've learned something about human nature. People try hard to cover up hurt feelings and sorrows. We often pretend we have the world under our control and nothing ever gets us down. Now you've heard my tale of woe, and you've learned about your Uncle Rory too. He had a sad, lost romance and may not have been the brash, carefree gigolo he pretended to be. But I admit he certainly did fool me."

Before I had time to digest her advice and confession, she set the automobile in gear and pulled onto the road.

"We must make tracks if we're going to stay on schedule. While I concentrate on driving, why don't you think back over today's events? I'm sure you have plenty to say."

Relief spread through me, pushing aside the sadness caused by her story. I had sunk so low that gloom and doom veiled my whole world. That was a new feeling for me, and I didn't like it. Much better to press my aunt with questions and try to solve the mystery of Uncle Rory's murder.

It had to be a murder, not a mere accident. Such a tumultuous life couldn't have ended with an act of carelessness.

Running through the day's happenings, I returned to one question that had gotten no answer.

"What do you know about the Chicago boss?" I asked. "Remember, Frankie referred several times to a man named Al. Glenda and Vivian explained about Johnny Jack Nounes, but not about him."

"Afraid I can't help. I know nothing about Chicago. It's too far away, and I've never been there," she said. "What I can do, if you want, is telephone a cousin who lives in Chicago. He's a lawyer and may know more about the world of gangsters than your average fellow."

"Gosh, that would be swell."

"Walter. Must you speak like that? Your slang is horrid."

I ducked my head.

"I'm sorry."

I hesitated long enough to make my remorse seem real, then prepared to ask another question. Actually, my thoughts shouted *hallelujah*. Lapsing into my customary mindset and returning to my practice of asking questions felt great.

What a relief. I really did feel *swell*, a word I was now forbidden to say.

Trying to keep the glee from my voice, I said, "I've come up with some possible suspects. Shall I list them for you, Aunt Ida?"

CHAPTER TWENTY-SEVEN

AUNT IDA PUSHED down hard on the gas pedal, increasing the Buick's speed as it came out of a turn.

"If you insist, I'll listen to your list of suspects. But first, tell me why you're still convinced that someone murdered Rory."

How could she ask that, after all we'd just gone through together? I choked back a snicker, knowing she wouldn't appreciate being laughed at.

Stripping all sarcasm from my voice, I said, "Consider all the ne'er-do-wells Uncle Rory worked with." Then I couldn't help myself; I did laugh. Quickly I added, "Not to mention out-and-out bad people. *Lawbreakers*. We met plenty today."

"Rory broke the law too."

"I realize that and don't condone his behavior. What's that old expression—no honor among thieves? I liked Uncle Rory, despite everything. But that doesn't mean I believe everything he did was good."

"That's a relief. I thought you were completely swayed by him."

"Sure, he was charming, and I think deep down he was a good man. But he was in a dangerous business and hung around with nasty characters. We saw that firsthand today, and we're lucky to be going home unscathed."

Aunt Ida coughed.

"At least we can agree on *that*." She flicked her gaze at me and turned back to the road again. "I thought taking you to Galveston would make you reconsider your fixation on murder. Now I feel guilty I've helped entrench you deeper into your theory—"

"You have no need to feel bad. Now, let's see." I spread out the five fingers of my right hand and wiggled them in front of our faces. "By my count there are at least this many suspects or *groups* of suspects. The number is *five*. Even people who told us they liked and appreciated Uncle Rory are on my list. Maybe they lied."

"Oh, Wallie." She added layers of indignation to the pronunciation of my name as only she could. "At least your analytical ability remains intact after this upsetting day."

My aunt's praise—even left-handed as it was—warmed my heart.

"However..." She hesitated for full dramatic effect. "It stretches credulity to believe criminals from Galveston could skulk around Gunmetal, kill a man, and escape without being seen. Don't you agree?"

My heart no longer felt warmed. The moment of basking in Aunt Ida's praise certainly passed quickly.

"*My* credulity is not stretched, Aunt Ida. Sounds to me like bootleggers move around the state all the time. Certainly Uncle Rory did. They even move *between* the states; that Chicago connection is real. I set out to discover if anyone had motive to kill him, and I believe I've done that." Something gnawed away at me that I couldn't shrug off. "Next I'll consider other questions."

She pursed her lips.

"Now what?"

"Like who had the means and the opportunity to murder Uncle Rory."

Despite the sound of the engine and the roadway noise, I heard her groan. When would my aunt learn that giving up was not in my character?

"Do you want me to be the kind of woman who gives up, who quits?"

"All right, tell me who you suspect," she said. "Or do you want me to guess?"

"I'll tell you, and I'll begin with those I deem likeliest to have committed murder, then go down my list from there."

"A logical approach."

Another compliment. This time I knew not to trust it. Probably a tactical maneuver on her part.

I held up my right forefinger.

"Topping my list is any member of the Downtown Gang. Any rivals of the Maceos could have had a business motive to get rid of Uncle Rory, especially if he was as effective as the Maceos say he was. Then, in second place"—I held up two fingers—"is anyone who works in the Maceos' gang. That includes the brothers themselves."

"You surprise me, Wallie. The Maceos stated categorically how much they appreciated your uncle and his skills."

"Of course they sounded sincere. But they engage in illegal activities and play rough, so that qualifies them for my list. How can we trust such shady characters?"

"Hmm, I see. Go on."

"Perhaps someone who works for the Maceos wanted to get rid of Uncle Rory in order to take his place. Could be someone we didn't meet today."

"All right. Members of the two rival Galveston gangs take your first two spots. So who fills the next three on your list?"

"Next come the Chicago gangsters. We don't know much about them, but they seem tough and unscrupulous. I wouldn't want to tangle with them."

"They scare you more than the Maceos?"

"Sure do. But maybe the difference is simply how the two thugs from Chicago behaved. For all we know, Sam Maceo's suave manners could hide an evil heart."

"You know why I hate to think that, but you could be right. And so, what about Vivian's estranged husband?"

"I was coming to him. Maybe he went to Galveston to identify her new boyfriend. His whole visit could have been a ruse while he was actually reconnoitering and planning how to kill Uncle Rory. Herschel had motive. No man wants to be cuckolded."

She gasped.

"Walter, how do you know that word?"

"English literature. Shakespeare wrote about cuckolds."

My head felt like it was on a swivel as I turned again to hide my smirk.

"You do read a lot." Aunt Ida's tone sounded grudging. "So that's it for your top four suspects. I must say your choices are obvious. Who is the fifth?"

That stung. Really, there was no pleasing the woman. I was darned if I did, and darned if I didn't. Just when I thought my aunt was conversing with me adult-to-adult, she stings me with another insult. Luckily for me, I held the trump card

"In fifth place is a mysterious stranger," I said. "Did I tell you about the man who loitered across the street from our house a few days ago?"

She let out a loud noise—one that I had to characterize as a squawk.

"What are you talking about? I know nothing about this. Did you keep this from me on purpose?"

When I didn't answer immediately, she exploded. "Well,

did you?"

"I did not."

Feeling unfairly accused, I fought to keep my tone level. I proceeded to describe in detail my encounter with the man who said he was on his way to Austin.

"He could've been a scout for one of the gangs, and now we know there are at least three who could be interested, two in Galveston and one in Chicago. I saw this man before Uncle Rory died, and Clayton saw him afterwards." Another thought hit me. "You want complete details, right?"

"Yes."

"With Holler's help, I found a cigarette butt in the carriage house after Uncle Rory's death. No one can smoke in Poppa's house, and Uncle Rory never smoked, so"—I twisted in the seat to look full-on at my aunt and spoke with what I hoped was portentousness—"how did a cigarette end up near the murder scene? Only his killer could have left it there."

Aunt Ida let out an exasperated *harrumph* and shook her head. I feared the car would swerve dangerously again, but she held it straight. "That is so thin," she said, "that it cannot be called evidence. Also, if this stranger was connected to Rory's death, why would he stay in Gunmetal afterwards?"

"I have a theory."

Aunt Ida groaned. "I'm sure you do."

"Some boss could have sent his minion to kill Uncle Rory, and then he stuck around to see if his handiwork was successful."

"What do you mean?"

"Someone tried to make the death look like an accident. The stranger wanted to see if the Gunmetal police declared Uncle Rory's death an accident."

"My oh my, you do have an active imagination."

"I can't put my finger on why, but the instant I saw that strange man, he seemed suspicious."

"Your father should limit the number of Sherlock Holmes

stories you're allowed to read."

Anger flared in me.

"Poppa would never supervise my reading."

"Perhaps he should."

With our conversation on the verge of veering down a contentious path, I decided to make peace.

"Now, Aunt Ida," I said, "let's not argue. An hour ago you said you wanted me to learn the ways of the world. Reading is clearly safer than engaging in adventures like the kind we had only this morning."

"Point taken." She cleared her throat. "Yet at the risk of annoying you, I need to ask another question about your suspect list."

I doubted her motive yet said, "Sure, go ahead."

"What about Vivian?"

"Vivian?"

"Since you insist on making a list, I suggest you include her. She could very well have had a motive too."

I mulled over her suggestion.

"I can't see it. In theory I agree that she could've been so hurt when Uncle Rory left her that she wanted him dead. Still, Vivian appeared genuinely surprised and saddened by the news. In fact, I believed everything she told us."

"We don't know her. Who's to say she's not a good little actress, adept at faking her feelings? Those young women, Vivian and Glenda, live in a brutal world that you and I know nothing about. Who knows how far their feelings and actions stray from the norm—or at least what you and I think of as normal?"

"I suppose. For that matter, there might be many people involved with the characters we met today who could have killed Uncle Rory. What a depressing thought. Still, our excursion to Galveston taught us at least one thing."

"What's that?"

"Uncle Rory was involved in dangerous work with crooked characters. How many people have been murdered in the Galveston rackets? His death could be just one more killing, one among many."

"But you mustn't forget the alternative."

"And that would be what?"

"His death might be what it appeared to be at the beginning—an unfortunate accident caused by his own carelessness."

My shoulders drooped.

"All right. I may not *think* an accident happened, but I will concede that it *could* have."

She patted my knee.

"Now, dear, simply because you don't want to believe it doesn't mean it isn't true. You seek an excuse for your uncle's death, one that doesn't involve his own stupidity."

After my sharp intake of breath, she added, "Or clumsiness. I guess that's a kinder way to phrase it." She hesitated before adding, "I need to clarify something. Don't take my willingness to explore your ideas as agreement. I don't think that a murder took place. I merely wanted to understand your reasoning. You have a good mind, and I confess that I enjoy sparring with you."

"Is that what you call it?"

We exchanged glances and laughed.

As our conversation lapsed, I realized that my brain hurt; it needed a rest. I had listed possible suspects based only on motive. My mind boggled at the thought of figuring out means and opportunity.

Drowning in thoughts of death and calamity, I needed the vistas of nature to soothe my soul. However, the passing landscape didn't offer much. Oak trees and ash had replaced the rice fields just north of the Galveston Causeway, and several pecan trees grew in the midst of a large field of cotton. I'd been so caught up in our dramatic conversation that the changes in the terrain never registered on me.

"When will we see Sugar Land?" I said.

"I chose a different route for the trip home," Aunt Ida said. "More direct since we didn't need to drive through Houston. Wharton is up ahead. We'll stop there and buy gasoline."

I slid down in the seat and shut my eyes. If I napped, the trip would pass more quickly. I was dozing—on the very edge of asleep—when Aunt Ida launched into a description of the glories of Wharton County.

Later I awoke to hear her say, "And that's why this area will be hit by a boom."

Straightening up, I rubbed my eyes. "What was that again?"

"Discovery of a large salt dome will spur development in this area."

Good grief, what did I care about salt domes? To be polite, I pretended to be interested.

"Why is that important?"

"When the Spindletop gusher blew in 1901, geologists learned that salt domes could contain oil. Ever since then, they've searched for salt domes."

She babbled on about oil and sulfur until we reached Wharton.

It cheered me that she was happy and returning to themes from her school teacher roots, but her talk of minerals bored me like a bad preacher in church.

Finally we reached Wharton. While an attendant pumped fuel into the Buick, I stared through the window at the small town. On the square across from us, a young man and woman stood in front of a massive, three-story stone courthouse. They gazed into each other's eyes and swung each other's hands back and forth.

I immediately thought of Dewey. I hoped I could see him tomorrow or, better yet, tonight. Ah yes, love. Sweet love.

Shakespeare got it right in *As You Like It*. "The sight of lovers feedeth those in love."

I sat upright, startling my aunt midlecture about the production of sulfuric acid, when I said, "I forgot to ask you about Uncle Rory's girlfriend, the one he regretted losing. Do you have any idea who she was?"

"Mercy me, child. You do ask the most extraordinary questions. Now, let me think a minute."

She frowned, as if debating her answer.

The filling station attendant tapped on her window, and she cranked it down.

"That'll be one dollar and sixty-three cents," he said.

She took the money from her purse and paid him, then stared into space again.

While she dithered, I pulled two cookies out of my own purse, where I'd stashed them after eating lunch at the Chop Suey Club.

I tried to munch surreptitiously but didn't succeed.

Aunt Ida swung around and glared at me.

"You know you are not to eat in the car. You're getting crumbs all over my new automobile. Please finish your snack outside. And be sure to shake off your clothes and hands before you come back inside."

Good grief. I spotted no more than two or three crumbs between my feet.

"Yes, ma'am."

I expect I sounded a tad sulky. I got out of the Buick and stood in the fumes of spilled gasoline and finished eating the cookies. I became so irritated that I decided to curtail any conversation for the rest of the journey home.

However, after we hit the road again, Aunt Ida surprised me by returning to my earlier question.

"I don't know anything about Rory's Texas girlfriends," she said. "During his last years in Gunmetal, I was teaching in

Yoakum."

"Darn it." I gnawed on a ragged cuticle. "Now I'll have to ask Poppa. I don't really want to bring it up with him."

"Maybe the girlfriend lived around Beaumont, back when Rory worked as a roustabout in the Spindletop field."

My spirits picked up a little.

"That would still fit what Susanna Weston told you—that he pined for a girl he left behind in Texas. Beaumont could be the place."

"That is not precisely what I said about the conversation and—"

"Close enough, and my own interpretation anyway."

She pursed her lips, and her hands tightened on the steering wheel.

"Now, Walter, we are *not* driving to Beaumont. That would ask just too, too much of me."

I laughed, and my shoulders relaxed.

"Yes, ma'am. Even I know that would be a wild goose chase. Hmm, but now that you mention it..." When a horrified look spread across her face, I hastened to add, "Just kidding. Really."

After a minute, I said, "I sure wish I knew if the special girlfriend and the dreadful thing Uncle Rory did were connected."

"You'll never know. And now, Wallie, let's give all this talk a rest. I'm played out and need to concentrate on my driving."

The rest of the trip was uneventful. By the time we drove past the sign announcing the city limits of Gunmetal, my place in the universe had returned to normal. The wild events in Galveston felt like a dream. Not quite a nightmare, only a dream.

"It's good to be home again, isn't it?" I said as Aunt Ida turned the Buick onto Orth Street. I rummaged through my purse and made sure I had all my belongings. "Thank you for this trip. I'll always remember our time in Galveston."

Despite a few flare-ups, I had learned a lot about my aunt and never felt closer to her than I did in that speck of time.

Dusk had set in, and lights were on inside our neighbors' houses. I was still fussing with my purse when Aunt Ida startled me by shouting.

"Wallie! What's happening up ahead? Can you tell?"

I scrutinized the street. Half a block away three automobiles sat parked at the curb. A crowd lingered on the sidewalk in front of our house.

A shot of nerves ran through me.

"Isn't that Sheriff Finch's car?"

My mind flashed to the night Uncle Rory died.

Poppa.

What if something had happened to Poppa?

CHAPTER TWENTY-EIGHT

AUNT IDA STOPPED the car near the house. I flung open the door, hurled myself out to the sidewalk, and ran down the street.

"Wallie, wait."

I paid her no heed.

The crowd near the street recognized me and pointed toward my backyard. Partially hidden by bushes, another group was bent over a lump on the ground. I ran straight to them, and they looked up as I skidded to a stop. Too late, they moved as one to hide what lay behind them.

A body was sprawled on the grass, a cowboy hat lying beside the left arm.

Was it Poppa's?

There was blood. Lots and lots of blood. It covered the head and torso of the corpse.

My breath came in gasps.

"Is that"—I pointed—"is that my father?"

Sheriff Finch grabbed my arm.

"Step back, Miss Walter. Get hold of yourself. That's not

the judge."

I peered at the men near me, not entirely sure I believed that Poppa was unharmed. "Where is he? I don't see him."

Doctor Dillenbeck stepped up.

"Your father is still at the courthouse. He'll be here presently."

In the waning light, I didn't recognize the dead man.

"Who is that?"

"No one knows," the sheriff said. "Probably just a stranger passing through town."

This second death in such a short time unhinged me. I threw all caution aside and spoke my mind freely.

"If he has no connection to Gunmetal, then why did someone kill him? That makes no sense."

And then it hit me.

A stranger passing through town.

I wrested my arm from Sheriff Finch.

"Let me look at him. I may have seen him before."

Aunt Ida appeared at my side and shoved me back from the body.

"Walter, settle down and control yourself. Go inside the house now. This is no place for ladies."

"But I think I've seen that man before."

She tugged on my sleeve, but I jerked away.

"I won't leave." My voice came out in a shriek, and startled faces gaped at me. "I told you Uncle Rory was murdered, and y'all laughed at me. Now look at—"

I broke off when I saw my father walk up behind the sheriff. Deputy Misak was with him.

I rushed over to Poppa and threw my arms around him.

He patted my back, murmuring, "Calm down. Take it easy."

He acted like I was one of his dogs. I reared back and glared at him full on.

"Tell him, Poppa. Tell Sheriff Finch about the stranger from Missouri. That looks like him, right there. I knew something was suspicious when I saw him watching our house last week. Now he's lying dead on our lawn."

"Now, Wallie, I—"

"Remember, I wasn't the only one who saw him. Clayton noticed him too and thought it odd enough to mention to you. Don't you remember?"

Too late, I realized my voice had escalated back into a shriek. Ordinarily I would have been embarrassed at my behavior. Perhaps it was the accumulation of the day's events, building up in me, piling on, one on top of the other. Yet for once I simply did not care what people thought of me.

"That's enough, Walter," Poppa shouted in a voice I'd never heard before.

"She's overwrought." Aunt Ida turned to Dr. Dillenbeck. "Will you help me take her into the house? She's still upset about her uncle's death—and now this."

Dr. Dillenbeck moved toward me.

"Of course."

I appealed to Poppa with beseeching eyes, hoping for help, but he turned his back on me.

He turned his back on me.

Aunt Ida grabbed one of my arms, and Dr. Dillenbeck took the other. They hustled me to the front of the house and up the steps to the porch.

Wrenching my arms away, I marched to the porch swing and sat.

"I'll stay right here, thank you very much. I want to watch what's going on."

I made sure my view from the swing included the men in the yard.

"Will you go inside," Aunt Ida said to Dr. Dillenbeck, "and get her a glass of water?"

"Madam, do not mistake me for a nurse," he said. "Excuse me, but I have a body to examine."

Even in the dim light, I could see Dr. Dillenbeck's scowl. I doubt he was used to taking orders, especially from a bossy female.

He stomped down the steps and across the lawn. As he joined the group beside the body, Aunt Ida went into the house. With her gone, I breathed more easily. When she returned with a glass of water, I sipped at it.

Holler was whining pitifully. Scraping sounds indicated his nails were making scars on the beautiful oak door. Soon he began to howl as only a beagle can.

Aunt Ida marched to the door, opened it a crack, and shouted, "Shoo, shoo." In a louder voice, she called, "Athalia? Will you please take this dog away?" She turned back to me. "Honestly, your family and its dogs."

She huffed and settled beside me on the swing. I shifted to face her and shook a finger at her. The shock on her face made me realize how unacceptable my behavior was.

Get a grip on yourself, Wallie.

In a quiet but intense tone, I explained my position.

"Now you *must* admit I'm right. Clearly this new death is a murder, not an accident." My words began to pick up speed. "*Now* you must agree that this second death makes it more likely that Uncle Rory was murdered."

Holding my breath, I watched Aunt Ida closely. Both of my legs jiggled up and down, and the old wooden swing creaked in protest.

I didn't mind, but Aunt Ida did.

"Quit that."

She pressed her hand firmly to my knee.

I stopped jiggling.

"Look what you've done," she said. "You've spilled water on your dress."

"I don't care. What I want to know is if you agree with me."

She hesitated.

"Well, do you agree or not?"

She stared into the darkness, then spoke slowly, picking her words with care.

"This new death does force me to admit your hunch might be correct."

I ignored *might be correct*, focusing instead on her grudging capitulation. A sense of deep satisfaction spread through me. I tried to be gracious in victory, using my hand to hide the smirk that spread across my face.

From the street came the sound of an approaching motor car. Dewey parked his father's automobile in front of my house, got out, and started toward the first group of people, our curious neighbors. I hurried to the edge of the porch and yelled Dewey's name.

He waved.

The mere glimpse of him thrilled me. Plus I was grateful to him. His arrival saved me from saying something obnoxious and boastful to my aunt. I always enjoyed being proved right—one of my failings, no doubt.

As I waited on the steps for Dewey, my heart flipped and raced. Who cared if he heard about the murder on my street and only came to investigate? If he hadn't come to see me, that didn't matter. Besides, I'd only just arrived home. He was here now, and there was so much to tell him.

I heard Aunt Ida slip inside the house behind me.

She must have sensed I wanted privacy to talk to Dewey. Thank heaven she approved of him.

Dewey sprang up the steps and joined me on the porch. He stared at me, holding his hands rigid at his side. His posture made him look tense, but his eyes told a different story. I imagined that they held longing and hope.

In a flash I realized he had no idea what I'd decided during my trip. How could he know that I was considering him a likely candidate for marriage?

But now wasn't the time for a full confession or even a declaration of ardor, for that matter.

Still, I needed to offer a small but encouraging sign.

I held out my hand.

"Oh, Dewey, I'm so very glad to see you."

The smile on his lips spread to his eyes. As they crinkled, I fancied that a deep comprehension shone from them.

"I missed you, Dewey. There's no one else I would rather see right now than you. No one."

He grabbed both my hands. We began to swing our clasped hands back and forth, back and forth, just as the couple in the town square of Wharton had done earlier that day.

"Will you sit with me?" I freed one hand to gesture at the swing. "I've got so much to tell you—all that happened on my trip—and now there's that horror out there."

Dewey glanced at the cluster of men, then looked back at me.

"For you, I have nothing but time."

We rocked on the swing together. Although delighted to see him, I didn't dare sit too close to him. I'd had enough of Aunt Ida's wrath for the day.

"What's going on out there?" Dewey ran his hands through his hair, an uncharacteristic gesture. I judged him to be agitated. "Someone telephoned me," he said, "and said there was another death on your property. I rushed over to see what was what. I was afraid it was your father." He gulped. "Most of all, Wallie, I was afraid you'd returned from your trip, and *you* had been killed."

"Oh, Dewey."

Our eyes sought each other and held.

"Aunt Ida and I only returned a few minutes ago. We

turned onto our street and saw all this commotion. I was like you—afraid Poppa had been killed. Thank heaven my family is safe. But something bizarre is going on, that's for sure."

"Are you frightened?"

"Yes, but I have a theory."

I plunged into a description of the gangster world Uncle Rory had inhabited. I was deep into my adventures in Galveston, when Aunt Ida peeked out the door.

"Why, hello there, Dewey." Her voice held an attractive lilt rare for her. "Shall I bring y'all glasses of lemonade? And Athalia made her famous molasses cookies."

"Thank you," I said. "That would be lovely."

My aunt amazed me—intent on matchmaking while a dead man lay nearby.

She disappeared into the house, and Dewey and I inched closer together on the swing.

He fingered the neck of his shirt.

"I worried about you while you were gone. Thank goodness you're back home, safe and sound. The few days of your trip felt like years."

Footsteps pounded up the front steps. Again our tête-à-tête was interrupted.

Deputy Misak stood before us on the porch, his Stetson in his hands.

"Your father sent me, Miss Walter. He says you'll want to know what was in the stranger's pocket. We found an address book. It has names of places the sheriff says are speakeasies in Galveston. Don't know why you'd care or what it means. Do you think it's important?"

"Hallelujah."

His words filled my soul with glee. For a second I recalled the station attendant pumping gasoline into my aunt's Buick. Just like her automobile, I was topped up with energy, filled to the brim.

I had to do something with all the bubbling zeal.

I turned to Dewey, put my arms around him—albeit somewhat timidly—and hugged him.

He hugged me back.

Because the deputy watched us with googly eyes, I couldn't allow the hug to last long. I tugged at Dewey's hand and pulled him down the steps.

"Let's go see."

Deputy Misak followed us down the sidewalk and out to the backyard, where Dewey and I joined the men huddled around the body. Off to the side, Poppa and the sheriff were going through a small notebook. It had a red cover and looked well-used.

I scolded myself for wanting to grab it, clenching my fists to keep them from reaching out and snatching. How could I convince Sheriff Finch to let me look too? My half day in Galveston had taught me so much about sinful locations and the people there. Even if the sheriff knew a lot, I might be able to fill in some gaps for him.

"Wish me luck," I whispered to Dewey. "I've got to see that little book."

He held me back, then patted my shoulder.

"Be sweet."

His advice brought me up short. I'd been prepared to barge in and demand my rights, but I quickly changed my strategy.

Moving to Poppa's side, I stood calmly at his elbow, watching him and the sheriff flip through pages. Occasionally they stopped to read.

After a time, Sheriff Finch noticed me.

"What do you want, Miss Walter?"

I pointed at the book in his hands.

"Is it true that book includes Galveston addresses?"

He looked at Poppa, who nodded.

The sheriff said, "That's right."

Attempting my most demure smile, I said, "Maybe I can help. My aunt and I were in Galveston earlier today and learned a few things about the work Uncle Rory did there."

Poppa's eyes widened.

"You did what?"

The smile that had been on his mouth wilted into a grim line.

"We didn't have a chance to tell you. We stopped in Galveston to pick up Uncle Rory's things. We thought you might want them." I fluttered my eyes at him, just a little bit, trying for a look of innocence. "I thought I might be able to help."

Swinging back to the sheriff, I said, "*You* are the expert, of course. I just want to make sure whatever I know gets transferred to you. I want to be useful to your investigation if I can."

I had difficulty talking like this to the sheriff, but I seemed to recall Sherlock Holmes—or maybe it was Dr. Watson—wheedling a lawman this way. Or had I just picked up this ability by watching wives use feminine wiles on their recalcitrant husbands?

"Mighty kind of you, Miss Walter." Sheriff Finch touched his hat. "Are you angling to take a look-see of this here book?"

I allowed a grin to spread across my face. What could it hurt?

"Why, yes, thank you."

I held out my hand.

When the sheriff passed the book to me, I reined in my emotions. Jumping up and down and shouting *yippee* would not be ladylike. Aunt Ida would go into conniptions if I leapt for joy.

Few of the pages contained notations. It didn't take long to thumb through them. I noted the Maceos' barbershop and its street address. Also the Chop Suey Club with its phone number. Toward the back, one name—written in bold letters and underlined—stood out. *Alphonse*. Beside it was what looked like a telephone number—Calumet 5-7277.

A tingle ran down my spine.

"Does the name Calumet mean anything to you?"

I looked at Poppa and Sheriff Finch in turn. Each man shook his head.

Deputy Misak stepped forward.

"Hey, I got an aunt lives in Calumet."

"Where is that?" I asked.

"Pretty far from here," he said, "on the south side of Chicago. Maybe the dead guy had relatives up that way too, like me."

The tingle started up again and ran up and down my spine, up and down without stopping.

The south side of Chicago.

That was news indeed.

CHAPTER TWENTY-NINE

KNOWN FACTS ABOUT the dead man raced through my head. Some of them meshed with other details I learned in Galveston.

Mentally I put them all in a package and tied it up with a pretty bow. I would offer this gift to the sheriff and see how he liked it. I would not leap to conclusions. None were warranted yet. Other than to say the corpse had suspicious connections to bootleggers in Galveston and Chicago.

Five people stood in a knot centered on the address book—Poppa, the sheriff, the deputy, Dewey, and me. I returned the book to Sheriff Finch.

"I have background information on a few names and places listed in there. Would you like to hear it?"

The sheriff took off his Stetson and scratched his head. An unfocused look came over his weathered face as he stared over nearby treetops. Clearly he was concentrating hard, whereas usually he was so offhand and casual.

He shot a look at my father, who shrugged as if saying, "Go on. It's your choice."

"So tell me whatcha got," the sheriff said.

Unable to contain himself, he rolled his eyes.

Looking at Dewey for encouragement, I started my spiel. "My facts don't point at any conclusions. I do believe, however, that they are suggestive and well worth looking into."

"So tell me, damn it." Sheriff Finch ducked his head and shuffled his feet. "Beg pardon."

I ignored his cursing and continued, unfazed, remembering how Sherlock Holmes stated his facts and theories quite calmly.

"This book holds the names of two people my aunt and I met today, also the names of business establishments they own. They are brothers Rosario and Sam Maceo, and they run a barber shop and a place on the pier called the Chop Suey Club. They deal in illegal liquor. Uncle Rory worked for them."

Sheriff Finch's face twisted.

"Rory worked for these guys, you say?"

I nodded.

"All right. What else you got?"

Now things were going to get sticky. Poppa would not be happy with what I had to say next.

Making a face, I screwed up my courage.

"While Aunt Ida and I were talking to the Maceo brothers this afternoon, two thuggish men from Chicago came to see them."

Poppa said, "Why were you—?"

Sheriff Finch waved his hand, quieting my father.

"Why do you call them thugs?"

"Aside from their speech and behavior, they talked about a rival gang that wanted to cut into the Maceos' business. Now, here's the really interesting part." I drew myself up to my full height and eyed each man in turn, making sure they hung on my every word. "The Chicago men referred several times to someone they called the big boss. His name was Al. And the dead man's book lists an Alphonse with a telephone number in

Chicago, in Calumet."

I stepped back from our circle and gave the men time to let my information sink in.

Then I said, "As I stated, none of this is conclusive. But it certainly seems suspicious to me."

Poppa spoke first.

"What are you doing, Wallie? I don't understand you."

I sought the right words to make him appreciate my opinions. I shut my eyes, all the better to block out their disapproval and concentrate on my explanation.

"I got angry when Uncle Rory died. He had a hard life. Some of it sounded awful, no matter how attractive a gloss he put on it. He seemed so unhappy. It was unfair that he got cut down right when he'd come home to Gunmetal.

"The way he died didn't sit well with me. It made more sense that he was murdered than he'd been unlucky or careless. And if someone did kill him, I wanted justice for my uncle— who was, after all, your flesh and blood too, Poppa."

I hung my head.

In a low voice, I stated my conclusion. "There was no one to stand up for Uncle Rory. That made me sad. Made me mad too. That's it. Now you have it all."

One solitary tear straggled down my face. Still looking down at the ground, I brushed the tear away with an impatient hand. It wouldn't do to look pathetic in front of these men.

When I raised my head, I was surprised to see Sheriff Finch observing me. He didn't look angry either. Rather, his expression was kind. He offered me his hand.

"Thank you, Miss Wallie. Whatever your reasons, you've done us a service. You've given me information that I'll be glad to follow up on."

Knock me over with a feather. I had not expected recognition.

I handed the address book to him.

"Thank you, Sheriff. As I said, I'm happy to help."

Not knowing what to do next, I glanced at Poppa. Perhaps it was only my imagination, but his chest seemed fuller, and he looked taller too. Maybe I had made him proud.

"Come inside." He took my arm. "We can leave these men to finish their grim duties."

As if in a dream, I walked back to the house beside Poppa—with Dewey following close behind. Poppa held the door open, and we proceeded to the parlor. Aunt Ida stood by the mantel. Her hands were fluttering at her throat. Athalia brought in lemonade and molasses cookies.

Despite the strain showing on her face, Aunt Ida uttered pleasantries about the refreshments, but her attitude made me want to scream. It was as if nothing of any consequence had happened.

As if no second murder victim lay out on our property.

As if Uncle Rory had not died in our carriage house.

As if there had been no exploits in Galveston.

Were these folks expecting life to carry on as before? I certainly was not.

And then...then I looked more closely at the people around me. Each showed signs of strain. Aunt Ida's fingers plucked at an imaginary thread on her skirt. Poppa chewed on a fingernail. Dewey's gaze darted around the room. Athalia didn't say a word, only offered the cookie platter and tiptoed out of the parlor.

Holler bounded into the room and ran to Poppa, who pushed him away. Surprised and chastened, my poor darling puppy slunk over to me and curled between my feet. Oh, we were a jolly bunch. At least I now recognized telltale indications that the latest death in Gunmetal was affecting everyone.

We sipped our lemonade and munched our cookies in silence. Holler didn't even beg for food. Every once in a while, a shout went up outside, and we could hear one of the sheriff's men yelling to another.

Poppa stood.

"What we have here is a—" He stopped and exhaled loudly. "Well, I don't rightly know what to say. I don't know what we have other than the obvious. Gunmetal officials have, at minimum, one murder to solve. That is certain. And, yes, Wallie, you could be correct. Maybe two murders."

He walked to the fireplace, where he rearranged a pair of candlesticks that stood on the mantel, then swung around and faced me.

"I must admit that threads appear to connect my brother to the dead man out on our lawn, threads we cannot ignore. Perhaps someone murdered Rory after all. We don't know by whom, and we don't know why, but suspicions mount that it was murder."

He returned to his chair and sat.

Tenting his fingers in front of his chest, he said, "While on the one hand I'm proud of your tenacity and applaud your ability to dig up information, on the other hand, Wallie, I fear for your safety."

"But, Poppa, I—"

"Let me finish. Because I worry about your well-being, I want you to promise that you'll give up playing at detective. You've done enough—indeed, far more than you should have. Thus far you have experienced dumb luck. Despite consorting with gangsters, you were not harmed."

He shot a nasty look in Aunt Ida's direction. "I'll discuss your part in this with you another time." Poppa swiveled toward me, and his eyes were unflinching. "And now I demand—I demand, you hear me?—that you stop your investigations at once. Do I make myself clear?"

Even though I seethed inside, I managed to reply through clenched teeth.

"Yes, sir."

"Do I have your solemn promise?"

I mumbled my response.

"I couldn't hear you."

"Yes, Poppa."

His face changed—a loosening of the skin around his eyes and an upward tilt of his lips. I watched some of the strain fade from his features.

His shoulders fell, and he ran a hand through his hair.

"Now then, I ask both of you, Ida and Dewey, to support my position. Wallie respects you, and you two are often in her company. Please help her toe the line. She will have difficulty obeying me, and I cannot keep an eye on her when I'm at the courthouse."

Ire rose in my chest, and I gasped. How could Poppa do this to me? My aunt had only just begun to treat me like an adult. Dewey might think I wasn't trustworthy.

"You insult me, Poppa. I'm no silly little schoolgirl, but you're treating me like one. And I certainly don't need jailers."

His voice rolled through the room like thunder, making Holler run.

"I've just lost my brother. I cannot lose you too."

CHAPTER THIRTY

WITH HEAD BOWED, I stared at my lap and mulled over Poppa's admonition. I understood his point of view, I really did. And yet I was still insulted. My hands shook, I was so mortified. How could he chastise me like that, especially in front of my aunt and beau?

I had to maintain my composure. I pushed my hurt feelings down, way down into the bottoms of my shoes. I wondered if anyone noticed a muscle was jumping in my cheek.

Silence ruled the room. Within minutes after Poppa's forceful speech, the grim party broke up. Both my aunt and my beau departed, making their excuses and scurrying out as fast as it was polite to do so.

On her way out the door, Aunt Ida leaned toward me as she passed and said softly, "Take heart."

Likewise, Dewey took my hand and whispered in my ear, "I'll telephone you tomorrow."

And they vanished into the night.

When the front door closed, Poppa and I met each other's eyes.

"My duty is to protect you. I trust you understand that." His voice was soft and kind.

Again I restrained myself. My answering nod was slight, almost nonexistent.

"Good night, Poppa."

My heart thudded and my cheeks burned. Avoiding further discussion with him seemed prudent.

He planted a kiss on my forehead and trod down the hall to the stairway.

I left the front hall and returned to the parlor. Through its large bay window I watched the sheriff's entourage of three automobiles progress down the street. I assumed they were transporting the stranger's body to—well, where did murder victims go?

One fact I knew for certain—a body no longer adorned our lawn.

I stood quite still and listened for sounds to indicate Poppa's whereabouts. Athalia had gone home for the evening long ago, and our old house remained silent. As silent as the grave where the stranger would soon end up. I shivered.

After delaying a few minutes, I gathered Holler in my arms and started up the stairway. I stopped halfway to the second floor.

A compulsion gripped me. I needed to assure myself that I was my own woman, so I slipped back down the stairs and into the dining room, heading straight to the decanter of bourbon. Poppa had left it on the sideboard after he shared it with me the night of Uncle Rory's death. I might be forbidden to investigate, and I'd promised to abide by that. However, I hadn't promised to stay out of Poppa's bourbon.

Setting Holler down, I poured an inch into a crystal goblet, gazed at the prized Kentucky sour mash, and took a swallow. The alcohol burned all the way down. But in a strange way it made me feel vindicated.

I would make my own decisions. I could be myself as well as a good daughter. Carrying the glass carefully up the stairs, I allowed Holler to navigate the stairs by himself.

Once in my bedroom and seated at my writing desk, I set out to update my journal. I firmly believed that every detail of my trip to Houston and Galveston was burned into my brain forevermore, yet a little voice in my head whispered that those important events might dim with time. Maybe that would happen even more quickly than I imagined possible. It would be better if I committed all my memories to paper.

I pulled Holler's basket close to my desk, got him settled, and took another sip of Poppa's bourbon. Then I began to write in my journal. Eventually my litany of events filled twenty pages.

Muscles in my shoulders felt tight, and my neck was sore. How long had I been writing? My glass was empty, my journal was full. The clock on my bedside table showed that it was one in the morning. In his little basket at my feet, Holler snored softly, occasionally twitching and whimpering. I imagined he dreamed of romping through grass and chasing little field bunnies. I turned off the lamp and climbed into bed.

Sleep, however, eluded me. I rolled from one side of the bed to the other. My thoughts raced and wouldn't slow.

How could I fall asleep after the day's events?

I'd crammed a year's worth of living into just one day. Only that morning Aunt Ida and I had motored out of Houston and on to the sinful city of Galveston. There we met two sets of gangsters and two genuine floozies, although I had to confess that the women showed themselves to be rather nice, given their, um, work milieu.

But that wasn't all, oh no.

Aunt Ida had spilled an important secret about her past.

Another man was murdered on the MacGregor property.

Poppa reprimanded me in a way he had never done before.

And Dewey Brandon and I were inching toward an understanding that our futures would be intertwined.

My goodness, such a day. Only the last event, however, produced unalloyed happiness. Safe to say, my emotions were muddled. My thoughts spun in crazy circles.

In reality, despite all these raucous events, I had actually accomplished something difficult. People whose opinions mattered to me had finally recognized the validity of one of my ideas. When I originally suggested that someone murdered Uncle Rory, everyone scoffed. Now Poppa, Aunt Ida, and even the sheriff himself all had to agree that I was not a foolish young woman fantasizing about evil. Unfortunately, though, my time to savor success before Poppa humiliated me had been brief.

Despite my promise to Poppa, I still wanted to pinpoint the likeliest murder suspect. I abhorred an unsolved puzzle. As sleep crept near me, I wished with all my heart that Poppa had not berated me.

The next morning I slept later than usual. If Holler hadn't pounced on the bed, demanding to be let outside, I might have slept until noon.

My reflection in the mirror showed that the tumultuous events of the day before hadn't changed me. I was surprised— and a little disappointed—that I bore no outward signs of my experiences.

Maybe if I looked older, people would stop treating me like a child.

After donning shirt, riding pants, and boots, I clomped down the stairs with my puppy bouncing along beside me. I had no fear of running into Poppa. Given the lateness of the hour, I knew he was at work. I greeted Athalia in the kitchen, grabbed a biscuit, and took Holler outside to do his business.

When he finished, he loped into the carriage house, and I followed. I sat on a barrel and watched my dog sniff every part of the building. Staring at the spot where Uncle Rory died, I realized how consumed I'd been by the mission to prove he was murdered. A good night's sleep had set my head straight, and now a new reality set in. One that depressed me.

Even I had to admit that Poppa was right. My sleuthing job was at an end. The lawmen needed to take over and use my information for their own investigations. There was nothing left for me to do. And in truth, identifying and tracking a murderer was a dangerous undertaking.

My emotions had cycled through annoyance, satisfaction, and humiliation. And soon, I predicted, boredom. I must resign myself to ordinary, humdrum living.

I stood and whistled for Holler, but he didn't come leaping toward me.

I whistled again. When he still didn't come, I yelled his name. What a bother.

I searched all over the backyard, peeking inside buckets and baskets, his usual hiding places. No puppy. I rushed inside to the kitchen and asked Athalia if she had let him back into the house. She hadn't seen him.

I began to worry. I hoped Holler hadn't ventured into the Carsons' yard or run off down the street. I went outside again and crossed to the neighbor's property. Holler failed to appear. I saw no indications he had been there, no obvious damage to the neighbors' lawn or to their precious garden.

Holler had never disappeared before.

I walked around the neighborhood, alternately whistling and yelling for Holler. One elderly neighbor enjoying her front porch hadn't seen him.

My worry grew. What if Mrs. Carson found Holler in her garden again, caught him, and did something bad to him? I shut down that line of reasoning. It would only lead to sickening conclusions.

There was nothing else for it; I had to ask Mrs. Carson if she had seen Holler. I didn't relish the prospect.

I had never stood on their front porch before, let alone been in their house.

Carefully I walked along the line between my home and the Carson place. My neighbors were adamant that no one should set foot on their land. I had broken that rule only once and learned my lesson. Since that time long ago, I had never transgressed again.

My stomach lurched when I began the march up the sidewalk to the Carson front porch. I banged on the door, turning back toward my house to keep an eye out for Holler. Waiting for a response jangled my nerves. How I wished nice Mr. Carson and not his wife would answer the door. I watched the doorknob twist.

The door opened a sliver, just enough for me to see that the lady of the house wore a blue bathrobe and had a white towel wrapped around her head.

"Why, hello, Wallie. This is a surprise."

Her tone, if not her words, cheered me immediately. She didn't sound angry. Given our history, that was a first.

"I hate to bother you, but have you seen my puppy? He isn't in your garden. I checked already."

Her lips twisted.

"I haven't seen your unruly dog, I can assure you of that. I haven't been out of the house all day. It is rather early to make calls, you know."

"I'm sorry I bothered you."

I turned to go.

"Wait," she said. "I'd like to show you something. Please come in for a minute."

CHAPTER THIRTY-ONE

MRS. CARSON'S INVITATION surprised me. No, it *shocked* me.

It intrigued me too. This lady had lived next door for all of my twenty-three years, but I knew nothing about her. I was accustomed to thinking of her house as a vacant hole where nothing ever happened. Mr. Carson was always pleasant, but his wife talked to me only when she was furious with Holler.

Demurring seemed like a good strategy. I didn't want to appear too eager.

"Oh, I mustn't intrude," I said and smiled.

"Please, do come inside."

She opened the door wider, and so I slipped through.

How delicious. I forgot all about trying to find my dog and relished the feeling of excitement gained from entering forbidden territory.

"I hope you can overlook my appearance." She gestured at her bathrobe. "I had barely finished washing my hair when I heard your knock."

She pointed to an armchair beside a lamp table. "Won't

you have a seat?"

She selected the matching armchair on the other side of the table for herself.

I sat on the edge of my chair and took stock of the room. One floor lamp cast dim light, and the curtains were drawn. If she lived like this, in a house akin to a dark cave, no wonder she was gloomy and dejected all the time.

"Here's what I wanted to show you."

Mrs. Carson picked up a framed photograph that sat between us on the table and passed it to me.

"That's me and my dog when I was about twelve years old. When I was growing up, I always had a dog. My folks were dog people like y'all are."

Holding the photograph close to my face in order to see it in the scant light, I made out a tousle-haired girl posed in a photography studio. She was patting a white terrier that sat on her lap.

I looked up at Mrs. Carson in surprise.

Mrs. Carson nodded and smiled. She had a lovely smile. I had never seen it before.

"I wanted you to understand that I really do like dogs," she said. "I imagine you think that I hate them, and I—"

"No, I think—"

She waved her hand to cut me off.

"No need to fib, Miss Walter. I know what you think and why you think it too." She pulled her bathrobe tighter across her chest. "I also want to explain why I don't have a dog now. Floyd can't be anywhere near them. He can't breathe around them and has always been like that. That's why I can't let your puppy come into our yard. If Floyd even gets near a dog, his throat closes up."

Why hadn't she told me that before?

Mrs. Carson leaned forward in her chair, and an eager look came in her eyes.

"Now tell me what happened last night at your place. I heard quite a commotion over there but couldn't tell what went on. Floyd wouldn't let me go see."

So that was the reason she'd lured me into her house. I glanced at a clock on the wall, not wanting to linger while Holler wandered alone outside.

In an effort to be polite, I gave a rapid rundown on the stranger's murder, concluding by saying, "I've enjoyed visiting with you, Mrs. Carson. You've been so neighborly. But now I need to go. I must keep searching for my dog."

Mrs. Carson's face fell, and her shoulders drooped.

"I understand, but I hoped we could talk longer. I don't get out much, as you probably know."

From outside came the sound of a door banging shut. I looked out a window in time to see Mr. Carson walk away from his tool shed and out to the back of his yard. He held Holler in his hands.

I leapt to my feet.

"Your husband found my dog. I must go now. I'm sorry."

Mrs. Carson also rose, flapping her hands. "Oh no, poor Floyd. He'll get sick."

In her agitated state, she knocked over several framed photographs that stood on the table. Two fell at my feet.

I picked up the pictures and replaced them on the table, glancing quickly at both. I squinting at the second, pulling it closer to my face, unsure that I saw what I thought I did.

The photograph of a young woman matched the one from Uncle Rory's wallet.

I went on alert. I didn't know what this signified, but I had the good sense—for once—not to ask any questions.

Even if I'd wanted to question Mrs. Carson, she had already left the house in a rush. I followed her out the door and across the yard. As she reached her husband, he sneezed and clutched his chest. Holler jumped from his arms and raced to me. I scooped up Holler and held him tight as he cuddled into my neck.

Despite his sneezes, Mr. Carson managed to say, "I found your dog out back in my tool shed. I chased him all around in there when he wouldn't leave. You weren't outside. I finally caught him and was taking him to your house. Excuse me, I must—"

A violent sneezing fit overtook him. He proceeded to sneeze, by my count, nine times.

"Floyd, you better go inside." Mrs. Caron turned to me. "I told you he can't be around dogs. I can't imagine why he decided to pick yours up."

With Holler wiggling in my hands, I could care less at that point why she always shooed him away. I was awash in delight that he was safe. I rubbed his ears while he licked my face.

"You bad boy. You upset me very, very much. Where have you been?"

I looked up to see Mrs. Carson escort her husband to their house. Once they were inside and their door was shut, I walked home on slow feet, keeping a steady pace. Actually I wanted to race as fast as possible back to the safety of my own home, but I was trembling and didn't want to drop Holler.

By the time I reached my backdoor and entered the kitchen, I was panting.

Holler leapt from my arms and ran to his water bowl.

I collapsed onto a chair and put my head in my hands.

Athalia stared at me openmouthed.

"Child, what's come over you? You seen a ghost?"

My laugh was harsh.

"What a good question. Maybe I did just that."

Wait. Athalia might know something.

I raised my head and stared at her.

"How long have you known the Carsons?"

"Oh mercy, a mighty long time."

"Even back before I was born?"

"You bet."

"Then perhaps you can tell me about their family."

"What you want to know, Miss Walter? I knows plenty."

Vibrations of anticipation shot through me. Without disobeying Poppa, I might be able to solve a small mystery. Asking Athalia questions about the past surely wouldn't count as disobedience.

"Was there ever a young woman living over there in that house? I don't mean Mrs. Carson when she was a young lady. Someone completely different. Someone with pale skin and very light hair. Does that ring a bell?"

Athalia dried her hands on a dish towel and joined me at the kitchen table. I drummed my fingers while she gave my question some thought. I'd be so disappointed if she didn't recall someone who fit the bill.

"Seems like I does remember a girl like that. Back before you was born."

"Did Uncle Rory know her? Were they friends, good friends?"

Athalia pushed back from the table and glared at me.

"Now why you ask me that?"

If I confessed the reason for my curiosity, would she refuse to confide in me? Or should I be my usual self and tell her everything? I decided to make a full declaration of intent.

"Oh, Athalia." I heaved a huge sigh. "On our way back from Houston yesterday, Aunt Ida and I took a detour through Galveston to pick up Uncle Rory's things. We ran into some people he worked with."

"Uh huh," she said.

I thought she sounded dubious.

"Oh, all right. I wanted to find out more about my uncle and his life there. I met his current sweetheart—the one who proved to be his last. She said he had always regretted losing a girl he adored. Now, I don't know where that old flame lived when he knew her. The only thing I've been able to figure out is that she probably lived in Texas. She could even have lived right here in Gunmetal."

I glanced out the window and at the Carsons' house.

"Maybe even right over there."

I leaned closer to Athalia.

"But here's something really interesting." I stood and walked around the kitchen a few paces. "In Uncle Rory's things I found a folder that held three small photographs. One showed a young woman, and I just saw that same picture in the Carsons' house."

Athalia's body twitched, and she waved her hands in the air.

"You been over there, inside that house?"

"Yes, I went over to ask if the Carsons had seen Holler, and Mrs. Carson invited me in. While I was there, I saw a photograph."

Athalia's hands flew to her cheeks.

"I don't know. Oh, I don't know."

"What is it?"

"Don't know if rightly I can tell you these things."

"Oh, for heaven's sake, Athalia. Think of all the secrets and gossip you've told me while we sat right here at this kitchen table. You know I won't tell anyone. Besides, what can it hurt after all these years?"

"Some folks says that house be evil. Don't know 'bout that, but folks do likes to keep their secrets, dontcha know?"

"I understand that, I guess. But if you tell me, then I won't tell anyone else." I shook my head in wonderment. "Good grief, those people have been neighbors for decades. It always seemed odd that I know so little about them."

"One thing I knows, sure enough. It be a sad old house. All those Carson folks have bad luck, and it do go on and on and on."

"I'm all ears."

And I was.

I hadn't realized before the strength of my overwhelming desire to learn something substantive about our longtime neighbors.

CHAPTER THIRTY-TWO

THE KITCHEN GREW quiet; the only sounds the tap dripping and Holler breathing. Actually, I fancied that I heard my own heart thumping too.

Athalia stood.

"I got to work on some vegetables."

From the icebox she pulled out a large bowl filled with green beans.

"I can snap while I talk."

"Let me do some too."

It didn't seem right to watch Athalia work while I did nothing. I removed a bowl from the cabinet and took a portion of the beans from her.

Now the sound of fresh beans snapping broke the quiet.

Athalia began to hum, then asked, "How far you want me to go back?"

"As far back as you think would be useful for me to know about."

She snorted.

"Don't know why you want to know 'bout old stuff

anyways."

I ran my fingers through the beans.

"It's like this. Nothing is unimportant when it relates to a crime. I pay attention to clues the police might not bother with. There are connections between folks that are important, for example. Sherlock Holmes taught me that."

She raised her eyebrows.

"Do I know him?"

"No, ma'am. You probably don't. He's a fictional detective who works in London, England. I've read all his stories. Holmes always solves murders before the police do."

Her laughter pealed through the room.

"And you wants to do that too?"

Pursing my lips, I tried to stifle my hurt feelings.

"I don't know why not. I can't see that Sheriff Finch and his deputy are doing very much to solve Uncle Rory's murder."

"Course not. Don't even think it be a murder. Ain't that right?"

I had to shrug that off.

"Guess so. But they definitely have a murder to solve now. That stranger out there was killed by someone. It was no accident."

"How'd he die?"

"Not sure. I only got a brief glimpse of the body. Seemed like it was stabbed or hacked."

"Lord have mercy."

I shuddered at the memory.

"You wouldn't believe the amount of blood."

"Oh, Miss Walter. You always been a nosy child."

"I prefer to say that I'm inquisitive."

"Just a fancy word for nosy, I reckon."

"Might could be." I snapped several beans, then leaned forward. "So what can you tell me? Why do you say the Carsons always have bad luck?"

Athalia rubbed her forehead.

"Some folks ain't able to keep their babies alive. Carsons be like that. They had babies and they died. Mr. Carson and his wife lost all three of theirs. And Mr. Carson, he had brothers and sisters. They all died save one."

"Was the one who lived a brother or sister?"

"Sister. Pretty little thing. Name of Faith. Think that be right."

"Did she have dark hair?"

"No'm. Yellow."

Excitement rose in my chest.

"Wait right here. There's something I want to show you."

I ran as fast as I could upstairs, retrieved Uncle Rory's treasured photo from my bedroom, and rushed back into the kitchen. I placed the picture in front of Athalia.

"Is this Faith?"

Athalia nodded vigorously.

"Sure enough, I believe it is."

Satisfaction that felt like a warm bath enveloped me.

"The house in the picture looked familiar, but I couldn't be sure."

Athalia picked up the photograph and examined it closely.

"That the Carson house. It looks different 'cause those bushes grown up around the front since then."

"What happened to the Carson girl, Athalia? Where is she now?"

"Miss Faith be dead."

The words punched me in the stomach.

"No wonder Uncle Rory felt bad. How did she die?"

Athalia's eyes were full of concern.

"What difference does it make, Miss Walter? Why do you care?"

Her question knocked me back. What did any of my suppositions prove after all?

So what if Uncle Rory's long-ago girlfriend had lived next door and was now dead? Would I tell Sheriff Finch I figured that out? No, of course not.

"It's like this, Athalia. Sometimes puzzles stick in my mind until I can solve them. Yesterday I learned that Uncle Rory had a sweetheart he loved and lost and then pined for. Well, ever since I heard that, I've wanted to know who that girl was. I can't get this out of my head. Maybe she lived right over there." I waved in the direction of the Carson house. "And now you've told me her name was Faith."

The wave of my hand knocked some beans off the table. Holler roared into action. He grabbed a bean, escaped with it to a corner, and chomped. He would eat anything, even a raw green bean. Silly puppy.

I pulled my attention back to the conversation.

"So figuring this out with your help, well, that means I can now go on to wonder about something else that strikes my fancy. I do like solving mysteries. Big ones or little ones, I can't help it. I guess I'm just nosy, as you say."

For several more minutes, Athalia and I worked on the green beans, snapping the ends off. When we finished, she ran water in the bowl to wash them.

"I got us a nice ham hock to cook these beans with."

"Cornbread too?"

She pointed to the skillet waiting on the counter.

Holler begged for more food, but I shoved him gently away with my foot.

"Want to know what puzzle I'll try to solve next?"

Athalia nodded.

"You gonna tell me anyways."

We exchanged smiles.

"It's like this. I think the man who died yesterday was sent by gangsters to keep an eye on Uncle Rory. However, if that's the case, then what was he doing here yesterday? Uncle Rory died more than a week ago, yet the stranger still hung around. Does that make sense to you?"

"No'm, it don't."

"Not to me either. I'm very curious about that."

"What you doin' to find the answer? Your pappy wants to keep you safe."

"You're right, Athalia. I promised not to go poking around anymore, and I'll keep that promise. Still, I'll keep wondering about these two murders." A sly thought entered my mind. "But I can keep trying to work things out in my head. That won't break my promise."

Out in the front hallway, the telephone rang.

CHAPTER THIRTY-THREE

I RACED INTO the hall to answer the telephone, Holler dashing along with me.

"Hold your horses. I'm coming."

Maybe it was Dewey. He promised to call today.

But when I heard the voice on the other end of the line respond to my greeting, my heart fell. It was Poppa, and I wasn't ready to talk to him yet. My feelings were still bruised from his harsh treatment the night before.

"Sheriff Finch just left my office. I thought you'd want to hear his news."

He sounded matter-of-fact. Although I still harbored bad feelings, he didn't seem to. Afraid to exhibit any curiosity about the sheriff's investigation, I didn't reply.

Poppa said, "Don't you want to hear what he said?"

"Of course."

"The sheriff telephoned the police in Chicago. Turns out that gangster boss is an enterprising thug name of Al Capone. He's causing problems for the police by killing rivals as he builds up his own criminal gang and increases his territory."

When I stayed silent, he went on.

"So this means, Wallie, that you unearthed an important clue. It also means that the two men from Chicago you met in Galveston are capable of extreme violence. What a blessing that you and your aunt made it home safely."

The elation I felt at providing a substantial clue warred with the resentment I still held in my heart over Poppa's treatment.

Don't be childish, Wallie, I told myself.

But to Poppa I only said, "Thank you for telling me. I appreciate it."

I waited a few moments, and then, when Poppa didn't continue, my curiosity got the better of me.

"What else did he tell you?"

"I knew if I told you that you'd want to know even more. I opened a Pandora's box. So let's make a deal. Will you *renew* your promise to quit sleuthing?"

"I will, I promise. Now please, please tell me."

"Sheriff Finch says the dead man on our lawn carried a document with his name and address. Even though it was soaked with blood, it was legible. Turns out the Chicago police knew this man. Donny Sorrento, age thirty—a Kansas City criminal and a known associate of Capone. The Chicago police were surprised that a Capone henchman was way down here, so far from Chicago, but also glad that Sheriff Finch contacted them."

The phone went silent. All I could hear were crackles down the line.

Then Poppa quietly said, "Your persistence made these connections possible." He blew out a breath. "Maybe I should be happier about your achievement, but I still confess that I'm terrified you'll get hurt."

"I'm glad you told me, Poppa."

"When you're a parent yourself, you'll understand."

"I suppose so." For an instant my thoughts strayed to Dewey as the potential father of my unborn children, but I dragged my mind back to the subject at hand. My father's words went a long way toward raising my spirits. "So has the sheriff developed any theories about the murders at our place?"

"We didn't get into that. Even though Finch said nothing explicit, he seems at a loss about what to do next. These murders present unusual challenges for a small town lawman."

"Then what if—"

"Stop. Don't you dare start up again. I will not stand for it."

"I wasn't going to start anything. I only wanted—"

"Not another word. You'll make me regret that I called you."

"Sorry, Poppa."

Although he couldn't see me, I hung my head. No doubt he would be glad to see my contrition. I always hated to disappoint him. But why had he dangled this news in front of me? He should have realized I'd rise to the bait. I felt hard done by.

He cleared his throat.

"I'm sorry too. I didn't want to get upset with you again. So on another topic, have you talked to Dewey today?"

"Not yet, but he did promise to telephone. The day's still young."

"Then I'm sure he will. I like that young man. I see a nice future ahead for you two, if that's what you want."

That brought me up short. Poppa had never ventured a word in a matrimonial direction before. His words were high praise for Dewey. At least this was one subject that Poppa and I could agree on.

"Tell Athalia I'll be home for supper earlier than usual. And now, I must return to my duties. Stay safe and be good, Wallie."

"Goodbye, Poppa," I said softly.

I hung up the receiver and stared into space. Holler spun around my feet, and I bent to pet him.

"Lucky for me I didn't tell Poppa my own news."

Holler didn't reply, so I whispered in his ear. "You're right. Mine was small compared to what the sheriff learned from his call to Chicago. Who cares anyway if Uncle Rory's old girlfriend once lived next door?"

The telephone rang again. Its peal came so close to my ear that I yelped.

This time I heard Dewey's voice, and my spirits took wing. I'd been afraid Clayton was calling again, even after I'd told him several times to stop.

"How're you doing today, Wallie? Hope you got a good sleep last night and recovered from yesterday's upsets."

"I'm better, thanks. Will you come over and visit later today?"

"You bet." His voice took on a chipper tone, and I imagined his grin. "How about I drop by after work? My boss is shutting the law office early today since he's got an event this evening."

"You're the hardest-working law clerk I know." An idea flashed to mind. "Why don't you stay for supper? You must try Athalia's wonderful cornbread, and I even helped with the green beans."

I hoped this was all right with her—and Poppa too. I should've checked before I issued the invitation, but I wanted to nail down Dewey's acceptance.

He agreed eagerly. After a few more minutes of happy talk, Dewey said he needed to return to work, and we said our goodbyes.

I no sooner hung up the receiver than Aunt Ida announced her arrival at the front door with her characteristic *bang, bang, bang*. Without waiting for someone to answer, she let herself in.

Holler ran to her and jumped on her skirt. He ought to have learned by now that she detested that. It never worked well for him, yet still he kept trying.

"Why don't you train your dog to behave? He's old enough to know better."

"I'm working with Holler, trying to teach him better manners." I thought of something cheery and smiled. "Holler is also learning some new tricks."

"Never mind that." Aunt Ida took off her jacket and hung it on the coat tree in the hall. "Come to the parlor. I need to talk to you."

Gosh darn it. My spirits flagged, and they had scarcely had time to soar after I talked to Dewey. Now here was my aunt treating me like a grade-school child again. And I'd been so hopeful she'd change after our heart-to-heart talks during our trip. My emotions couldn't keep up with all that had happened to me since Uncle Rory hit town. I was buffeted about, pushed hither and yon over and over again.

Dutifully I followed her into the parlor. She sat on the settee and patted the cushion beside her.

"Please sit."

I didn't want to, but her request was trivial, so I sat.

"How do you feel this morning? Are you recovered from last night?"

Her frown indicated concern.

Dewey asked those same questions. Maybe both of them were truly worried about me.

I smiled.

Aunt Ida's expression brightened.

"Ah, now I see your lovely smile. You must feel better, and I'm so relieved. I couldn't sleep for worrying about you. I know your father's approval means so much to you."

I seized the opportunity she laid in front of me.

"Look, Aunt Ida. I'm a grown woman—old enough to vote. Yet Poppa treated me like a child last night." I ducked my head, avoiding her gaze. "Sometimes you do the very same thing."

"We only want what's best for you, Wallie dear. We want to keep you safe."

"I only want the best for you too, but I don't tell you what you can and can't do. About time you recognize I'm old enough to make my own mistakes and learn from them."

"Not if it means you risk mortal harm. Young people often underestimate the possibility that bad consequences can happen to them. When you've seen as much of life as your father and I have, then you'll see why we worry."

Too tired to argue further, I decided to change the subject. A deep breath in and out helped me regain my composure.

"Poppa just telephoned with news from Chicago. But don't you worry, Aunt Ida. I'll keep my promise to him and won't do anything risky. However, that doesn't mean I'll stop trying to figure out who committed the two murders."

She nodded and murmured that she understood. Although I doubted that she did, I told her about Al Capone and his henchman, Donny Sorrento, watching her face closely as I relayed the news. When I came to the part where Sheriff Finch said that Capone was a dangerous gangster who was bumping off rivals, her eyes widened.

"How extraordinary. I hope we don't see anyone related to those Chicago men ever again—or to the Maceos either, for that matter."

"I hope so too."

But after I agreed with her, I immediately wondered if my statement was true. But what did it matter anyway? Those gangsters would either see us again or they wouldn't. My wishing for more adventure wouldn't change anything.

I'd given my word to stop sleuthing, and I intended to keep it. I'd never again seek out gangsters, thugs, murderers, rumrunners, or anyone else of their ilk. And that was final.

But thinking about them was another matter altogether.

"Aunt Ida." I lowered my voice to a confidential tone. "Here's a question I've been pondering. Mind you, it's only mental work, nothing active. Still, I can't help wondering."

"About what, child? Say what you mean."

I stood and walked to the window. All was peaceful now. Our property showed no signs it had been the scene of two murders. Yet dark storm clouds were moving in from the north.

Keeping my gaze on the outdoors, careful not to look at my aunt, I explained the puzzle I was trying to solve.

"Why did Donny Sorrento stay in Gunmetal after Uncle Rory died? I can spin a theory to make some sense of the reason Sorrento came here in the first place; he must have followed Capone's orders to keep an eye on Uncle Rory. Maybe it was part of Capone's plan to beat out rival gangs or even to expand his territory into Texas."

I returned to the settee and sank onto it. Holler nuzzled my feet. I patted him absentmindedly.

"But I can't for the life of me figure out why Sorrento would hang around Gunmetal after Uncle Rory died."

Aunt Ida snapped her fingers.

"I've got it. Maybe there's another bootlegger in town. Maybe he caught Capone's interest, for whatever reason— either to work with him or against him. Perhaps to build Capone's own territory or maybe to get rid of Capone himself?"

"That seems possible." I sank back against the cushions. "At least it's a reasonable supposition."

She threw her head back and laughed.

"This is all your fault, and look what you've done. Your enthusiasm for solving crimes is rubbing off on me."

We both chuckled. It felt good.

Then I remembered I needed to ask her about Faith Carson.

CHAPTER THIRTY-FOUR

OFF IN THE distance, thunder rolled.

Aunt Ida jumped up. "If it's going to rain, I must get going."

I sprang up too and stretched out a hand to her.

"Please wait. I want to discuss something else with you."

She sat on the settee again.

"All right, but let's be quick."

"How long have you known Mr. Carson?"

"For as long as I can remember. Why do you ask?"

"And do you recall his sister Faith?"

Aunt Ida didn't answer right away. Her eyes glazed and then she blinked, giving me the impression that she was thinking hard in order to pull up her recollections.

Finally she said, "I believe there was one sister who survived for a time. That family lost so many children. I had moved away to teach in Yoakum by the time that sister died. Faith lived longer than Mr. Carson's other siblings. People said they came of bad stock—said it was the Carsons' Indian blood." She edged forward. "Is that all? I don't want to get caught in the rain."

"What's this about Indian blood?"

"Floyd Carson's grandfather was Kit Carson. Surely you know that?"

I nodded.

"Of course. Everybody in Gunmetal knows."

"His grandmother was a full-blooded Cheyenne. Back when Floyd Carson and I went to school together, all the boys thought his connection with a famous scout and Indian fighter was exotic, but it scandalized us girls. Floyd got teased a lot, and I always assumed that he resented his name. Some of the teasing was mean-spirited. You know, like saying his grandma was a dirty Indian squaw, things like that. I felt sorry for Floyd being so scrawny and quiet." She stood. "Now I must be off."

"I'd like to ask——"

"Wallie, your questions will just have to wait. I don't even have my umbrella with me." She went into the hall and retrieved her jacket, pulling a pair of deerskin gloves out of a pocket. "When I spotted the dark blue sky this morning, I figured a norther would blow in, so I've got warmer gloves. Just wish I had remembered an umbrella."

Before I could offer her mine, she gave my cheek a quick peck, startling me with the unusual mark of affection. Then she threw open the front door and left with great speed.

Darn it. I moped because my talk with Aunt Ida was cut short.

Still, there was no longer any hurry to find answers. I was off the case. It was in the hands of the sheriff and his men. All I had left was avid curiosity.

"Let's go, Holler." Off we flounced to the kitchen. I told Athalia that Dewey would join us for dinner and that Poppa expected to be earlier than usual, adding, "Aunt Ida says a blue norther is coming in."

"Oh lordy. I hopes Mamadell takes in my plants off of the

porch." She wiped her wet hands on her apron. "Now then, what about dessert?"

We discussed the virtues of several different recipes, settling on Mamadell's buttermilk pie. Then I went upstairs to write down every word Aunt Ida had uttered about the Carsons. I also made notes about Al Capone and Donny Sorrento.

An idle thought wandered through my mind—what if one day I used these characters in a murder mystery of my own? I'd name my fictional sleuth Sherleen Holmes, maybe make her a long-lost American cousin of the famous Baker Street consulting detective. Maybe I could use my fascination with this case for something productive someday.

My bedroom window's northern exposure provided a good view over the backyard. While I updated my journal, from time to time I checked on the advancing storm. The wind whipped up, and tree branches banged against the side of the house. The temperature dropped in my bedroom, and I pulled my favorite sweater from the wardrobe.

While I sat warm and cozy, Holler whined and rubbed against my feet. At only six months, he had yet to experience weather extremes that hit Texas in the autumn. The blowing wind seemed to disturb him. After a few minutes, I took pity on him and patted my lap. He leapt up and curled on my stomach. My left hand petted and calmed him while my right hand kept writing.

Once I finished updating my journal, I noticed my trousers were wet from Holler's slobbering mouth. I patted my shoulder, and he climbed up.

"Stay," I said.

I drew a large handkerchief out of my pants pocket, used it to dry his mouth, and patted my trousers. The hanky was damp—not wet—so I returned it to my pocket and Holler to my lap. He weighed too much to stay on my shoulder for long.

I took a fresh sheet of paper from a drawer and wrote a

brand-new name. After transcribing it two more times, I sat
back to admire my creation.

Wallie Brandon. Wallie Brandon. Wallie Brandon.

I giggled. Going even further, I imagined the formal
announcement of our engagement in the local newspaper. *Walter
MacGregor to wed Dewey Brandon.*

I clapped my hand over my mouth and giggled again. Folks
who didn't know us would be unable to tell the man from the
woman.

An earsplitting crash in the backyard made me jump.
Through the window I saw the side door of the carriage house
flapping about in the wind.

What a bother.

I needed to shut the blasted door. Poppa detested it when
stray animals sheltered among his carefully arranged tools in the
carriage house. He couldn't keep out field mice, but he drew the
line at orphaned cats. He was as bothered by them as Mr.
Carson was to dogs.

I rushed downstairs, grabbed a jacket, and found Athalia in
the kitchen. She wore a jacket too. I grinned at her.

"You must really be cold. I've never seen you so bundled
up inside before."

"I be fixin' to walk to the store to—"

"Don't do that. You'll freeze to death."

"I wants tonight's supper to be special. Won't take me long
to run to the store."

She rushed out the back door while I stood there in the
middle of offering to go myself. I shut Holler in the kitchen and
followed Athalia down the back steps.

The wind howled, and Poppa's hunting dogs howled back
from their kennel. I yelled so Athalia could hear me.

"Let me go to the store for you."

Shaking her head, she trudged toward the street, waving as
she went. I waved back, and we went our separate ways.

Even with a sweater underneath, my jacket wasn't warm enough for the abrupt drop in temperature. I clutched the lapels to my neck and dashed to the carriage house. Once inside with the door closed behind me, I found the torch that Poppa kept near his work bench. Its beam helped me search out any cat or other critter that might have scurried into the comparative warmth of the place.

I was inspecting a basket of firewood when I heard the door open and shut. Without turning around, I called out to Poppa.

"You weren't kidding when you said you'd be home early for supper. This must be a first."

When he didn't reply, I straightened up and spun around.

Mr. Carson stood ten feet away. He stared at me with unblinking eyes.

"This is a surprise. What're you——?"

"Are you all right?" he said.

Our words tumbled out and overlapped each other.

I chuckled.

"Let's start again. Yes, I'm fine, and what're you doing here?"

He stepped closer.

"I was out in my tool shed doing some *important* tinkering," he said and winked, "when I saw you rush outside. I was afraid something was wrong. So much has happened over here lately that I thought I'd better check on you."

"Aren't you kind? Nothing's wrong, other than that door." I pointed to the one he had used. "The wind forced it open. It was banging back and forth, and I came out to fasten it shut."

"And how about your puppy? I hope he's safe inside."

"He is, so you needn't worry about running into him. Your wife says if you're around dogs, you get sick."

He shuffled his feet and grimaced.

"That's been a problem all my life. I always wanted a dog. For companionship, you know."

Speaking of companions, what about your sister?

While I tried to come up with a way to raise the subject of Faith, he pulled a small pouch out of his jacket pocket.

"You mind if I smoke?"

I gestured up at the hay in the loft over our heads.

"Seems to me it would be a fire risk."

"I'll be right careful."

He took out papers and began to roll a cigarette.

"I didn't know you smoked, Mr. Carson."

"Only the odd cigarette now and then. Anita doesn't like it."

I remembered the cigarette Holler found in our carriage house the night Uncle Rory died. It didn't seem likely that Mr. Carson had left it there, but if he had, then I had even one fewer clue to the murderer. Darn. Still, since he was here, I could ask how he felt about my uncle. I had boldly confronted Sam Maceo, and my method worked well with him. Why not do the same with Mr. Carson? After all, he was no gangster.

I took a step closer to him. In response, he backed up. He didn't have an intimidating bone in his body.

"Did you and Uncle Rory play together as children?" I asked.

Mr. Carson's hand stopped halfway to his mouth.

"Why do you ask?"

"The first time I met my uncle was last week. Now I wonder what he was like. Maybe you can clue me in."

"Well, I, uh—" His cigarette completed its journey to his lips, and he took a long drag. His hand trembled. "That was a long time ago. Your uncle and I, uh, well, we weren't especially good pals or anything like that."

"He liked your sister Faith well enough, though."

His head snapped up. "Who told you that?"

"His current girlfriend knew about her. She mentioned it to me."

Mr. Carson narrowed his eyes.

"You said you knew nothing about your uncle and wanted me to fill you in. So how come you know his girlfriend?"

"I went to Galveston to pick up his belongings. While I was there, I ran into that woman."

He nodded slowly.

"So that's where you were. I noticed you weren't around for a while."

"Yes, my aunt and I had a nice road trip."

How odd that he wondered about my whereabouts.

He stubbed out his cigarette on the heel of his boot and kept the butt in his hand.

"Say, we're going down to Port Aransas tomorrow, me and my wife. Gonna celebrate our anniversary. I planned a little surprise for her and wonder if you'd help me with it. I need the lady's perspective."

"Sure, I'd be glad to help."

"All right, let's go."

He turned to leave the carriage house.

"Wait. Not right now, not in this storm. Can't I come over tomorrow?"

"We're leaving tomorrow. Has to be now."

He opened the door, and the wind blew it out of his hands. He ran back to me and gave me a gentle push.

"Come on. Won't take but a minute."

I made a snap decision. Whatever this favor was, it would be small. Mr. Carson was always nice to me, so what could it hurt to be nice back?

Together we ran from my yard into his. By the time we entered his tool shed, we huffed from the cold wind, and our hair was disheveled. Thank goodness the rain hadn't begun yet.

Mr. Carson stamped his feet and blew on his hands.

"Whew, this here's gonna be some storm."

He flicked on an overhead bulb that hung from the rafters.

The interior of the shed was roomy; I had never been inside it before. What he called a tool shed was bigger than our carriage house. Mr. Carson was a house painter, and he evidently stored the tools of his trade here. I saw tarps and paint cans but no obvious gift for his wife. What required my female expertise?

A crack of lightning hit nearby, startling me.

"You may not be able to drive to the Gulf tomorrow, Mr. Carson. The storm may keep you here."

He leveled an odd look at me.

"Oh, we *will* leave tomorrow. I haven't booked any painting jobs all week. I'm determined to go."

He walked to the corner where his Studebaker sat, opened the driver's door, and brought out a cardboard box from beneath the front seat.

"This here's a gift for my wife. I want to make sure Anita will like it. What do you think?"

He opened the box and drew out a pale pink shawl. It was such an exquisite creation that I gasped when I saw it.

"How beautiful. Mrs. Carson will love it."

Actually, I feared she might not. The shawl was made of woven silk and quite elegant, not her style. She was as plain as a house wren, but perhaps she'd enjoy a touch of glamour.

Mr. Carson came toward me with the shawl spread open.

"Let me see how it looks on you."

I backed up. This was getting odd. For the first time I worried about being alone with this man. The wind was making a terrific noise, and the dogs were howling. If I screamed for help, no one would hear me. No one was even inside my house.

My goodness, my imagination was getting the better of me.

This was the result of Poppa and Aunt Ida warning me not to court danger.

I clasped the torch tightly and held it at my side, ready to strike if necessary.

You're a silly goose. Mr. Carson has always been kindness itself to you.

"No, please. It wouldn't be right for me to wear your wife's new shawl."

Taking another step backward, I bumped into a wall.

He had me trapped.

CHAPTER THIRTY-FIVE

SOMETHING INSIDE MR. Carson seemed to shift. I couldn't comprehend how it happened, but suddenly menace radiated from him. Peering at him more closely, I noticed that his eyes were glazed over and unfocused.

He murmured words I couldn't understand.

"What did you say?"

"Faith." He stared at the shawl. "Faith had a dress just this color. Her hair was like yours—blond and shimmery. Maybe that's why I always liked you." He rubbed the shawl against his cheek. "Color is very important to me. Pink was her favorite. Do you really think Anita will like this?"

Every muscle in my body tightened. Whatever was wrong with Mr. Carson, I didn't want to make it worse. Still, I had to say something. Maybe I should try to keep him talking and then dash out of the shed when his focus wandered.

It wasn't much of a plan, but it was all I could devise on the spot. I clutched the torch more tightly and moved it behind my back. He didn't seem aware of it. I certainly hoped he wasn't.

"What was your sister like? You must've been devoted to

271

her."

He shut his eyes, and I prepared to bolt. Then he opened them wide. His expression brightened.

"Faith was my little sister. Mama and Papa said I should always look after her. She's in heaven now. I know she is."

The poor man. A lump rose in my throat.

He licked his lips.

"She, uh, she was my best friend. 'Here comes Floyd and Faith,' that's what they always used to say. Wherever I went, she went too. I couldn't have a puppy like you have, but I had Faith."

I didn't like the sound of that. A girl was not a dog. I couldn't help myself. I had to reply.

"But she wasn't a pet. I hope you didn't treat her like one."

He sneered.

"No, dummy. I did *everything* for her and kept her safe always. Like Mama and Papa told me to do. If they'd told me to look after their other babies, why, I bet I coulda kept them safe too."

"They died from disease, didn't they?"

"I think so. Ones that were older than me, those died before I was born. Them I don't know about. But the younger ones got sick and died."

"So one day Faith got sick too? Was that it?"

"No." The word burst out of his mouth. Once he yelled, he kept on doing it. "She wasn't sick. But she made me sick. Sick at heart. Your damned uncle changed her. That's what did it."

I shrank back against the wall. This was more than I bargained for. The light was dawning on me, albeit slowly, that my nice neighbor might not be as kind and sweet as I'd always thought him to be.

I looked right and left, searching for something to draw his attention away from me or to give me anything else to talk about. Anything but my uncle and Mr. Carson's dead sister.

This line of questioning was getting me into deep trouble.

I was more frightened now than I'd ever been in Galveston. And that was saying something.

He thrust the pink shawl at me.

"Here. Take it."

I caught it. Silly of me, but it was too beautiful to let fall on the dirt floor.

"I advised Faith not to take up with Rory, but she wouldn't listen. Then I warned your uncle." A momentary sneer flashed across his face. "I warned him so good that he lit out of town and was gone for decades. My Bowie knife is a fine persuader. I heaped guilt on him too, threatening to tell the town how he had sullied my sister's body."

Where was he going with this? Tears flowed down his checks now.

Shaking his head and sighing, Mr. Carson said, "When he left town, I doubt if Rory knew that Faith was pregnant. I didn't know then either. If I hadn't run him off, then he could have married her. It was my fault, what happened after that."

He balled his fist and pounded his leg repeatedly.

Rolling out in front of me was the story of a small town tragedy. I *had to know* how it ended.

"May I ask you some questions, Mr. Carson?"

He recoiled but nodded.

"How did Faith die?"

"She drowned. No one else knew she was expecting a child. She asked me to help her."

I pictured a young woman stepping into a stream and drowning herself. Like Ophelia in *Hamlet*. Yet somehow that picture didn't seem right. I shied away from asking for particulars, though, not sure that I wanted to know. Not right now anyway. The answer might prove to be too dangerous. Everyone in town knew of the stiff morality of Floyd Carson.

"Mr. Carson, did you talk to my uncle last week?"

"Not really."

"What does that mean? I don't understand."

"When I saw Rory go into the carriage house, I went over to your place to see him. I thought I'd have it out with him. Tell him how he ruined Faith's life, and mine too come to think of it. When I saw his feet sticking out from under the Model T, I flew into a rage. You saw the result."

Clamping my mouth shut, stifling my shock, I was too stunned to move.

Then I realized that my chance to flee had arrived. Mr. Carson hung his head and stared at the ground, lost in his sordid thoughts. I inched sideways but didn't get far.

"Where do you think you're going?" Mr. Carson was yelling. "I can't let you leave now."

So this is what Poppa feared would happen to me.

Curiosity always killed the cat, just like everyone always said. I'd thought I was so smart. Well, I wasn't. Instead, I was the cat. The stupid ol' cat.

Damn.

Mr. Carson said, "You know you shouldn't swear. I'm surprised at you, Miss Walter."

I hadn't meant to speak out loud.

"Well, hell's bells, what does it matter now? You're going to kill me anyway."

His arms went wide.

"How do you know that? I don't even know that myself."

I exhaled loudly.

"I'm not stupid. I can work it out for myself. You just confessed to murdering my uncle, and unless you want to go to jail—which I assume you'd like to avoid—you can't let me leave."

"Gosh, I'm impressed. You worked that out pretty darned quick. I hadn't quite reached that point myself."

"My aunt says I read too many murder mysteries. But

maybe I haven't read nearly enough of them. I should've known not to come into this shed with you."

His eyes grew wide.

"I wanted your opinion about Anita's gift. I didn't mean you any harm. I really didn't."

"Methinks thou doth protest too much."

His mouth fell open and he stared at me.

"What?"

"Oh, never mind. I was just showing off. So where do we go from here? What're you going to do now?"

"Don't push me," he shrieked. "Can't stand being pushed."

"I'm sorry."

He rubbed his head as if it hurt.

"Well, I ain't figured out what to do with you yet. You were always kind to me, and I appreciated it. I liked you. Why did you have to be so blasted nosy?"

I wobbled a little, remaining silent while he was quiet too, evidently pondering his options.

He rubbed his hands together.

"Let's see. Considering my present situation, I could always tie you up and leave you over there with my work things." He gestured toward his painting supplies. "Then there's drowning, an accident, and my Bowie knife."

Was that his repertoire for murders? That amounted to three, perhaps even four methods—all of which he may well have tried with some success.

My scalp prickled. He had confirmed my suspicion—he had drowned his own sister. I'd think about that later, but who did he knife?

Donny Sorrento? Really?

For once I was at a total loss for words. Scrawny, moral little Mr. Carson? I didn't know what to do.

Well, I could breathe. I *needed* to breathe. I did it slowly.

While I concentrated on breathing, I also had to try to

control my eyes. My gaze was darting around the room, and I didn't want to give away how panicked I felt.

Mr. Carson looked up from his fingers and stared at me as if surprised to see me in his shed. His head tilted. "Why are you holding Anita's shawl?"

How curious.

"You just gave it to me. Do you want it back?"

"Yes, please."

He reached out his hand and grabbed it when I held it toward him. Then he nuzzled the shawl against his cheek again.

He'd said the shawl was for his wife, but he seemed to associate it with Faith. Whatever was happening to him, he was confused.

Had he slipped into madness? Perhaps he was ill in his head and that explained the murders he'd committed. I had flared up at him, letting the MacGregor side of me run wild, but now I must revert to kindness. That might help get me out of the jam I'd gotten myself into.

Something had to work. It just had to.

Searching for a topic that would distract him, I kept returning to the death of Donny Sorrento. That was my own craziness—a totally unsuitable subject. Yet it loomed so large in my head that I couldn't nudge it aside to find a better one.

There was always Faith. She appeared to be at the center of this tragedy. If I got Mr. Carson talking about her, his trance-like state might repeat. Then I'd rush him, hit him on the head with Poppa's torch, and race out of the shed.

All right then, I had a new plan—a slight variation of the old one.

"Tell me about your sister. Faith must have been a very special young lady. What did she like to do? Read? Play the piano?" I looked at the army of paint cans standing in rows. "Did she paint or draw?"

Mr. Carson fingered the shawl. "Faith loved to paint. She

always talked about colors and how they made her feel. Even though I was older, she taught me so much."

"Was she much younger than you?"

He shook his hand. "Just a little more than a year. We were close, very close. We got along so well."

His expression became so dreamy that I almost expected him to float up to the ceiling.

That darned Donny Sorrento kept bubbling up in my thoughts. I decided to give in and ask about him. I knew it was a risk, but I didn't want to talk about Faith anymore. I was losing patience, needing to get myself out of this blasted shed and run for help.

"How about the stranger who died on our property last night? Do you know anything about him?"

A cunning look came into Mr. Carson's eyes. He twisted his head and looked out a window, then shot me a sideways glance.

"He wanted money. I promised to pay him, and he came back to get it. It wasn't right to prey on a family's sorrows. Not right at all. I showed him."

"I don't understand."

"Think of a color. A dark, dark color. The worst color there is."

"Well, Mr. Carson, I must say that I do like puzzles, but I'll have to think on this one for a little bit. So I—oh. I think I see. Do you mean the color black?"

Grinning like a child, he nodded vigorously.

"So the stranger saw you go into our carriage house the night my uncle was inside, working on Poppa's Model T? He was blackmailing you, wasn't he?"

"He was." Mr. Carson tossed the shawl onto a bench. "And now, Miss Walter, let's go get my Bowie knife. We have business to attend to."

CHAPTER THIRTY-SIX

MY CAPTOR RUSHED toward me. His right hand grabbed my left arm. I didn't resist but grasped the torch more firmly with my right hand. When he pulled me toward the door, I moved the torch low and around to my side. Then I felt something dangle from my pants pocket.

A picture of a slobbering puppy rose in my mind. I'd put my hanky there after wiping Holler's mouth. Why, if the handkerchief found its way to Mr. Carson's face, he'd be even sicker than he was right now. A different kind of sick. A useful kind.

I had to bring the handkerchief out of my pocket and rub his face with it.

The wind howled more ferociously than ever. If I waited to make my attack until we were outside, then it might be easier to maneuver without Mr. Carson understanding I was trying to escape.

Meantime, I needed to keep his mind busy with my eternal questions.

I aped a solicitous tone.

"Are you sure this is a good idea?"

"I have no choice."

"Of course you do. There are always choices. That's what you learn in church every Sunday. You are a good God-fearing Christian, aren't you?"

He squeezed my arm so hard that I squealed.

"Don't talk about that."

"I'm sorry. I won't bring church up again. But I know how much your religion means to you."

"Shut up. Shut up. Shut up."

We stood beside the door. With his free hand, he reached out and opened it. Rain and wind gusted inside.

I kept my thumb and index finger tight on the torch and used the other fingers to clutch my handkerchief. When Mr. Carson turned to see what had slowed me down, I thrust both the torch and the hanky into his face.

He yelled. The torch hit his nose hard, and I squashed the hanky into his face even when he jerked his head away. He used both hands to shove me.

I fell back but still held the torch and the hanky. I must have hit him harder than I'd thought; his nose was bleeding. His hands flew to his face, and he gawked at the blood that dripped onto them.

"Here, let me help you."

I came at him with the dog-smeared cloth, intending to do even more harm than I'd done already. As I'd hoped, he was confused and thought I meant to help.

He let me rub his face with the cloth. I used my right hand, and now held the torch in my left. Stepping back to examine my handiwork, I watched Mr. Carson's eyes turn red and begin to water. He sneezed several times, and then he coughed. He doubled over and kept coughing.

I slipped past him on the side, picked up a length of wood, and exited through the door. The wood slid easily into the door handle and would keep him from opening the door from inside.

That was only a stopgap; I had to act fast. Lights were on in both my house and the Carson house. Rain fell hard, and wind whipped my hair and clothes. I hightailed it across one backyard and into my own. By the time I reached the back steps to my house, I was gasping for breath. After a short breather, I ran up the steps and burst into the kitchen.

Athalia screamed when she saw me.

"What's happened to you?"

Holler began to bark.

For a second I leaned on the back of a chair.

"Can't explain now. Must call the sheriff."

I ran down the hall, slipping on my wet shoes, but managed to stay upright. Holler followed me, continuing to bark. Shouting into the telephone receiver, I called up an operator.

"Get me Sheriff Finch. It's an emergency."

Sheriff Finch wasn't in his office, but Deputy Misak was there. I told him what had happened and begged him to rush to the Carson property. He assured me he would hurry.

Next I called Poppa, but he had already left for home. All I had to do now was wait for reinforcements. I slumped against the wall, trying to catch my breath and slow my thudding heart.

Athalia watched me from a few feet away. Holler swirled around my feet. He didn't understand what was happening but seemed to know I was upset.

One more deep breath, and I could move and speak again. I scooped Holler up to my chest and spoke over his head to Athalia.

"You heard what I told the sheriff's man on the phone?"

"Sure enough, I did. What we do now till folks come to help?"

"I'll get my deer rifle. I'll go back and make sure Mr. Carson stays in his shed. You better stay here and tell anyone who comes what the situation is. I expect Poppa will be here soon too."

Within five minutes I returned to stand guard outside the shed, my rifle at the ready. Mr. Carson coughed and pounded on the door. Occasionally he managed to yell. Rain poured over me, and I quaked with the cold but stood my ground.

Deputy Misak arrived minutes later, followed by Poppa a short time after that.

Quickly I sketched in what had happened, giving enough details that they understood the seriousness of the circumstances.

When Poppa told me to go back to our house, I gladly fled the scene.

Athalia had made hot cocoa and had a quilt ready to throw over my shoulders. No sooner had I seated myself at the kitchen table than a knock came at the front door. She scurried off to see who it was.

Next thing I knew Dewey loped into the room. When I managed to stand to greet him, he folded me into his arms.

"You've had enough excitement for today, don't you think?"

I buried my nose in his nice, warm, dry neck.

"Enough for a whole month."

I was delighting in Dewey's embrace for the very first time, when the sheriff interrupted us. He led me into the parlor, where he questioned me for an eternity, until my tired mind began to produce gibberish. I believe he mumbled something about my persistence paying off and helping to find a killer. With that, he released me.

I excused myself and crawled upstairs to bed.

My adventures left me plumb tuckered out. I was so tired that I even left Holler downstairs to sleep overnight in the kitchen. Yet although my body was limp with exhaustion, my mind kept whirring. I tossed and turned for a long time, replaying the night's events. When I finally slept, I became one with the bed. Without Holler to wake me up early, I slept late the next morning.

The rain still fell.

The sky was still dark. And I awoke at ten thirty.

Goodness me, I felt like a real slug-a-bed.

Self-indulgence seemed the order of the day. I ran a brush through my hair and pulled on my pink chenille robe. Ambling into the kitchen, I hid a big yawn with my hand when I joined Athalia.

She stood at the sink, staring out the window that overlooked the Carsons' house. When she heard me, she turned and grinned.

"You been needin' some rest, you been on a tear here lately. Whatcha want for breakfast, eggs or waffles?"

Too exhausted to stay upright a minute longer, I plopped down at the table on the nearest chair.

"You choose. It's too big a decision for me to make this morning."

"It ain't really. It almost be afternoon." She set her cast iron skillet on the stove. "Don't you fret none. Be all right just this once to be lazy."

I planted my elbows on the table, needing to be propped up or I might fall over.

"No, wait. I do know what I want to eat. I'll have both eggs *and* waffles."

The kitchen was too quiet.

"Where's Holler?"

"He be in with Mister Walter, in his study. Want I tell him you be awake now?"

Before I could answer, she shuffled from the room.

Within minutes, she returned, with Poppa and Holler leading the way.

Holler jumped into my lap, and Poppa stopped on the other side of the room and studied me with a fond expression.

My hand covered another yawn.

"You were right, Poppa. I did get into a heap of trouble by being nosy. I don't want to talk about it now, though. At least Mr. Shakespeare proved right once again."

Poppa pulled out a chair and sat next to me.

"Right indeed, thank heaven. 'All's well that ends well.'" He smiled when Holler licked my hand and nestled under my chin. "Athalia has kept watch on the Carson house for me. She's counting the number of church women going in and out."

"Yes, sir. I kept careful count. Make it seven so far." Athalia beamed and waved a scrap of paper at me. "Got all the ladies' names down too."

Mention of Mrs. Carson drew my interest. "Have you figured out if Mrs. Carson knew anything about her husband's murders?"

"Sheriff Finch believes she was in the dark about all of them. That's not conclusive yet, but her behavior indicates she's in total shock over his crimes. I can't help but feel right sorry for the woman."

"So the members of her church are rallying around her? For sure Mrs. Carson will need their ongoing help—after her husband has gone for good."

"The church ladies support her now," Poppa said. "If my experience is anything to go by, however, soon those women will turn out to be fair-weather friends, scandalized when Mr. Carson's murders stick to him. At this point in time, they probably believe that he's innocent of any evildoing."

A shudder ran through me.

"He's not right in the head. He killed the person he loved dearly, so there must've been a big war waging in his soul all these years. Sad, sad."

I rubbed my cheek on Holler's sleek fur and gave him a squeeze.

"When I checked in with Sheriff Finch this morning,"

Poppa said, "he noted that Floyd Carson continues to act strangely. He's not coherent, babbling a lot."

"He's in jail and will be tried later?"

"Yes. Obviously I won't be the presiding judge."

Bang. Bang. Bang. Aunt Ida's knock carried all the way to the back of the house. I wasn't sure if I could face the onslaught of Poppa and her at once. I expected a coordinated duet of chastisement for my foolhardy actions.

Into the kitchen she waltzed. For once she didn't stand on ceremony. She hadn't stopped to take off her coat, so when she bent to hug me, I got wet.

"I'm so glad you're safe, you precious girl." She kissed my forehead, then straightened. "You may be precious, but you are also darned infuriating. We *warned* you that you were getting in over your head. But, oh no, you refused to listen."

"Please, Aunt Ida, I can't—"

"Have a seat, Ida."

Poppa stood and pulled out a chair for her.

Athalia bustled over.

"Better hand me your coat, Miss Ida."

"Thank you." Aunt Ida took off her deerskin gloves, passed them to Athalia, followed by her wet coat. "Shall we move into the dining room?"

I jumped up.

"Good idea."

Anything to jar us loose from the topic Aunt Ida had begun. Later I'd have the fortitude to withstand recriminations from both Poppa and Aunt Ida, even in concert. But today I needed to recuperate.

Once we were settled in the dining room and Athalia had brought in coffee, Aunt Ida reported on the gossip around town. Understandably, folks all over Gunmetal were abuzz with the report of Mr. Carson's arrest. The local newspaper had already sent their senior reporter to interview Sheriff Finch. The town's telephone operator reported that big city journalists were due in from Houston and San Antonio shortly.

A frown creased Poppa's forehead.

"This poses a problem. Wallie, I'm not keen to have your name plastered all over newspapers throughout Texas."

"Mercy me, no." Aunt Ida sounded incensed. "You know the rule. A lady's name should only be in the papers a few times during her entire life. For birth, marriage, and death announcements. Now I might also amend that to include the winning of prizes for best flower arrangements and the like. But that is all."

"Maybe I could adopt a nom de plume," I said. "I could call myself Sherleen Holmes."

She shot me a withering glance.

"That is not amusing, Walter."

Ducking my head, I murmured into my coffee cup.

"Just a small joke, Aunt."

Then an idea hit me with great force, and my head popped up.

"Consider what would've happened if I hadn't insisted that Uncle Rory's death was a murder. He would've had no justice, no justice whatsoever. Plus we would've lived next door to his murderer for years and years."

I sat tall in my chair and stared defiantly at Poppa and Aunt Ida.

"I deserve to be proud of myself. I hope you two will also be proud of me. I set out on a mission and proved my point."

My father and aunt sat back in their chairs, exhibiting shock at my forthright statement.

But I was not finished yet, oh no.

"I hasten to add, however—"

"Wait." Poppa held up his hand. "Your aunt and I have something to say."

He looked at her, and she nodded.

"We have agreed that although we can't condone your risky behavior and hope you never exhibit it again, we also are proud of you for—"

My voice came out in a squeak.

"You are?"

Poppa said, "Yes, we are. You didn't back down in the face of opposition. No one believed your theory that Rory's death wasn't an accident. Yet you persevered."

Aunt Ida said, "Even when you were made fun of as a meddling young woman who didn't know what she was talking about. That takes real fortitude, Wallie, so good for you."

With both Poppa and Aunt Ida beaming at me, tears came to my eyes.

"Thank you. Your praise means so much to me. I don't know what to say."

They burst out laughing.

"Now that is a surprise," Poppa said.

I brushed away a tear that was dribbling down my cheek, trying to come up with something to reassure them.

"Well, actually," I began.

They laughed again.

I grinned.

"I really don't plan to gallivant around the great state of Texas looking for wrongs to right. This was a very special case. My alter ego, Sherleen Holmes, has had one outing—and one outing is enough. You can rest assured of that."

Privately I doubted my own words, but I needed to reassure them. After all, none of us could foretell the future.

I pushed back my chair and rose from the table.

"And now I'm going to telephone Galveston. I'll try to find either Vivian or Glenda at the Chop Suey Club and—"

"Why would you do that?" Aunt Ida said. "That's not necessary."

"I believe it's only fair to tell them that their information helped solve the murder of Rory MacGregor."

As I turned on my heel to walk to the telephone, Poppa and Aunt Ida began talking in excited tones to each other. I was glad to miss that, although they'd catch me up later, alas.

Luck was on my side. Vivian answered the telephone at the Chop Suey Club. When I told her about Mr. Carson's actions and explained what part his sister Faith had played in Uncle Rory's death, she whimpered and let out a few sobs. Then she pulled herself together quick enough and thanked me for calling her.

"But I called to thank *you*, Vivian. Without your information on my uncle's lost love, he might never have received justice. I'm so grateful to you."

"But you were very kind to telephone, Wallie. We were all wondering what you'd uncover but didn't feel like we could bother you. Can you tell me more about the associate of Al Capone who was killed by your neighbor? Might be I can shed a little light on that matter."

I revealed all I knew about the mysterious stranger and his blackmailing of Mr. Carson. Then I added, "If you know any reason Mr. Capone sent Donny Sorrento to watch Uncle Rory, it might put the final piece in the puzzle."

"I don't remember the man's name," Vivian said, "but I do know that Al Capone sent someone down from Kansas City to keep watch on your uncle. Then Capone sent Frankie back down here again by train. You remember him, don't you?"

"Of course. How could I forget Frankie?"

She laughed. "Frankie was supposed to locate the man from Kansas City. During that man's last call, he said Rory MacGregor died and that he wanted to get to the bottom of it before he returned to KC. After that, there was no more communication. Now the Maceos can tell the guys in Chicago what happened to their operative."

"But why did Capone want Uncle Rory followed in the first

place?"

"Oh, sorry. I forgot to mention that," Vivian said. "A big shipment went missing, and it looked like an inside job. Only two guys could've engineered the robbery, and Rory was one of them. Right after Donny Sorrento checked in for the last time, the real culprit was caught. Capone wanted Sorrento to quit tailing Rory and return to Kansas City to work on another operation." She started sniffling again. "Rory's luck finally ran out."

"You got that right." We listened to each other sniffle for a while. Finally I remembered how expensive long distance was. "Say, Vivian, I really do thank you for all your help. Tell Glenda hello from me. I'll never forget meeting you two, and I wish you luck—all the luck in the world."

"Goodbye, Wallie, and many thanks."

I hung up the receiver, guessing I would never talk to her again.

In a somber mood I returned to the dining room where Poppa and Aunt Ida had their heads together in deep conversation. They looked up and stopped talking when I entered the room.

I filled them in on Vivian's news.

Poppa laced his fingers together and gazed at me over the top of them.

"So, no dangling threads remain. I hope that is the conclusion to this quite wretched tale. I also hope that our lives can return to normal. My job is to be a law-abiding citizen of this community and to ensure others also uphold the law."

He unlaced his fingers and pointed at me.

"Your job, Walter MacGregor, is to stay out of mischief and to use your extensive intellect in ways that will enhance our community yet keep you on the safe side of law and order." He placed a hand on Aunt Ida's arm. "Your aunt believes I should censor your choice of reading material, but I believe your good sense will win out. I hope you understand that Sherlock Holmes is a fictional construct and that there need never be a genuine Sherleen Holmes."

After crossing my fingers and concealing them beneath the table, I said, "Oh, Poppa, I couldn't agree with you more. And while I expect we'll discuss these days for a long time to come, if you'll excuse me now, I feel in the need of a nap."

I stopped by the kitchen to pick up a tray with my ever-so-late breakfast and carried it to my room. I finished the food off with dispatch, slept for three hours, and rose to freshen up. Discarding the chenille robe for my usual costume of shirt and riding britches, I bounced down the stairs with a degree of energy that had been lacking earlier.

I was progressing through the hall on my way to the kitchen when someone knocked on the door. It didn't sound as if Aunt Ida had returned, so I went to answer.

Dewey stood on the porch with a bouquet of flowers in his hands.

He held the flowers up to his nose and sniffed.

Eyes twinkling over the top of the bouquet, he said, "Thought you might need a congratulatory gift. Or perhaps even some cheering up. In any event, I wanted you to have these, together with my sincere appreciation for our, uh, our friendship. I believe it will only grow over time."

I accepted the bouquet.

"Thank you, Dewey. I agree with you. Still, I have to give you fair warning. I can't guarantee that I'll always be sweet, as you wisely advised me to be just a day or two ago. If we can proceed on that basis, then, please, do come inside."

"Don't worry, my dear Wallie. We understand each other very well."

He winked at me, crossed the threshold, and gathered me into his arms.

—THE END—

Kay Kendall

Notes on Fact and Fiction

THE ONLY LIBERTY I took with Texas geography in this book was to add the fictional town of Gunmetal near the real ones of Cuero and Yoakum.

The topography of Houston and Galveston I did not change, and most buildings stood in 1923 as I have described. The great storm of September 8, 1900, did indeed destroy much of Galveston, at the time a thriving place boasting the nation's first electric street lights. The loss of 8,000 lives still stands as the deadliest natural disaster in American history. The criminal masterminds, brothers Rosario and Salvatore Maceo, built their empire of vice in the city afterwards. Al Capone did send henchmen down from Chicago to see if he could horn in on the Maceo's burgeoning crime success, but nothing came to pass from that foray.

Theodore Roosevelt's Rough Riders were recruited in San Antonio at the Menger Hotel (still in existence), and the casualties from the Battle of San Juan Hill are as I have reported them.

Characters developed from my own imagination—some

inspired by my Texas forebears—I have placed within the historical setting of 1923 in southeastern Texas as accurately as I can. Kit Carson did have children with his Native American wife, and they had grandchildren. The one I depict in this book is fictional, however.

Sadly, since I wrote this book, the history of Sugar Land, Texas, has altered. Recent archeological digs have unearthed many gravesites of convicts who were used as virtual slave labor. Their remains bear the marks of their cruel servitude. The model company town that Isaac Kempner developed grew atop these inequities.

History provides a fascinating yet fraught study of human nature.

Kay Kendall

Acknowledgements

ALTHOUGH I CAME late to writing crime fiction (although not to reading it—oh, no), I've been happily submerged in this new chapter of my life, befriended and amply supported by the members of the crime fiction family. Total immersion works well, not only in learning a foreign language, but also in acquiring a new career.

My mysteries found a wonderful home at Stairway Press, which brought forth my debut book, *Desolation Row*, in 2013. Publisher Ken Coffman runs his company like a creative collective and allows his authors input in areas that large houses don't offer. Helping bring my mysteries to readers are my talented and copasetic editor Beth Hill, marketing guru Chris Benson, cover artist Guy D. Corp, and administrative wizard Stacey Benson. (Note: the Bensons aren't related.)

On most Wednesday evenings I huddle with my writing group as we pore over our latest pages together. I owe immeasurable thanks to these writers for their constructive critiques: Laura Elvebak, Kay Finch, Julie Herman, Bob Miller,

Amy Sharp, Anne Sloan, and member emeritus Dean AKA Miranda James. We all appreciate Susan Hairston for opening her home to us for our gatherings. These friends were unstinting in supporting the adventures of Austin Starr's grandmother as portrayed in this book.

Houston is blessed with the superb Murder by the Book, where I began a decade ago learning more about the broad crime genre and its many sub-genres from the knowledgeable staff there. I also began attending local meetings of Mystery Writers of America, where friendly writers offered sage advice on how to delve deeper into mystery writing. MWA is overseen nationally by tireless executive director Marjory Flax, and I currently serve as the Southwest Chapter president and sit on the national board.

Another supportive organization is International Thriller Writers, which welcomed me into its debut authors program in 2013. In my class I found great friends, including Daco Auffenorde, Marjorie Brody, John Clement, T.L. Costa, A.J. Colucci, Mary Louise Kelly, Barry Lancet, Melissa McGregor, Jenny Milchman, Lynne Raimondo, Robert Rotstein, Michael Sears, Terry Shames, Patti Sheehy, Colby M. Zampa, and James M. Ziskin. I enjoy reading their new books and meeting up at conferences like ITW's own ThrillerFest, administered by executive director K.J. Howe, who is herself now an award-winning thriller author.

In sum, I acknowledge the support I've received from Mystery Writers of America and International Thriller Writers, while saluting my colleagues noted here who've made my mystery writing life a delight. To them I also add—write on!

About the Author

KAY KENDALL WRITES award-winning historical mysteries. In her previous career, she also earned awards for her international public relations projects, working in the U.S., Canada, Russia, and Europe. Kay and her Canadian husband live in Texas where they have rescued abandoned pet rabbits for twenty years. Currently their household includes three bunnies and one bemused spaniel.

CPSIA information can be obtained
at www.ICGtesting.com
Printed in the USA
FSHW010312160719
60019FS